Christopher

First published by Jacana Media (Pty) Ltd in 2021

10 Orange Street
Sunnyside
Auckland Park 2092
South Africa
+2711 628 3200
www.jacana.co.za

© Nozuko Siyotula, 2021

All rights reserved.

The financial assistance of the National Institute for the Humanities and Social Sciences (NIHSS) towards this publication is hereby acknowledged. Opinions expressed and those arrived at are those of the author and are not necessarily to be attributed to the NIHSS.

ISBN 978-1-4314-3159-5

Also available as an ebook.

Cover design by publicide
Editing by Helen Moffett
Proofreading by Lara Jacob
Set in PSFournier 9.8pt /14.5pt
Printed by XMD Books, Cape Town
Job no. 003870

See a complete list of Jacana titles at www.jacana.co.za

Christopher

Nozuko Siyotula

For my grandparents –
Noluphato and Mnqabande, still the Thina flows,
and
my nephew Sigurd Siegemund
– the hope of all things I write.

Family tree

Vuyolwethu "Vuyo" Aitken (nee Fani)
- married to Christopher
- daughter to Mxolisi Fani and Nontsikelelo (Nonti) January
- niece of Nobantu ("Romance") January
- great-grandchild of Theodore "Groot Pa Katjie" January
- granddaughter of Theodore ("Teddy") January and deceased Reverend Fani
- niece of Beryl, Khanya, Tsitsi January
- grandniece of Ou Takkies

Nontsikelelo (Nonti) January
- married to Mxolisi Fani
- younger sister to Romance
- granddaughter to Ma and Theodore ("Groot Pa Katjie") January
- daughter of Theodore ("Teddy") January, the last-born child of Groot Pa Katjie
- cousin of Beryl January
- mother-in-law of Christopher
- grandmother of Eliyah and Elijah
- niece of Ou Takkies

Nobantu ("Romance") January
- daughter of Theodore ("Teddy") January, the last-born child of Groot Pa Katjie
- cousin of Beryl January
- elder sister of Nontsikelelo ("Nonti") January
- sister-in-law of Mxolisi Fani
- aunt-in-law of Christopher
- niece of Ou Takkkies

Mxolisi Fani
- married to Nontsikelelo ("Nonti") January
- brother-in-law of Nobantu ('Romance") January
- son of deceased Reverend Fani
- adoptive son of Alf
- father of Vuyolwethu ("Vuyo") Aitken nee Fani
- son-in-law of Theodore ("Teddy") January

Christopher Aitken
- married to Vuyolwethu ("Vuyo") Fani
- son-in-law of Mxolisi Fani and Nontsikelelo January
- nephew-in-law of Nobantu ("Romance") January

Theodore ("Groot Pa Katjie") January
- patriarch of the January-Miya clan
- father of eleven children, last-born is his namesake, Teddy
- grandfather of Nobantu ("Romance") January and Nontsikelelo January
- great-grandfather of Vuyolwethu ("Vuyo") Aitken nee Fani
- granduncle of Ou Takkies

Grandmother Bhele
- matriarch of January-Miya clan
- referred to as Mam'Bhele
- mother of eleven children
- grandmother of Nobantu ("Romance") and Nontsikelelo January
- great-grandmother of Vuyolwethu ("Vuyo") Aitken nee Fani
- grandaunt of Ou Takkies

Beryl, Khanya and Tsitsi January
- cousins of Nobantu and Nontsikelelo January
- Beryl, daughter of Theodore January's older brother
- Khanya, daughter of Theodore January's brother
- Tsitsi, daughter of Theodore January's brother
- aunts of Vuyolwethu ("Vuyo") Aitken nee Fani
- granddaughters of Theodore ("Groot Pa Katjie) January

- nieces of Ou Takkies

Ou Takkies
- illegitimate son of Zola January, eldest son of Theodore ("Teddy") January
- grandson of Theodore ("Groot Pa Katjie") January and Mam'Bhele
- uncle of Nobantu ("Romance") January and Nontsikelelo January
- granduncle of Vuyolwethu ("Vuyo") Aitken nee Fani

Kleintjie
- nickname for Theodore January Junior, also called Teddy
- maternal grandfather of Vuyo
- nickname is also used for son of Ou Takkies
- "distant" nephew of Nonti, Beryl, Khanya and Tsitsi
- "distant" relative of Vuyo

Prologue: A January by the sea

Christopher died.

I'm thinking of that moment. That niggling sensation which seems to precede all major shifts in our lives. We all know it; we have all been there and always, sometime before or afterwards, we realise that we had long seen it coming.

It's finally quiet. The only voice I can hear is my own. Laced on my tongue are the affirmations I have to say out loud, to manifest the healing that must sprout from the darkness, to find for us new hearts in which to live, and to heal what has been shattered.

Christopher died.

Christopher is dead.

Christopher.

Sunday

We were told of the coming time.
A time for us all.
A time when the fires would be stamped out.
A time for great-grandfather finally to be the man he had dreamed of his whole life.
Time for the virtues spoken of in folktales – of the slyness of jackals, and the fortitude of estranged village girls determined to not be stuck in the realms of the spirit world.
Time for the reaping and sowing of blood.
A time for us all.
As a child, I bathed in my insecurities.
I called myself shy, but that was an arrogance that hid my fear of being known.
I petted my crazy mother and comforted my broken father.
I am a January, the first to be called to the harvest.
I could survive it all; then it all became love.
Now, it has become courage to accept that I know nothing at all.
I know that I am here.
I know that we are all here.
I know that I see you, as you do me.
I know that all of it is meaningless.
I know that all of it is for a purpose.

Vuyolwethu "Vuyo" Beatrice Fani

When I was younger, death was all I saw.

Until Romance's arrival.

She picked me up in her arms. "A big girl, how old are you now?"

Romance is my aunt and the elder sister of my mother. A tall, dark woman with a soft but commanding voice. A figure of natural authority. I opened the kitchen door one morning and there she was, washing the dishes as she sang a song before turning to me with a smile that filled her face.

"Nine."

"Nine years old. You look just like my father. Do you know about Groot Pa Katjie?"

I shyly shook my head.

"He died the year you were born. He came to see you, and when you came out, he said, 'This is my Beatrice, she has given me joy at the end of my long life.' Nobody knew where he got the name from." She smiled thoughtfully and sat me down.

Her eyebrows were knitted like mine, but her tar skin was quite unlike anything I had ever seen. To this day, one of my favourite things is to sit close to all of her and just take in her abounding beauty.

I regarded this large woman as she moved about swiftly and expertly around our kitchen. She was saying a great many things and laughing at her own jokes. I had never seen somebody from my mother's family who looked like her. She was her own sort of rose. I loved her from the first. I knew instantly that she was as wild as my mother, but unlike my mother, who spent a considerable amount of time controlling her natural inclinations by being tactful and measured, Romance bashed about in a brazen sort of way that could grate your nerves while simultaneously drawing you closer to her.

"I have come to deal with your mother. She is in the shower now. Have you eaten?"

I shook my head.

She clicked her tongue: "Well, I don't speak the language of mutes, and last I checked there was nobody called 'Fool' in this house."

I bowed my head at the reprimand. "No, I haven't eaten."

"Am I a dog that you address me like that?"

"No Aunty, I haven't eaten yet."

"Good. I am Romance, your aunt. Now go fetch your mother upstairs, she desperately needs to eat."

"Yes, Aunt Romance."

"Already sounding like a child!" she shouted after me as I climbed the stairs to go tempt the tempest into unleashing her wrath.

I am writing this in the dead of night. I am in our beach house, the one Christopher left to me. It is quiet outside but for the dark waves that crash ceaselessly against the shore, and I'm unsure of how it came to be night in what has felt like one long day that began a decade ago. The wind is making the windows whistle, and as I turn my head to follow the noise, an invisible hand snuffs out the candle.

An omen.

I came here three days ago. It wasn't that long a drive, but Ma and Romance had invented all sorts of horrors that could befall a woman like me, a heavily pregnant woman grieving the death of her husband. If it wasn't the ghosts of the night, it was some witches' brew, and if not that, well, *things like that* were just not done.

But I could feel the wind of the ocean brushing against my cheeks and calling out to me. I would stand gazing at the Thina river, and it would whisper to me: "Meet me at my end." The longer I stayed in the village, the stronger the call of the wind, the more vivid my dreams. I had to leave. I had to come here, now, before my children arrived.

Grandmother said to me in a dream: "We know about life because its mystery is revealed in death, and in the end, we go back to the beginning. This is our faith. Do you not have faith, child?"

I haven't had these thoughts in a long time.

They have been flooding into my head since I came to this place.

The chickens were the last straw.

Romance and my mother had dragged me here to where the Thina bends to flow down to the ocean, in a village high up in the mountains where time never moved, but the sun kept its daily promises.

They were always watching me here, in the village. During the day, it was Aunt Tsitsi and Aunt Khanya, who cooked me too much food, and who sat having rambunctious chatter as they ladled large servings onto ever-available plates. At night, Aunt Beryl and Ma kept vigil with their subdued conversation that snapped and popped like a spinning record. Romance was the colour in between; but the chickens were too much.

Before we travelled to the village, relatives and sympathisers had descended on the home Christopher and I had shared, where Romance and my mother took turns shuttling them in and out.

Always a candle has to burn – that was the rule for a grieving soul. Since that fateful morning I had done nothing but comply with customs of which I knew nothing. At first it was because I didn't care, and the ceremonies of sadness appealed to my sensibilities because I could choose what disposition to have and with whom. Romance's annoying church people were meted out indifference. Christopher's friends and colleagues were met with quiet strength. My father's relatives I enjoyed, and I often sat with my cousins until they were dismissed by my mother at dusk. She would enter like the suspicious avenger she had become since Christopher's passing, light the candle in the bedstand, and then flop down into the wingback chair and gaze out at the setting sun. After a while she would stand and ask me the same questions: "How do you feel?"

"I don't know." This I would change to "OK, I guess", depending on the company.

"Are you hungry?"

"I could eat."

"Have you thought about what I said?"

The answer to this last question had many variations, namely:

On a good day, "Not today, Ma."

On a bad day, "I had a difficult day, I don't want to talk about it."

Every other day, "Why? All my doctors are here and it would be too difficult to find another doctor somewhere else. Also, isn't it dangerous?"

She would reply, "Dangerous to give birth? Like all the other women in history?"

To which I would reply, "I'm not sure."

She would exit the room at this point.

Some months later, once my immediate grief had lifted slightly, my mother came to my room at dusk and repeated her questions.

I had grown accustomed to re-entering the world without a chaperone, and the days I didn't feel like being the pitied widow were becoming more frequent. The bulk of my battle was getting through spaces that led to enquires after Christopher – the grocery store, the gym, a dental appointment – people who felt somehow attached to our existence, but to whom I had no true allegiance. Their tortured expressions on hearing the news, followed by their mandatory condolences and the courtesies on my end were in the beginning the more difficult experiences I had in trying to make sense of his death. The moment I thought it was safe to return the places we had frequented, he appeared to remind me that it was he who owned these spaces.

In time though, perhaps these unassuming faces whispered to each other through the vine, because the questions all but disappeared. Those who knew gave me dull smiles when we crossed paths, and those who didn't saw nothing inviting their pity; but it still bothered me – their eyes darting from my face to my protruding belly. It didn't escape me. Pity would not be what met my children as they entered the world. I didn't know much about nurturing, but I knew that I didn't want that for them.

My mother asked the last question routinely, but was genuinely surprised by my answer this time: "We can go."

She clasped her hands at her breast. "I think it will be what you need. I need a month to organise everything, and get Anele not only to do the cleaning, but the house-sitting for some months."

"I will ask about doctors there and get a good referral."

My mother nodded and left the room.

A month later, Romance, Ma and I packed up her Jeep and drove to the homestead of Groot Pa Katjie, my great-grandfather, whose home was perched high up in the valley on one of the many bends of the Thina River. He was the grandfather who visited me as a ghost in my dreams. I had never laid eyes on him, but I had been lent his hazel eyes in this life.

From the homestead, you could see the mountains rolling out into the horizon enclosing the remote village that was still a thriving community, largely made up of relatives and some favoured neighbours. Tatomncinci Gerrie lived there with his family now, but no member of the extended family needed permission to arrive and spend the night.

Many tales were told about Groot Pa Katjie, who passed away the year I was born. My favourite was about his horse Phelandaba, who literally kicked to death anybody who sought to threaten Groot Pa Katjie. Phelandaba lived to be very old, outliving Groot Pa Katjie, and when we were younger and all the cousins came to the homestead from all over the country to spend the Christmas holidays, our parents spent their days shouting gruesome threats to anybody who dared to enter the part of the kraal where Phelandaba was kept, or to try to ride him. Our parents told us of the boy who had tried to steal him but ended up dead, his neck broken, body twisted, and legs upturned after a horrendous fall. Nobody had felt any sadness for the boy, a notorious upstart from a neighbouring village who must have thought that Phelandaba's temper was an old folktale, and decided to acquire for himself a strong golden stallion as a prize.

One morning I found my father drinking his coffee on the verandah that looked out over the kraal, and asked if we could go watch the boy charged with brushing and feeding the temperamental horse. He picked me up and walked over to the kraal. The young boy, Klein-Kop as he was commonly referred to, was already dipping the brushes he used to groom the horse into the flea disinfectant.

My dad traded jokes with the small boy. He was one of Tat'Zola's many stray children that he could not deny, given that Klein-Kop had the trademark threaded eyebrows and fair skin of all January offspring, our inheritance from Groot Pa Katjie. That morning was the first and only time I ever touched Phelandaba. Klein-Kop had allowed me to feed him after assessing that the mood of the horse seemed predictable. I remember I reached out and touched the blond hair that cascaded down from the ridge of his neck like a waterfall, and he had blinked his black marble eyes as he chewed the clumped vegetables from my small hand.

That was the last memory I had of the village until the afternoon my mother's white Jeep was spotted in town some seventy kilometres away. The bus driver had told the young boys who worked in the yard packing groceries, and they had casually mentioned it to the taxi conductor, who had joked about it with the petrol attendant while filling up his taxi, who had told Skhova who was in town collecting Mam'Thembu's pension at the bank. Skhova had married an elder cousin of the January clan, thereby becoming an uncle to Romance and Ma. When the whispers of our arrival found his ears, he had set out to find us.

The town was really just a few dilapidated buildings built on either side of the national road cutting between them. There was a Shell garage that was constantly packed with rickety buses and taxis. The latter were actually vans that the locals referred to as 'springboks', 'bokkie' for short. They were given this name as they could travel fairly fast on the often badly maintained gravel roads in the network of villages spread out along the mountain range. The drivers knew all the villages that official maps never listed by name, and which clans lived where, and earned their commission carrying as many loads as possible during the day. In a bokkie, people with knockout stenches were crammed in with gas tanks, goats, chickens, eggs and all other goods purchased in town, packed both inside and on top of the van. Those who didn't want to endure this paid the sum total for all the seats the driver could fill in one load. The driver of the bokkie was also bound to your time, which is what made the arrangement particularly convenient. This service was mostly used by people who had moved to the cities (and now earned better) when they returned for the big holidays like Easter and Christmas. Sometimes the wealthier locals paid the lump sum if they too had many groceries, particularly if there was going to be a funeral or a ceremony of rites.

Skhova had paid for a bokkie early that morning when he had arrived in town, as he had many errands to run. When the taxi conductor told him of our arrival and where we had last been seen, he came to find us.

"I refuse to call you uncle," Ma said excitedly as she gave him a hug. He had found us packing goods into the trailer Ma had hired from the wholesale shop owner. I was resting in the car, and he had offered me a kind greeting after he had surprised my mother.

"I won't force you," he laughed as he picked up some of the blankets and other wares Ma had bought at the wholesale shop. "We knew you were coming, but nobody told us the day. I caught your scent in the air."

"Exactly how a January arrives anywhere. Anybody who meant us harm can try again on a different day. Evil never sleeps," Ma said, stuffing some smaller items into the corners of the trailer. This casual contempt for the world was typical of how my mother's side of the family spoke. Romance came round the side of the car where Skhova and Ma were standing trading stories.

"Well, if it isn't our uncle," she said, breaking out in a wide smile.

"Oh, I just told him I won't call him that," my mother added as Romance and Skhova embraced.

"He has even gained weight," Romance joked, pulling at his glistening cheeks, "our wife is keeping the pot full. Who would have known that you two would grow from throwing rocks at each other to this, our uncle?"

They stood by the car chatting for a little while longer until he excused himself. He was the first of a thousand relatives who would hear of our coming and descend upon us at Groot Pa Katjie's homestead.

The cousins of Romance and Ma all came to Groot Huis, the biggest hut in the homestead. Groot Huis was built for Mam'Bhele to have room in which to do her sewing. It was originally the name of the big hut in the middle of the homestead, but came to be the name we gave to the entire homestead, as it was from there that the January-Miya family was reborn. It from here that my great-grandmother governed over the family.

All around the walls of the big hut were straw mats and sponge mats laid out on recently waxed linoleum tiles. Groot Huis was bubbling over with such excitement that I forgot I was sad. Everyone had my face – knitted brows and wild thick hair. Ma was smiling, laughing even. People performed stories that ended with raucous tears of laughter. Though the men were smaller in size than the women, they had an air of dignity, and were given the honour of addressing and welcoming us – which turned out to be the real reason for the gathering. Tat'Gerrie stood up and quieted everyone present. The candle that had been lit at dusk flickered on the wooden cabinet under the window.

Tat'Gerrie cleared his throat: "My children, as a father, your father, the only one left to you in this life, I find it important to say something when we as a family are facing moments in our lives that feel beyond us. When our last born" – he flapped his hat towards my mother – "when she called me a while back to say she was bringing the child we see here" – he pointed to me – "to deal with this tragedy, I was very overjoyed. She had remembered our ways. Your mother remembered our ways." He said this looking me in the eyes, and I nodded inadvertently. "She had remembered that the spirit of a January is always healed by other Januarys. There is power in being together." He shifted his weight from one leg to the other. "This is your home. The children you will birth will have their navels buried in that garden out there, where the navels of everyone who is in this room are buried. This is our way." He stood stoically for a brief moment before continuing, "However, I also know that you have the spirit of Pa Katjie because he gave you his eyes. He said from the Undying Lands: 'This is the one who will take this family further.' You cannot escape it." He cleared his throat again: "You cannot escape it. You must not be deferred by our limitations."

At this point he gazed at me solemnly and lifted his index finger: "Now, I didn't plan these words, they are coming to my mouth from my heart, meaning they are coming from those who want you to hear what it is that I am saying. Only you will know what to cling to and what to let fall by the wayside. My job is to be the messenger. A January's resilience is a bright beautiful thing, it has no match. None."

For this last statement he received affirmations from the room. "And you are nothing if not a January." He pulled his handkerchief from the breast pocket of his shirt and wiped the corners of his mouth. "I'm done," and with that, he sat down. The room was filled with blinking blank eyes, and Romance began singing our great-grandmother's favourite Xhosa hymn, after which we prayed. The hilarity picked up again soon afterwards, and dragged on until early in the morning.

The homestead was a machine that never slept even after some of its inhabitants had retired. As we rested, Ma and I, while Romance could be heard shouting instructions to "the stupid boys who had let the pigs run into the garden", the January clan woke up to keep the wheels churning. The store, cattle, sheep, the ploughing and daily chores – these all chugged along like a well-oiled train, and that's how so many days melted into one.

Most days I sat under the acacia trees that lined the fence on the perimeter of the homestead, and watched the deceptive tranquillity of the Thina River. The several nieces and nephews of various uncles and aunts regarded me with curiosity. The braver ones asked direct questions to clarify the gossip they heard around the village from neighbours who had seen me stretching my legs or escaping the company of those charged with my care.

"Can I touch your belly?" asked one of the young girls.

"Sure," I replied. She stepped up to me shyly and placed her small dirty hand on my belly. Her hair had not been combed in days, and she was clearly enjoying the rebellion. It would soon be the Easter holiday break, but some of the children had already begun their holidays.

"How many children are in there?" she asked.

"Two."

And her eyes opened wide: "Really?"

I smiled at her innocence. "Yes, really."

On other days the children didn't care for me at all, but when their friends asked about me, they answered their questions without tact: "That is our older sister who lived overseas and her children are from overseas" – not exactly the truth, but also not exactly a lie.

Aunt Tsitsi and Aunt Khanya, my caretakers during the day, were their own brand of special. Both were animated and short-tempered, with a strong affinity for the other. Each of their conversations was held at the highest volume. They were the government of the homestead, the ones who made decisions about which business ventures the family could undertake, and who would be employed. They assisted with the business accounts and also resolved any family disputes that arose. Most of their days were spent verbally abusing those around them who didn't walk fast enough or speak up for themselves. They were rural women who wore long dresses and head scarves, but were also strategists who understood not only the world, but the people around them. In the mornings they came to enjoy their mid-morning tea in the room where I spent most of my time if I wasn't outside.

"Yoyo?" Aunt Khanya called out to me by my nickname, sticking her head in the door.

I lifted my head. "I'm awake."

"OK good, come sit with us." I fought my annoyance at being disturbed, but slid off the bed and made my way to where they were sitting outside the room. They had laid out straw mats and were sorting red kidney beans to make umnqusho later that day. "Sit here, my child," Aunt Khanya said, pointing to the sponge mat she had dragged out of Groot Huis for me. I felt a pinch of guilt for being annoyed.

They continued their conversation: "Listen Khanya," Aunt Tsitsi said at highest volume, picking up where she had left off once they were sure I was comfortable, "we arrived there to help those ungrateful people. Two days before the wedding and there was no baked bread in sight."

"No!" Aunt Khanya exclaimed.

"No cut wood for the food!"

"No!"

"No slaughtered animal."

"No! No! No! A disgrace if you ever heard of one."

"It was worse if you were there," said Aunt Tsitsi, throwing some of the beans she had in hand into the five-litre bucket at their feet. "We vowed not to leave because imagine what they would say about our family after that – look at them, their family has fallen, they can't even throw a decent event!"

"And you know that's how it is."

"Exactly. The women from that family are city girls. All of them had those devil's claws for nails, with no knowledge of how to make food from a vegetable. Honestly, I wondered how our brother found such a wretched woman."

"It's the education, it messes with their heads," Aunt Khanya said, disgust all over her face.

"But to cook," Aunt Tsitsi let out a small cough, "what does *she* eat every day? Never mind feeding him, what about her own body?"

"These children think respect is a matter of politics. I will never be seen at that family's events ever again. What would it have hurt for them to learn at least one thing?" Aunt Khanya said in rebuke.

Aunt Tsitsi nodded, then added: "I blame our brother, and it doesn't help that he comes from the line of the Januarys who are known for being quite dense."

"Who? Sebenzile's brood?"

"It could only be," Aunt Tsitsi lamented. "Very dense. Wasn't he the one who was at Somandla's funeral changing his baby's nappy on the hood of his car?"

"Yes, and then he went ahead and handwashed the nappies afterwards."

"Which man who was there watching these wonders didn't love his child that he had to perform fatherhood so much? What is this foolishness?"

"It's as you say, Khanya, the education makes them go crazy – like they are the first ones to open a book. Do they know we also went to school?"

"I suppose it doesn't matter if it's in the village, but in the city, men learn how to wash nappies at school, that's the entrance exam."

This was typical of the conversations between them when they were not discussing what work needed to be done on the several January homesteads.

There were rare days when I was left to my own devices. On these days I would look out over the Thina, and it would remind me of my father when he taught me to overcome my fear of water by borrowing an old man's story. There was something about water that my mind connected with a negative spiritual element; it held only terrors for me. Its ability to be a habitat for a whole other world made me mistrust it. It was the only sport I refused to take part in at school, and at the age of nine I still could not swim, which at that point was a constant worry for my parents, who had grown up in villages where countless children were swept away by the strong currents of rivers due to their inability to negotiate their way out of the water.

My great-grandfather, Groot Pa Katjie, had a tale he told his children to warn them about the dangers of the great Thina river that flowed down in the valley: "There was once a boy named Mbiza who was a renowned liar. True to the meaning of his name, 'pot', he loved to stir the pot. He once broke into the house of an old blind man who was also hard of hearing. One night the old man had some lamb cooking on a pot over the fire. The man's only animal was a grey cat named Kati, for whom he used to leave the window of his hut open in the evenings.

"Mbiza, being the scoundrel that he was, had learned the old man's routine. One night he climbed through the window and said nothing when the blind man called Kati. He simply watched him, sitting as still as possible until he was convinced the blind man didn't suspect a thing. Mbiza closed the window so that the animal could not interrupt his plan. He found his way to the boiling pot and pulled out the largest portion of meat, wincing through the pain as he gulped large chunks of hot meat down his throat as silently as he could, until only a smooth bone remained in his hand. Instead of leaving the blind man some meat, he was overcome by greed and he reached down into the pot again and again until there was nothing left but a pool of boiling oil and lamb-flavoured water.

"In a panic, Mbiza searched around the room for something that could be mistaken as meat by the old man. He spotted dishcloths balled up on the rickety table in the makeshift kitchen. Silently, with the movements of a cat, he made his way to the opposite end of the hut, grabbed the dishcloths and threw them into the pot, then quickly left the old man's hut through the same window in which he had come.

"When the old man discovered this late that night, he knew Mbiza had to be involved. He reported the incident to the chief of the village, after which Mbiza was called to explain his whereabouts to the council. He was found to be at fault and was publicly whipped. This did nothing to deter his mischievous nature.

"A few weeks later, Mbiza was swimming in the oxbow bend of the river that flowed just below the village. It was prohibited by the chief to swim there, but naturally, Mbiza had ignored the instruction. As he pulled off his clothing, he found himself looking into the eyes of a creature he had never seen before. A beautiful girl with hair flowing all the way down her back and eyes like the blind old man's cat. The girl asked Mbiza why he had come to disturb her sleep. He found himself unable to answer, but immediately fell in love with her. She was a serpent-like creature that one could liken to a mermaid, and people hadn't seen those for hundreds of years. When Mbiza managed to break free from the trance she had put him in by looking into his eyes, he ran with all his might to report his sighting, but nobody believed him. Instead he was whipped once again for breaking the law set by the chief."

At the end of the story, my father would kiss my forehead and rock me until sleep became a friend again.

When I looked out to the Thina, I felt called by it; but unlike Mbiza, my destination was at the river's end. Nevertheless, at that moment in my life I was where I was supposed to be; despite the frustration I felt at the activity around the homestead, something in me felt grounded. I could feel the babies I was carrying moving around a lot more these days. My feet had become swollen, and I had to limit my movements as I easily became lightheaded.

On a quieter afternoon, I found an older nephew called Kleintjie washing his sneakers by the water tank. Kleintjie was the son of my mother's favourite uncle Ou Takkies, who had passed on years ago. Ou Takkies – who wasn't old as his name suggested, but was given his nickname because he was born with wrinkles that never did smooth out – had never met his child, but as with so many January children, the features were so distinct – knitted brows and wild thick hair – that he was immediately accepted when his mother had presented him to the family as a stray. Kleintjie was a typical January man, with a slight frame and tight muscles. His nickname had been given to him because of his baby face. He was a quiet young man, but his brows were constantly furrowed as though something had just annoyed him. That being said, he was kind and quick-witted when engaged. He saw me coming towards him in a slow waddle, and pulled out the rickety wooden chair he had made by knocking some pieces of disjointed wood together with nails.

"Am I not going to fall when I sit on that thing?"

"It won't be because of the chair," he replied, breaking into a noiseless laugh.

I smacked him on the head and eased myself down onto the chair. "Why are you not at school?"

He shrugged his shoulders. "I'm not good at it, and nobody wants us there."

"What do you mean? Who is us?"

He continued cleaning his green New Balance sneakers with a small light-brown wooden brush, bending over the enamel tub filled with soapy water. "School is for girls. If I want a girl I need to make money, and there is no money at school."

I smiled at this typical logic. "So how will you make money?"

"Right now I am working in the shop, supervising the driving boys with Tat'Gerrie, but I don't know, maybe I will go my own way. Will you stay here forever?"

"No."

"I heard your white man died?"

"Is that what they call him? My white man?"

"Well, was he not white?"

"He was," I replied softly, looking at the ground, "and he was my man."

"Then I guess they have reason to call him that," he said, scrubbing the bottom of the shoe. He lifted his muscled arm to wipe sweat on his forehead with the back of his forearm. "What happened to him?" he asked, bending back down to continue cleaning the shoe in hand.

I thought of the moment after my mother had called me to rush back from the shops "because Christopher–", but then the phone had cut out. She had spoken to me in that pinched panic tone that she had called me with when my father had had his first stroke. I knew something was amiss when the call dropped. My mind raced through all possibilities as I drove towards the beach house, where we were on holiday. The bottles of wine I had gone to buy clinked against each other in their rustling plastic bag. Each rut in the road was an opportunity for me to panic.

The night before we had sat as a family having a spirited debate about the political developments in the country, and what they would mean for the masses. The others had all drunk too much wine, which irritated my mother; she had left us on account of a manufactured headache after admonishing us and reminding us that my father would have found our behaviour appalling. This was in itself a lie, as my father used to enjoy nothing more than a good time. Romance was so drunk that she passed out in a stupor on a deck chair with her legs sprawled. When we finally decided to call it a night, we found dragging her to her room a sobering experience.

Later, after we had climbed into bed, Christopher coaxed me into making love, a messy intoxicated affair that was highly enjoyable, more for its audaciousness than its climax. He had fallen asleep with his palm flat on my stomach, as was his habit.

I pulled into the driveway and sped from the car into the house, where I saw him lying on the very deck where we had been sitting only a few hours ago. He was in his salmon-coloured swimming shorts only. Water was still dripping from his body, and his head tilted unnaturally to the left. I never reached his body because my mother and Romance pulled me away as the paramedics flashed lights into his eyes. What happened? What happened? What happened? It was all I could say of a life turned to ashes.

I remember that day in so much detail. Right down to when my mother asked me to close his eyes.

Now I said, "I don't know what happened to him, but he isn't here – that's the most important fact."

Kleintjie looked out into the valley with the Thina down below, the small wooden brush dripping water onto his jeans. "This is life," he said, which was his way of showing compassion. I smiled at him and said: "Yes, and once you know that a person dies a couple of times more after the moment they stop breathing and how brutal that feels, life becomes more significant."

"Then why do you look sad?"

I ignored his question and asked again, "Why are you not at school?"

"I told you."

"That's not a reason. I was one of six black students – three girls and three boys – at my first school. They didn't want us there, but that doesn't mean black people shouldn't go to school. In fact, us being there probably allowed for more of us to come in."

"It's not like that with men. Nobody values what we do or what we feel, and I am not going to cry like a child because it hurts to feel unwanted. I'm going to be a man. I am going to continue. So they say write this stupid test, do this do that to go to the versity, but what am I going to do there? The Down There Boys went to the versity, three years of writing tests, and they came back to the village with nothing. You know what they do now? They drive some of our bokkies, I am their boss. I make more money than them, and I should still be in school. All around the village, the versity boys sit and drink, and get lifted on weed. They start the fights that break out at ceremonies and when the chief asks questions, it's always the versity boys. So if I am a January and that means something in the world, why must I go to versity? Unless I want a white girl, like you wanted a white man."

I laughed. "So you think I only studied so I could move up in society with white people?"

"If your dead man isn't white, then I am wrong, but if he is, then I am right."

I considered him for a minute. He bent down again and began scrubbing another pair of multicoloured running shoes. There was so much he didn't know, and yet the bravado of youth had convinced him that he knew the truth of my life because I was now a thing of pity.

By now, Kleintjie was hanging the shoes in pairs on the poles of the fence. When he returned to the basin, I stood and said: "You don't know anything about this life." I pushed my hair out of my face with tears brimming: "And you should go to school." I walked away in a huff.

We moved to the suburbs after the famous election.

Being a witness to mass violence was exciting in the moment. The air was charged with change, but the way to achieve it created divides that pulsed not only through the people, but our leaders as well. Nobody was who or what they seemed. In trading stories, those who plotted vengeance often found the details they needed from the careless and feverish whispers of bodies burning at funerals and so-called spies gunned down at rallies.

The children even made it a game when the men with the machetes would come running down the road, burning with the bile of hatred for those who were not part of their tribe. The children would scatter, high up into avocado trees or the darkness of ceilings, screaming coded words to their friends whom they knew were targets. The targets would hide as they listened or watched the men ransack their homes and throw to the floor the plated lunches prepared for them by their unsuspecting mothers. Some mothers survived the attacks and proved they had no boys, but others perished with the swing of a machete, while long guns sprayed holes into the ceilings.

Oscillating between the normality in between such tragedies and the unpredictability of the exact moment of impending violence was how I spent my early childhood. It wasn't a tragic childhood by any account, although now I know that it's not natural to come to count on the death of a neighbour or a friend as an accepted way of turning the day. We were on the cusp of freedom; there were no rules on how to get there. Nobody was who they were raised to be; they just knew that times needed to change.

My parents were not urban, and had moved to what then qualified as South Africa from the then Transkei, the "independent state" of the Xhosa people. In the township we had lived in before, all our neighbours were Xhosa, so as a rule you never asked a neighbour what they were by way of ethnicity. My parents were more accustomed to asking to which clan a person belonged than where their people were from. The scandal of being neither what you purported to be, nor where you are were from, made everybody, particularly my parents, aware that there lay very present dangers all around them, disguised as friendly neighbours or harmless passers-by. I mention this to tell of the times and the company we unknowingly kept.

Some were uncovered as thieves through violent deaths even though they had performed gallant acts – like babysitting for those parents who could not be home until evening. They made sure we children were home and not on the streets. Others were cursed with the kind of beauty that is a commodity in a world of people who are up to no good, and which made them more of a prize to betting and bad men. The most important ones were the friends who died needlessly as collateral for times they had not created: people with whom you had shared the secrets and mischief of childhood about the adults among whom we lived.

One year, we – among them, friends we later lost to the violence – had discovered a couple making strange sounds in the backyard of a neighbour's house on New Year's Eve as the fireworks exploded overhead. Most of us were prohibited from going into the backyards of our neighbours as a precaution against being unintentionally exposed to other people's business. On this night, we had planned to uncover the object that stood in the corner of the yard covered with in dark green plastic. It appeared to be a car, but we didn't understand why it was parked outside when the man who lived there had a single garage, and used taxis to travel to work. The mystery of the object had burned in our imaginations since we discovered it. Among us were various speculations about what could be under the green cover, and New Year's Eve was the perfect time to satisfy our curiosity – the relaxed and distracted mood of the adults around us allowed us to slip away into the darkness.

We heard the sounds long before we saw the figures. The lady was standing upright with her skirt pulled up to her waist, and the man had his pants dropped to the ground. We could see the moon shape of his bottom squeezing into the woman, causing her to make sounds we had never heard prior to that night. Often we were cautioned against men as 'they only used women'; we didn't know if what we were witnessing was a man using a woman, but from the sounds she was emitting, it certainly did appear that he had the advantage. These and other events filled our escapades with random conjecture as to the true nature of the lives of the adults who framed our reference of the world.

Then came moments when the violence affected someone you knew and loved, and their death made such a huge impression on you that you vowed you would not forgive the violence that preceded it. There was no way out, though, and in those neighbourhoods, the ones where the winds of change blew stronger than anywhere else, we sat through the flames of the burning houses and the rounds of gunshots deep in the night. We knew that not all parts of the country were on fire, just the places where we lived; and when it was permitted by law for all races to live anywhere, we left. Not because we didn't love our community or value our way of life, but there was the call of the unknown, the impetus to flee from our neighbours' mirrored pain, and the promise of an equality most had thought too painful to dream about.

The recollection of those events has become disjointed over time, but it has remained immaterial to the weight of emotion that I still attach to so violent a severance from a place upon whose community I had come to depend.

After my mother had bathed me that evening, I lay alone on the bed gently rubbing my stomach. The only audible thing was the intermittent clucking of a chicken as it searched for a comfortable position on the stack of fifty-kilogram bags of flour in the corner of the room.

I knew the routines of the chickens in this hut. At dusk they would come in, following each other, and after some squawking and competition, they would settle down as my mother and Aunt Beryl came in to keep me company.

Tonight, however, there was lots of work to be done on the fields to prepare them for the planting season. The perimeter of the homestead was being strengthened as a rowdy bull had charged through it some days ago.

I didn't mind being alone. I hadn't been alone since our arrival some weeks back.

I don't know why Kleintjie upset me. He was like all the men on my mother's side; determined to be his own man. This was a trait to be proud of, but I had made him feel ashamed of his convictions. I was ashamed.

On the eve of motherhood, I hoped to have been more grown up than I felt – and at moments I did – but it was fleeting.

When I held my father's hand for the last time, I knew that his loss meant that I would carry a certain hollowness for the rest of the days of my life; no man would love me again without limitations. True love. Not the kind Christopher gave, which had me sitting on bathroom floors in the middle of the night in prayer with tears falling from my eyes as he tossed about on our bed. In those moments I knew I had grown into a woman without a father on the one hand, and a woman in love on the other, but it had not been as I had imagined. I was too young to lose my father's guidance, and too naïve to blossom in the full glare of a man's love. It was not them; it was my fault. My fault for gaining years in life but not living.

I thought of the oppressive silence that had grown to be my companion once we moved to the suburbs. It was a lonely place where noise of any kind was squashed by the silence of conformity. Each house had two or three children, and manicured gardens with tall trees, and homes with two or three garage doors, and two or three chirping birds at dusk and dawn. Even though we quickly consumed the new curriculum required for our adjustment and survival, urgently trying forget what we had left behind in the fire, it never felt like where we had come from. It felt like we had betrayed our friends

My parents did well in that new environment, but were constantly caught off guard when they were invited into the homes of those who regarded them highly. Satiated wealth had a quiet elegance to it that they had to learn both in speech and in manners. The delicate balance involved in being cultured but ambitious were lessons they could not have learned being black-rich in the case of my mother, or black-classy in the case of my father. It was not a syllabus taught in burning and violent neighbourhoods. It was these very nuanced lessons that fostered my dedication to the protection of my privilege, deciding to lose myself in a space where I was neither black or white, but what I believe I am now – an "I don't know".

At least Kleintjie knew what he wanted: to be respected and a man.

Ma came into the room with her laptop, rattling the dozing chickens: "There is going to be a braai, you want me to bring you anything?"

"I thought you were working the fields?" I teased.

"Never me. Besides I have a paper to present two weeks from now for some seminar at the university, and with the babies coming, I want to be ahead of the game."

I smiled. "Okay Professor! Well, I don't feel like anything."

She left, her bare feet making a *pat pat pat* sound on the polished linoleum. My mother's transformation when she was in the village always surprised me. Her blank cold face gained a shade of red, and her eyes danced with joy at the slightest thing. She remained the least animated of her relatives, but when she was among them it wasn't difficult to imagine that she was one of them, or that she was highly valued by them.

For the most part, tragedy had governed the ebb and flow of our relationship: it had severed our initial bond, and it had begun to restore it again.

"Do you know what happened to the lady whose children were killed by those men with machetes?" I asked my parents as we drove to the hospital, the rains pouring down.

"She moved to Cape Town. Why?" My father answered, craning to look back at me.

"I always wondered."

"An awful thing to wonder about," my mother said, all manner of disapproval lacing her voice. I nodded and placed my head against the window.

The windscreen wipers moved furiously on the glass as we drove in silence. My mother barely spoke, choosing to keep her eyes on the changing scenery.

We reached the hospital and shuffled through the parking lot in the pouring rain. I stood by myself in the waiting area with my white teddy bear pressed against my abdomen as strangers smiled at me, and nurses kept barking instructions at me not to touch certain objects, until I resigned myself to sitting on a red-cushioned chair. The pale fluorescent bulbs filled the room with a sickly white glow, lighting up people who were biting their nails alarmingly or holding cups of coffee to their lips for prolonged periods, a distant look in their eyes. My father had told me to wait for him in this room, politely requesting a nurse to keep an eye out for me; and she did, a salty side-eye.

Save for the rain, it had been a normal afternoon. Hot, uneventful and quiet. My mother and I had been sitting on our favourite sofa reading when she suddenly asked me to go fetch her dressing gown, even though she had already changed out of her pyjamas. I obliged. Things happened quickly after that. My father searched frantically for his keys. I was told to put on my going-out jacket, and my mother made yet another outfit change, and pulled her big hair into a bun.

I asked them if we were going to meet my sister, and my father handed me my teddy bear and said: "Let's get into the car, baby."

When we came home later that day, my mother had glazed-over eyes, and her face bore no expression worthy of mention. Though she didn't often smile or animate her face, I could still reach her when I needed her; but that afternoon, as the rains poured down, I lost her.

The following days, she filled the house with her presence, walking around in crumpled days-old clothes, shocking us with her rage. My mother has a wildness to her that forms part of the doctrine of how she was raised. She is terribly proud. Often you would hear her muttering to herself when she was annoyed with my father: "You know nothing of a January woman." And when shoring up her resolve in facing challenges, she would say "never count a January out." Failure, to her, was to be genetically defective, because she was a January. Being unable to carry my sister to term broke her so completely that she became somebody else – haunted by her body, the gravesite.

For a long while, I had no mother. For years, actually. Our interactions were governed largely by duty – do your homework, wash the dishes, change your clothes – that sort of thing. Hardly a relationship full of warmth and common understanding. We had always had periods of long silences before, because she was not a talker, but now our silences felt sinister. They made me scared to go near her.

One time, she slapped me across the face because I had let a pen run ink all over my white shirt. So hard, I didn't even cry. I looked up at her and blinked several times. She stood over me and watched as I crept up the stairs to my room.

That was the night my nightmares started. Each night I would fall easily enough into sleep, but when it reached its depth, I was ensnared by tremendous evils that danced so close to me it felt as though I would be locked in this alternate world forever.

I didn't ever tell my father that my mother had slapped me. I knew he would never forgive her, despite his relentless love for her: his only manifesto. She ruled him completely, but I was where his love for her ended. One word from me would have made him less tolerant of the emotional siege she had maintained since my sister's death. He believed it was our shared pain, not justification for unfettered malice. She also said nothing of it, and since that day an ocean-wide rift spread between us that placed us at odds with one other, even when we were seeking the same thing.

That first night of terrors, I screamed at the top of my lungs into the darkness of my room, and found that I had wet my bed when I woke up. My father came to sit with me, a vigil he repeated each night I screamed in terror, until his health began to be affected. He barely slept when I had my terrors; and he found no comfort in his wife, who walked around in a daze of disappointment.

My mother had loved her ideas more than she loved either of us. She was dedicated to the world in her head, which is why she was unable to let my sister rest after she refused to form in her body. She wrote my sister into all her books and carried her around to places she had no business being. She would comb her hair and hum a broken tune that we knew to be a lullaby to soothe a wailing child.

I didn't mind being left alone. Being alone is useful in that it illuminates your thoughts, provides a necessary pause for contemplation. To be a lonely January is not uncommon, even though we were raised to value the community of family. Often I felt I was watching my life while standing at an open gate. In the Great Out There, I knew I could find what I had been searching for all my life if only I could move my feet, but beside me stood my parents, the border around my thoughts. They needed me. I held them together. So the gate stood there, open, and in my mind I ran fast and hard out the gate and into the unknown, but my physical self grew ever more rooted, preoccupied with pleasing them and excelling in the little that I had been tasked to do to help them. I kept hoping they would remember what they had forgotten after my sister came to live with us – as the ghost that breathed through us all as she tried to escape the clutches of my mother. But we went on orbiting around each other, while simultaneously existing as the happy family snapped on postcards.

The chicken was on my head when I woke up.

I had dozed off listening to the excited chatter of my nieces, who were revelling in the anticipated break from routine as the adults sat outside watching the meat sizzle over the open flames. The aroma had filled the air, and there was the usual animated debate about whether switching on the outside lights would keep the cows from sleeping. The matter had been the controversy of the village since the lights had first been installed by Tat'Gerrie, much to the anger of the neighbours, who lamented that as usual, the Januarys had found a way not to conform.

The electricity project had been approved by the chief, who had met with the government officials when they made presentations about installing power lines that would run through the village, and the costs that would result for all the households. The whole thing had been celebrated as a hallmark of progress. All the families had signed up to have power installed in their homes, and soon afterwards, delivery trucks were constantly seen dropping off televisions, DVD players and other appliances to those homesteads where families had means.

There had never been any discussion of whether lights were permitted on homesteads, let alone where. It was just assumed that power was only for indoor lighting, with each neighbour copying how and where their other neighbours had installed power in their homes. Other homesteads installed electricity in only one hut, and lit the others with candles or paraffin lamps. So when one day a light beamed out from the top of the valley into the darkness below, all manner of complaints were forwarded to the chief. The prospect of frightened animals running off into the night was a favourite complaint, but they ranged from a possible rise in bewitchings to the inability to sleep. The outside light caused so much conflict that the chief – recognising that the usage of lighting had been a blind spot in the negotiations concerning the power project – kindly requested Tat'Gerrie to use the outside light only intermittently. It didn't make the complaints disappear, but it at least set a precedent. So when neighbours began installing their own outside lights, customs developed about when they should be used – at night when there was a ceremony or large gathering; during the holidays when many families returned from the cities and routine was flexible; and when it was the busy season for farm work – the sheep needed shearing or the fields were being ploughed in preparation for planting. The cementing of these customs, as it became common for the villagers to have outside lights, didn't curb the chatter amongst those who constantly thought of ways in which the outside lights disturbed village life – to the extent that it was still a topic of discussion whenever they were switched on. It was during one of these conversations, taking place right outside the room where I had been resting with the chickens keeping me company, that I had fallen asleep.

But now I felt the round soft flesh of something unnamed spread across the side of my face. I turned, unsure in which reality this was occurring. The strong smell of the chicken's feathers hung close to my nose, and as I turned my head, the chicken fluttered its wings and jumped into the air as if to take flight. Meanwhile, Romance was screaming at somebody. She sounded nearby, but all I heard were chickens screeching in panic. The two small girls who had been outside chatting about the possibility of blind cows were now hunched over my bed with their hands open, steadying themselves to pounce on chickens who were all too aware of their intentions.

In a fog I asked, "What's going on?" just as one girl leaped onto the bed and caught the chicken by the end of one wing. As it writhed in panic, she wrestled with it until she had wrapped her small hand around its neck and pulled back its wings behind its back. Then she hopped off the bed, chicken in hand, and made her way out the room.

All the while Romance shouted, hands on her waist, her frame filling the door: "The problem is that you don't listen. I told you hours ago to do this, and look now what it has come to, you have to be hopping about like an animal to do something that so simple." The other girl, a bit older than the one who had hopped onto the bed, followed with two chickens, one in each hand. Romance also had words to throw her way: "And of course the younger one follows the elder. The elder who should know better, but who sits and waits for everyone to follow them around. Do this, do that, have you done this, have you done that? You can see the fields are busy, but all you are good for is just sitting and waiting for forks to be pulled out your asses."

Finally Romance turned to me in her version of tenderness: "Listen, these children don't listen. We were never like this. Those chickens needed to be slaughtered hours ago. Now we will be up until all hours of the night waiting for the food to be served. Careless stupid children!" Then she walked out and closed the door, as if to give me privacy.

I was incensed. The footsteps of the little girl who had hopped onto the bed to catch the chicken were all over the duvet where her dirty feet had stepped, and the odour of their unwashed bodies clung to the air. There was no silence in this place. It might be a wonderful place for my mother and Romance, who could relate to its hubbub of activity, and knew how to situate themselves in it, but I wanted to be alone. I wanted to be in my own home. I was so enraged, tears sprang to my eyes. I missed Christopher. How could he leave me to do this all alone?

The last time I was this lonely was just after my father had passed away. He had spent the better part of a year in a hospital connected to the machines that kept him alive. The irony was never lost on me; in many ways, this allowed us the time to decide how we would keep him alive when the inevitable occurred. I would sit next to him as he stammered through sentences which I tried to answer with either the joy he could no longer express, or the despondency characteristic of those who found themselves rendered invalids after having lived a different life. It was a time of denying true feelings for the sake of appearing strong, and it was only once we reached the end of his road that we realised how little strength we actually had. During that time and after his passing, I wrote incoherent journal entries, trying to purge my pain. Remembering this made me want to retrieve my journals from my luggage.

I struggled off the bed, stepping on the white feathers which were the remnants of the chicken fight that had abruptly ended my slumber. In the closet by the door, I found my maroon case which held all my personal items. I pulled out my journals. Sitting on the edge of the bed, I paged randomly through one, stopping to read lines here and there.

August
Getting the beach house was a good decision. We spend all our days here swimming, cooking and chatting. He looks so happy here, maybe it's what he's needed all along. I feel tired

all the time these days, though, maybe I am getting old, who knows, but I think I might be pregnant. It's a suspicion, but I think he doesn't want children from the way he talks about them. Men that old are pretty settled in their ways. I am scared he won't react the way I hope. We will see – it could be nothing.

October
So I am pregnant after all, and he says he's happy. He was silent when I told him, then he bit his inner lip and nodded continuously. We took a walk on the beach that evening and he asked me if I wanted to move our life down here and away from the city. I need to think about it. What am I doing the city anyway? What am I doing with my life in general? I am more terrified of this child than he is. At least he knows who he is: I'm just beginning to figure it out.

No date
There were two heartbeats! Two. Christopher was so proud of himself, the doctor called him a "strong old dog", and they both cackled.

I closed the journal.
I am leaving, I decided.
I found my phone under the pillow and texted the domestic worker who took care of the beach house to ask her to leave the keys in the postbox at the end of the driveway. I wanted to be in my home, just for a couple of days. Even if *things like that* were not done, I was going. I had clothes and toiletries at the beach house. All I needed was someone to take me there, and I knew exactly who I would approach – but tomorrow.
I already knew the routine of the day. Ma would roll out of bed next to me at sunrise, blow out the candle on the night stand, and shuffle, groaning, to Groot Huis to get the wash basin. Aunt Beryl would come in soon afterwards with a large bowl of whatever the young girls had prepared for breakfast. A shapely woman with hands like puffed dough, she would negotiate her way onto the bed and sit

with me as I ate. Once I had finished, Ma would come in with the basin filled with warm water, and place it on the floor. By then the chickens (now last night's dinner), had left, and the room was filled only with the double bed where we slept, the wooden wardrobe by the door, and the stack of flour sacks. Ma closed the door and secured the lock. I undressed and placed my feet one by one into the metal wash basin, standing with my arms outstretched like I was on a cross while Ma washed my body. Afterwards I would dress in fresh clothes, and Ma would comb and moisturise my big mane, then plait two rows on my head. Sometimes we chatted, but most times all this happened in silence. The only silence I would know until dusk.

Ma was busy these days with her presentation, which had diverted her attention away from being attached to me, or ensuring that someone else was. Due to the planting season fast approaching, all the human capital on the various homesteads had been directed towards the fields. The boys worked the tractors. The girls did the chores. The women strengthened the fencing around the perimeters of the homesteads. The men sent the cattle to the abattoir and ran the daily operations of the shop. Everything and everyone had a place. It had been this way for decades. The certainty made me feel out of place, and seeing it in full throttle that morning made me feel even more determined to leave.

I had devised an escape plan. I packed all the things I thought I would need in a discreetly sized black backpack and put it in a small plastic tub normally used for kneading steamed bread. Walking out of my room, I saw that the homestead was buzzing with activity, people and animals vibrating with purpose. It was easy to go undetected, even in my state, because all attention was diverted to what had to be done by the day's end. The heat was already unbearable for that time of the morning, and one thick dark cloud had condensed in the distance, telling a tale of the storm to come.

The shop was further up the mountain behind the homestead, on the last flat plain before the dramatic lift of the mountain into the heavens. There was a natural staircase that had developed over time as people went up and down, framed by golden savannah grass. The shop had been built higher up not only because of the presence of the plain, but also because the road could be accessed from there without having to descend to the bus stop at the bottom of the valley. Buses couldn't make it up the mountain, especially if they were loaded with people and goods, but the bokkies, small trucks and some truly resilient sedans could, and did, even in the rainy season when the gravel road ate at the tyres and clogged them firmly in its red clay sand.

Fixing the roads was also work for the harvest seasons, when trucks would chug up and down to the town or the villages where the white farmers lived. It was mostly the young boys who did this kind of work. They organised themselves in gangs hailing from separate villages, and delegated sections of the road, mostly determined by the parts that wound through their villages. Then they would collect big rocks and lay them in the road so that when it rained, the clay and rocks would solidify into a solid platform that could suffer the loads that passed over them in the height of summer.

Many of the boys who did this kind of work in the village were from the bottom of the valley, and were referred to as the Down There Boys. They were young men who had no jobs; some were educated, and some were not. The work they could find in the village was largely seasonal; fixing the roads or picking and packing at the surrounding commercial farms owned by white farmers.

I didn't know how many there had been in the past, but the common lament from the older generation was always that were many more these days than were needed. In the off-season, basking in their high-season earnings, they caused mayhem that often led to knife fights or other skirmishes that had to be dealt with by the chief or families of influence in the village. There was often talk of the village being unsafe, which, from the way people talked, worried the elders. They tirelessly engaged the Down There Boys about drinking less, participating more in the community, not feeling hopeless, being determined, having respect for elders and the customs of their clans – but the Down There Boys simply attended these gatherings and left drunk, laughing at the suggestions made to them.

Three Down There Boys worked in the shop as packing boys, and as I waddled towards them, they stopped loading bags of cement into the open back of a truck parked in the large garage where the trucks were kept. They were amazed at my presence in that place – I saw it from the darting looks that passed between them.

The tall lanky Down There Boy extended a greeting: "How are you, Sisi?"

I was surprised by his deference, as we looked to be the same age. "Hello, can you tell me where Avumile is?"

The dark-skinned Down There Boy who was on the back of truck balancing the cement bags pointed inside the shop: "He is inside getting the papers. We can go get him for you so you can rest."

"Don't worry yourself, I will go to him."

The tall lanky Down There Boy shook his head. "There are many people there, maybe it wouldn't be proper for you to go there." He tried not to look at my belly as he said this. Understanding that there were customs of propriety in these parts of the world, and that I was still a married woman even if widowed, I acquiesced: "OK, I will wait here. Please bring me a chair so I can rest my feet."

The dark-skinned Down There Boy jumped down from the back of the truck and went to fetch a green plastic garden chair. He helped me to sit down, his armpits already ripe, and sweat on his taut gleaming skin. He was attractive; I smiled at this thought, which made him raise his eyes and turn his head away.

"What's your name?"

"Bavelile, Sisi," he answered dropping his voice and shuffling his feet, looking down at the Thina, which was much smaller from this vantage point.

I didn't know what else to say, so I searched around and landed on the huge rocks in the corner of the garage: "I hear it's the time for fixing the roads."

"There is a lot of work at this time of the year."

"That's good, right?"

He stopped moving for a second, then his body loosened up again before he nodded: "It's work, I guess." I became aware of my perfume wafting in the air between us, and turned my mind back to what had made me make this climb with my backpack shielded in the plastic bowl.

"Do you have many deliveries today?"

"Yes, we are going—" He was interrupted by the sudden appearance of an agitated Kleintjie. "And now? What is this?" he asked me, his permanently furrowed brows expressing genuine annoyance this time.

"Do you know how much trouble I will be in if Tat'Gerrie hears you were up here?"

I was trying to stand up from the plastic chair. The tall lanky Down There Boy was leaning against the truck with his hands in his pockets, revelling in the morning spectacular. Bavelile was standing to the side, unsure if he should assist me. I placed the backpack on the ground and tried to slide out of the chair.

Kleintjie continued, "Honestly, everyone has been treating you like an egg since you got here, but clearly you have more strength than we know because the woman is now travelling far and wide, making a spectacle of herself."

"Help me out of this chair," I pleaded, struggling to lift myself.

"For what? What are you doing here?" Kleintjie asked.

Bavelile tried to speak up: "Avumile, let's just help her so we can continue..." His words tapered off as Kleintjie shot him daggers with his eyes. "So we can all participate in this mess? What if she gives birth right here, will you be so helpful then? And also, who asked you?"

"What mess are you talking about?" I was angry. "Get me out of this chair!" I looked at Bavelile straight in the eye: "Both of you."

Kleintjie and Bavelile lifted me to my feet. "Please can you excuse us?" I said to the tall lanky Down There Boy and Bavelile. They looked at Kleintjie, then sauntered off into the distance.

"You will take me to my house, right now. I will stay there for three days, and on the fourth day, I need you to come and get me."

"I am not doing that."

"You will do it."

"And where will I you say you are?"

"You will be gone as well. You have loads of shipping to do, right? All along the coast, it's the season, right? You are going to collect some steel because the shop is running low, and when you come back you can tell them where I am."

"Do you know who Aunt Khanya is, and have you ever seen her angry? I am going to lose my job!"

"What job? You are a January, this is your inheritance. Those two boys over there are at work, not you."

"Is that how things work in your life? It must be nice to be a princess."

"Listen here, Kleintjie, you don't know anything about *my* life."

"No, and you just don't know anything about life in general! Can you not see how you look, why would you want to do that?"

Tears began to flow down my face in sheets. Kleintjie turned to see if anybody else was watching. "You can stop crying now, because I don't care about tears. What you are asking is wrong."

I continued to cry.

"When you stop crying, I will take you back down the mountain." He said this tersely, but the heaving of his chest gave him away. I continued to cry, but now it was calculated. He repeated his sentiments about his indifference, and I went on weeping, biding my time.

"Okay, stop," he said eventually. "I will take you."

I continued to whimper softly.

"But you must stop crying."

"I just need a couple of days and I will be back again."

"Okay, okay, just stop crying. Those two will finish loading the truck, then we will leave. They will come with us, I will leave them in East London to deal with some other business so they won't know where your house is. But I need the name of a doctor, any doctor, in case something goes wrong. Death always has a tail, and I won't be blamed for anything that should happen to you or your children."

"Nothing is going to happen."

"You don't know that!" he said angrily, "you don't know that." He stormed off and called the Down There Boys to finish loading the truck. An hour later, the small van was chugging along on the gravel towards town, with Kleintjie in nervous silence, driving me towards our beach home.

It took us three hours to get there via East London. At last, we were on the meandering road that always made Christopher rage with its countless speed bumps. I rested my head against the window, neither listening to the music nor Kleintjie's stories about the one time he had travelled to the big city with his mother when she had been alive. I was trying to decide whether he was a person who would have irritated Christopher. I knew when Christopher sighed loudly and tapped his left foot that he was unimpressed with whatever he was being forced to endure. He was too polite ever to be overtly rude, but when he was irritated, his disposition offended people so much so that perhaps it would have been better if he had said what was on his mind. This was an argument we often had.

As Kleintjie continued driving, he peered at me intermittently. In the end, I decided that he would not have irritated Christopher. He was a teenage boy with misguided ambition. He loved the family, and wanted to be respected. He loathed the conditions in which his peers existed, but he didn't know how best to address them.

After a period of silence, Kleintije told me about his father, Ou Takkies. "I don't long for him, but I hoped that maybe somebody would say you remind us of him in this way or that." He kept darting his head my way. My head was against the glass, my eyes glazed. I could feel the wind from the ocean pushing against the small van.

We approached the house, and as we drove down the gravel driveway, I could feel my heart beating in my throat. The house was a big dark shadow blocking the ocean, framed by shrubs that looked like creatures of the night. The last time I was here, Christopher had greeted me from the open front door as the taxi drove away. He was leaning against the door post with a cup of coffee as he patted the excited dog with his free hand, like in an advert. He had kissed me on the cheek when I alighted from the car. We had sat outside on the patio drinking wine until late, and had taken a walk on the beach, after which we returned home to make love and spend the rest of the night sharing our thoughts in whispers. It had been a long night. A beautiful night.

Kleintjie helped me carry my bags to the door. I thanked him, and he said: "I'm sorry about today."

"You don't have to be sorry."

"I do. A January by the sea is a powerful thing. No matter how I feel, if you have been called here, I have no right to question that."

I nodded and he drove away.

The truth: I had no idea why I had come. Every part of Christopher was here, but not in the way I had hoped. Christopher being dead now filled me with terror because I couldn't verify if he had got to the other side all right, or if he was in the eternal darkness of death, or if he had bargained his way into a heaven I wouldn't make it into. Would he remember me, or was that a selfish question? Where was he now, precisely? All that was here now was in the past. Christopher always loved to sneak up behind me, but now he was crawling under my skin, and the hairs on my neck were shooting up and my heart was beating fast. I turned the key in the door and switched on the light, wheeling in my luggage and closing the door behind me.

I heard all the noises in the house. The buzzing of the fridge. The dripping of water in the sink. The squeaking of the closet door that was ajar in the next room. The silence had its own life, when the waves weren't crashing on the shore.

In the months since Christopher had died, I had managed to create a strong narrative about my healing. I kept journals, and when I wrote everything down I believed I was moving forward, and that computing the despair on a page would make it lighter to bear. I met friends over coffee and watched them try to comfort me and empathise, and I made them believe they were doing a good job. The proverbial and almost inevitable wrestle with God ran parallel with all these other efforts to heal.

The wind started to blow more strongly and the curtains, where the window was slightly open, swelled. I slid onto the leather couch, feeling the tiredness of my bones. I blinked heavily as sleep crept in – or was it death disguised? I turned on my side and drifted into oblivion.

Later that evening, I awoke with a start. My heart was racing as I scanned the room, trying to recollect where I was. I wasn't sure how many hours I had slept, but it wasn't a restful sleep, it was one of necessity. To escape. The waves were thundering. The wind whistled through the trees as their leaves smacked against the window. I searched the drawers for a candle. Always a candle must burn when you mourn, Romance had said. Eventually, I found the only candle in the house in the lounge next to the ashy stub of burned lavender incense. The scent was mild but comforting.

I traced the words on the page of my journal with my finger. That was the reason I insisted Kleintjie bring me here. The hole left by Christopher could only be closed by him. I longed to laugh, not to test if I was still capable of such force of emotion, but because it was an honest and impulsive reaction to the ridiculous. I had to quiet my longings before my children arrived so they did not find a shell in the body of a mother. I feared that I might gift them, from the beginning, disadvantage from within – when the pressures from without were already numerous. Mostly, I longed to accept what could not now be changed: the fact of Christopher's death.

I should have known that death likes to leave no prisoners. As I sat on the couch in the lounge, I wondered at my conviction that this road to closure would be different.

I closed the journal and slept again on the couch.

That was three days ago.

Right now, I'm by the ocean. It is early morning. I am alone. I have been up all night, writing. The sun will be rising soon but for now, my surrounds are tinted with the navy of dawn. The surf rolls up the beach in a pattern I have been watching for what feels like hours. My eyes are raw and dry, and I wipe away the remaining tears from my cheeks as I walk into the rolling waves. Nobody is around. I turn and look at the houses built on the rock and sand surrounding the beach. Not a single light is on. The water is cold as I step into it. The wind blows lightly on my face as my feet sink deeper into the sand. With each crash of the waves on the beach, the water rises up my body. First my ankles, then my knees, now I am waist deep and losing my balance slightly. The white dress I am wearing feels heavy on me, and still the crashing of the waves, and now my body is floating. In the darkness.

All alone.

One of the last times I was here, it was New Year's Day. Christopher and I had been drinking all night on the patio of our house, this house, which is right on the beach. He loved to burn lavender incense when we drank, to add to the ambiance, but that night we were hardly fit to take in the sights and smells of our surrounds. The drunken messes we were, we stupidly devised an illogical plan to swim. I gathered dry towels from the bathroom, and he grabbed another bottle of white wine, which we had convinced each other did not make you as drunk as red wine. We walked arm in arm to the beach along a long pathway built from our patio down on to the fine white sand. It was still quiet; early morning, and most people would only just be turning in after the various parties they had attended.

Christopher ran into the water as soon as we reached the beach. I saw the water and panicked. "Come back, baby!" I had screamed. He was laughing. He was so happy it relieved my anguish. He waded into the water until it reached his waist, then turned to beckon to me. I hesitated. "Come, aren't you always saying you are a mermaid?" Just as he said that, a strong wave smacked his back and he disappeared into the dark waters in a long moment that gripped my heart with such a terrible fear I dropped the wine bottle on the sand and ran into the cold water just as he re-emerged. When he saw me splashing into the water, he laughed in a deranged sort of way, and told me that apparently only his death could make me adventurous. It was funny then.

Now I open my eyes in the water, my chest tight as the waves knock me about, and some water enters my eyes, stinging and forcing me to close them. *There you are, Christopher. Next to me, in our bed. It is early morning. You are reading. No, you are sleeping. No, you are writing. No, you are laughing. No, you are sulking. No, you are making love to me. No, you are whistling.* My eyes open.

I am deep in the water now. It is not a fact I have verified, just a feeling I have. I know if I try to touch the bottom now, it would be like dancing in mid-air. I am afraid but determined. My chest is still tight and my neck is strained. I close my eyes again and a flurry of thoughts rushes into my mind.

I see all of their faces. From the past and present. Romance with her untamed mischief, wild with laughter, cheated of a life and honoured for her ability to endure hardships. Christopher, the complicated. The love of my life, his ice-blue eyes, lifeless in the morgue. My mother, my oldest adversary. My father, my man for all seasons, cut down to size by sadness and bodily limitations, he could not overcome, leaving us with nothing left to pass down to our heirs but his abounding love.

My breathing becomes easier, but my eyes remain closed. I see them all floating next to me, and I can't hold onto them. They were all lent to me for my gain, and now they have left me to do what I must with the task I have been given. I see Christopher again beckoning for me to come into the water, to come to him. I stretch out my arms.

Friday

Mama grew to love the revolution.

It was the chaos that drew her in. The upturned tables and the burning buildings and women's screams muffled by the anger of shouting men. Their sweating skin, black, from the plumes of the smoke and from the dark blood that flowed through them. They coloured her mind with the glory of freedom. She held it like a lover and wrapped her firm thighs around the waist of its pulsating excitement. She enjoyed that she did not know what else was next. She had always loved the heat of a fire.

You wouldn't know it if you saw her, so meek and mild. Quiet in every corner of rooms she entered, but she was the kind whose pens scratched prophetic words to life. She worked tirelessly at perfecting the art of incitement. She only needed a thirsty mind to soak in her words, or a gifted orator whose tongue was able to mould her prophecies into life.

The pressure it takes to feed unborn generations she placed on her own shoulders. Under it all, she was a girl who was born into a freedom that wasn't documented because it had birthed itself in the lacunae created by prejudice. The tighter the grip was pressed on her people, the more things slipped through the cracks, the more she perfected her art until, being one with her pen, she gave birth to her baby revolution.

For hours she stared at her daughter in the midnight hours, praying fervently for her. She breathed into her the wildness of the wind and the cunning of birds that could trick invisible forces in order to soar.

Nontsikelelo "Nonti" Fani (née January)

"Almighty God, our heavenly Father, in penitence we confess that we have sinned against you through our own fault, in thought, word and deed, and in what we have left undone..."

...in what we have left undone...

In a movie, scenes happen much faster than in life. Seeing that pink mess, I longed for the movie version. It was all over the table, on the bed, on their hands and between my legs. In bed last night I could hear her talking to me in the sweet shrill voice of a child. A faceless beauty, nonchalant head in the clouds, lost as to which question she was going to ask me next.

This child was going to be mine, not her father's. I could feel it. She was conceived on a Saturday when I counted back; my favourite day. A day when you could be anything you wanted because you had nobody to report to. An adventure, she felt like an adventure. I wanted to show her the world, and so each day I took a different route home and narrated the way to her.

Other times I told her about where we grew up, her aunt Romance and I. Romance was then known as Nobantu. I have never really bothered to find out where this crass alias had its genesis. I just accept her as my sister, my elder sister. She led the way and suffered for us both, so I let her be Romance.

High up, on one of the many bends of the Thina River, you will find our grandfather's homestead. There is no other way to find where I grew up on a map. You would have to study the bends in the river and follow them until at some point you would look up and see four mud houses, all different colours, dotted along the sedimentary lines of the mountain. They are distinct for their pristine condition, with an organised kraal and well-maintained fence along the perimeter of the homestead. Even if you got lost in trying to find the correct bend in the river, you would be directed there to go sit and catch your breath to escape from the brutal beating of the sun – many strangers were found under the cover of the acacia trees that ran along the length of the homestead edge. And so you would climb the steps developed over time up the steepest part of the mountain until you arrived at Katjie January's homestead.

My grandfather was a coloured man whose family was originally thought to have hailed from a town named Makhanda, but he left that border town on missions that are until this day not quite determinable – save for what was later to become an urban legend.

The story goes that the resident drunks at the Koop Shop, the village tavern, had seen him strolling along the gravel road with a small parcel tucked underneath his arm. He was a slight man of average height, thick curly hair and brows so defined they were comical – curved, thick and joined in the middle. He had easy manners and was soft-spoken. His eyes were the amber colour of the water that crabs loved to hide in when girls surprised them at the pools as they collected water for the cooking in the homesteads. In those days, once a boy – which is to say, an adolescent male – had undergone the initiation ceremony, he was free to go off and become a man, which included getting a wife and acquiring his own assets.

My grandfather must have been sixteen when he arrived in the village; back then, this was considered the average age of a young adult man. He had made acquaintance with the drunks at the Koop Shop by asking for directions to the chief's homestead, after which he took leave of the men and proceeded in the direction they had pointed him in. The men were naturally amazed by this interaction, and found themselves prickling to find out what the meaning of the stranger's arrival could be.

By sundown, the villagers had descended upon the chief's homestead and looked with wonder at the stranger who sat composed outside the homestead. It was long into the night before the stranger was called in to place his request before the chief, who heard him out, but asked that he return in the morning. The chief had for his own reasons instructed that the stranger be given board for the night, and told to remain there until he was called to meet the council the following morning. This was wisdom on his part because he sent envoys out into the night, enquiring at the surrounding villages about the stranger. To have found this village, the stranger would have had to pass several other villages, and to have travelled for days to find himself in so remote a place.

The envoys came back with varying accounts of the stranger. He had first been seen two days ago in town, roughly some hundred kilometres from the village. He had been alone, and had gone around asking from where the buses that went to the village departed. In those days the buses only ran twice a week, on a Monday and a Thursday, for reasons nobody knew or cared to find out about. The stranger had arrived on Friday morning and was told by Nyawo, who had been working as the station manager since Jesus's birthday, that he had no option other than to hike or walk in the hope of appealing to somebody's mercy in order to reach the village. Nyawo had no reason to suspect the stranger of malice, since, as it was reported to the chief, the stranger knew who he was looking for, and in which direction he was headed. The designated envoy who interviewed Nyawo indicated that the stranger was seeking Ma Miya's daughter or her people because she was his great-aunt, whom he had never met on account of their family having moved to Katkop and then to Makhanda. Nyawo said that the stranger spoke with such ease and openness about his quest that instead of suspicion, he felt pity for the stranger, lost to his people, having judged him after that conversation to be an orphan. The envoy who interviewed Nyawo thus concluded that the stranger was an orphan of Ma Miya's people, who had probably come on hard times and was returning home. The council had been gripped, after this account, by a wave of sympathy for the stranger.

Then the second envoy spoke. He had interviewed two people: the driver who had given the stranger a lift, and a local coloured man Kevin, who had allowed him to spend the night in his home. Tyiwa, the local philanderer, said he had come upon the stranger trekking along the road towards the Pondo villages. Tyiwa, alarmed by the stranger's confidence in walking so casually through villages renowned for violent murders and robberies, stopped and asked where he was going. He could tell the stranger was of a different clan, although he had not pegged him as a coloured man. Hee spoke pitch-perfect Xhosa and the Hlubi dialect so well Tyiwa immediately gave the stranger his trust. Tyiwa said the stranger told him that he had once lived in these parts of the world, but had been away for so long that when he made the decision to walk, he based it upon his knowledge of the area as he had known it then. Tyiwa had been uncertain of the stranger's age; he appeared to be extremely young, but he gave accounts of events that had occurred in these parts of the world long before he could have been born. The stranger knew the characters by name, and whose clan they belonged to, and to whom they were now married. Tyiwa had provided the stranger with minor details where the stranger had incorrect or slightly outdated information. The second envoy asked why he had not suspected the stranger of being a spy, to which Tyiwa had replied that there was nothing to report about these parts of the world that the women didn't know and had already reported. The council accepted this account, and the second envoy continued his report on how the stranger had ended up spending the night at Kevin's home.

Kevin's family owned the wholesale enterprises in town, but his grandfather had settled away from town to enjoy the tranquillity of rural life. It was here that Kevin had grown up and now lived with his own family. His parents frequented the royal homestead due to their contributions to the community, so his testimony was weighted more heavily than all the others that were to be heard in the council that morning.

By Kevin's account, the stranger had been disappointed when he had parted from Tyiwa and discovered that he was not where he had intended to end up. Tyiwa had decided for himself that the stranger was mistaken about his ancestry and his destination, and that he had actually been looking for Kevin. The fact that both he and the stranger were coloured men no doubt informed Tyiwa's thinking. According to the envoy, Kevin had lamented to the stranger that he had been a fool to trust a man named Salt to get him anywhere. Tyiwa, on Fridays, was preoccupied with the many women he entertained in different villages. His mind had only been on that, and the stranger had wanted to go too far out for his liking; so even though he had begun the mission as a good deed, his carnal needs were far more pressing. So he dumped the stranger with Kevin, knowing that Kevin could instruct one of his employees to deliver the stranger to the village.

The second envoy said that Kevin had judged the stranger to be of no threat. He had reservations about his past, which is why he suggested that the stranger find the chief. According to Kevin, the stranger had wads of money and could not clearly spell out its source. The stranger might be a rich young man who had disobeyed a father's command, and now found himself a man without means. Equally, he could be a thief who had waylaid a stranger in the night and shaken him down for his last cent, and that was how he had come into the small fortune tucked underneath his arm. The latter thought was wholly ruled out on account of the young man's size and tender hands. Kevin even went as far as to insinuate that the stranger was so soft that perhaps he had not even known a woman yet.

The third envoy had been sent further afield, in the direction from where the stranger had come – Makhanda. From there, the envoy had ascertained that the stranger had boarded the bus to East London, thereafter making his way up north with the old buses that were driven by Ta'Grey. The driver had nothing of significance to note about the stranger save to mention that he had been quiet throughout the three-hour drive, and had spent the sojourn with his eyes fixed on the changing scenery outside, speaking to no one and doing well at not attracting attention to himself.

The council was swayed by these testimonies to suggest whipping the stranger until he confessed his true intentions for having come to this village. One of the elders suggested that he be put to the fighting fields to test if he was a skilled fighter – which might support the theory of his being a thief. The chief listened to all the suggestions being brought forward as the crowd swelled outside, wanting to see the matter settled. The stranger's request upon arrival – asking for land to build a homestead – was not what raised suspicion, but coupled with his race, it turned him into an enigma for the women and a threat to the men. Each turned to the other, asking questions of this hazel-eyed stranger who sat that morning outside the chief's residence as his fate was being decided.

The chief decided, after long deliberations that lasted until well after the day had turned, that the stranger would firstly engage in a stick fight with the village's best contender. Thereafter he would be interrogated by the advisors to the royal home about himself and his reasons for coming to the village. Finally, he would be given an audience with the chief to present his case. This way there would be clarity on all fronts.

The stranger was informed of the decision, and so it was executed the next day. He was thrashed by Nyathi in the stick duel, but it was remarked by all present that he was not as soft as had first been suggested. The duel, which had been expected to double up as a exercise for extracting information, lasted most of the morning. Nyathi was a big boy, like the bovine he was named after, and with thick boulders for arms attached to a shield of a chest, he escaped most duels without ever being struck. The stranger's slight build made him swift on his feet, and it was hard for Nyathi to counter his moves; for some time during the contest, the crowd was split on which contender would take the win. If the stranger had handled the simple technicalities of swinging the stick weapons more expertly, he would have been the victor. Once Nyathi had been declared the winner, the young girls bought out enamel jugs of water for the fighters to drink and to wash the sweat and blood off their backs, and plates of food for them to enjoy. Nobody spoke to the stranger; most were unsure what language he spoke, although the rumours were that he was fluent in three languages as well as the Hlubi dialect of the area.

The stranger was then moved to the Royal House where he faced the arduous task of providing the advisors to the chief with a clear and coherent story of his lineage; his purpose in having sought out the chief; and on what business he had come to the village. Nobody had access to this meeting save for the three advisors who hailed from the families which had advised the Royal House for centuries. The accounts of this interrogation are imprecise and scattered. Some said the stranger was tortured again in strategic parts of his body by the chief's bodyguards, which explained why when he finally appeared in front of the council, he looked as if he had just come from the duel with Nyathi. Others said that the three advisors treated him like a gentleman, but made it clear that they sought the truth from him and evidence to corroborate such truths; he was warned that if he was found to be a liar, he would face far graver beatings than Nyathi could ever mete out. After which, it was said that the stranger complied. The girls who sent food to the royal houses, and who were often used as spies by the prying women of the village, reported that the stranger had sat sharing jokes with the advisors as they all enjoyed the meal placed at their feet. They said that the stranger had an air of dignity about him. The growing perception was that he would be well received by the chief, which he was.

The following day, people were requested to gather at the Royal House. An announcement was made that communicated the following:

> *Theodore January was born to the house of Ma Miya, who had the misfortune of birthing twin boys. As per custom, the younger boy had to be smothered to prevent there later being a question over the inheritance of the homestead. But*

as the softness and cunning of women goes, the younger boy was smuggled away, first to Alice, then later to the coloured area in Makhanda, where he was raised by the midwife, Constance January, as his custodian. This was how he knew to find this place. The fair skin of the family made it easy for them to integrate with the coloured communities of that area; and as result, for two generations the Miya boy had been raised away from this place, although his people – the midwife so to say – had knowledge of his roots. For whatever reason, those that came before him had grown content with not being connected to the place of their birth but he, Theodore, was not.

After this preamble, the chief spoke directly to those listening: "I cannot hold a man back from returning to the place of his birth, especially when those who can tell the truth of the night when Theodore's grandfather was whisked away are still alive. Ma Miya knows her treachery, but that line died with the eldest twin, who sired only girls who have since left home and are now scattered in their own homes in various villages from here to Mthatha. So we find ourselves looking at Ma Miya, an ageing demented woman, who has no family save for this stranger. He has actually come to ease the burden that would otherwise fall on Ma Miya's neighbours in taking care of his kin. She has a grandchild who has come to remind her of her betraying the customs of our elders, but in this instance, she has won a prize. Now when we were worrying about who would bury the old lady who has grown violent with time due to her wounded mind, we have been given a young man who can begin to build up the house and the name of Miya again. Remember Tat'Miya, who with his proud graceful nature had nothing but wise counsel for all those he encountered. He had no hand in the deception of his wife, and for his sins, died without ever knowing that he had a son who could bear him sons. And so the mother's secret has been discovered. This is a moment to rejoice, for though the council usually considers matters of fallen perimeter walls, fruit trees beaten *by the weather and eaten up by festering worms, or livestock ruining neighbours' harvests, now we decide on Theodore's fate. We have agreed to allow him to build up the home of his grand-uncle who, had he known he had such a nephew, would have blessed him with every honour. The only thing the stranger asks is to be able to keep his surname so that those who might seek him may not find it such a difficult task. It has been ruled this is a fair request given what he, Theodore, endured during his interrogation; and so the stranger will live amongst us as a January, but as a known descendant of Miya.*

This news was well received for the most part. For the women, it was a time to swoon, as it had been discovered that the stranger had undergone circumcision according to Hlubi customary law, and was allowed to wed a woman in the village. Theodore had, with the announcement, become the most eligible bachelor in all the village.

The council dissolved the meeting, and the villagers headed back to their homes to attend to the day's work, but the topic of Theodore January remained a favoured way of passing the time. Some feared that Theodore was a seasoned thief who had heard that there was such a woman as Ma'Miya and had somehow solicited her secrets in order to execute this plan. Many believed that the chief had erred in this decision without accounting for how the stranger had come into the thick wad of money he was believed to have; but many were equally relieved that Ma'Miya had been taken off their hands. The woman's dementia had reached levels where her behaviour could not be predicted. She could be sullen and childlike in her tantrums when complaining about the portions of the food she was served, or out in the garden naked tending to the harvest. Her situation had become a bit of an embarrassment, and with people burdened by their own responsibilities, the issue of her burial had plagued her neighbours, as the chief would likely charge that affair to them.

From Theodore, eleven children were born, all of whom claimed their dual ancestry in various ways. Some remained January, others Miya; others became January-Miya or Miya-January, all endorsed by Theodore, who in time moved some of his relatives from Makhanda to live in the village. The Januarys were known for their fierce loyalty, much like the grandfather who had rebuilt a fallen house after hearing the tale of his true ancestry from an ailing midwife, refusing to allow his family to fall apart and for its name to disappear. The family was known for banding together against common enemies as much as they were for their fair skin and the comical eyebrows framing their light eyes. Theodore's genes carried right through until Romance and I were born. Romance came out as black as the night, like our mother: tall and fierce. I was born with normal brown eyes, but with skin fair like our father's and wild curly hair that flew in all directions even after the hottest comb had run through it.

I told the baby growing inside me all of these stories in the seven weeks I carried her until I was watching the news one Sunday morning, and realised I had not felt ill all week. It was a quick thought, and I held my belly to see if I could feel her, but I could not make a fair assessment. Mxolisi said the baby was a boy, but I knew she wasn't.

He already had his boy in Vuyolwethu. In their world together, I was a placeholder who held the title Mother. Having a daughter, my first daughter, had not been how I had imagined it. She was my carbon copy with the exception of the light cat eyes of a great-grandfather who, when she was born, held her up with his failing strength and gifted her the name Beatrice – the bringer of joy, his last joy on this earth before he died of old age that very year.

Vuyolwethu displayed the characteristic rebellion of January women since her birth. She didn't care for authority at school, but as she grew older, her rebellion became the subtle, more dangerous kind. She held back her true feelings in a calculated manner. I always knew who she was though; she came from my line of women and she could not scare me nor even please me easily. In our world, love was conveyed by gifting strength. If you could stand in the wind and not bend to it like a reed in the savannah, then you were the jewel of people's eyes.

That was how our mother had loved us. She had not rested on her abundant beauty, which she treated as trite. She could stop a man dead in his tracks with her wild hair shooting from her head like an unruly bush and her dark rich skin, but she lacked the timid nature of a lady, being instead a towering woman with the broad shoulders, full breasts and thighs typical of most of the women January-Miya men married. In our home, it was defeating the odds that was deemed beautiful. Compliments were showered on the lone star who managed to shine in unenviable circumstances – like Romance. My father's preference for Romance was a recognition of her untamed force, released into the world to fearlessly crash into all she encountered. Vuyolwethu, however, was born to a man who had the tenderness of doves; and because of this, she could not be corrected when her faults warranted reprimand. Instead, she grew to be a child who was a law unto herself – with me, her mother, her strongest adversary.

I had not even known I was pregnant with Vuyolwethu until my mother walked into my bedroom as I was dressing and congratulated me on my pregnancy, after which we learned that I had been with child for close to three months. My love for her had been delayed, but I had known from the beginning in the case of her sister. From the oily skin, heavy painful breasts, to the vomiting in the morning when she was still growing inside me, she had been a celebration from the moment of conception.

Then the pink mess. I asked to see it. The doctor said it would be a standard procedure. Standard, like every other thing. It had a metric measurement. Standard, uniform. I hate it when people use that ridiculous term, "standard procedure". The doctor had said these words after delivering the news of the death of my unformed baby. The procedure was scheduled for the following week, transforming my body, once an incubator, into a grave.

Mxolisi sat there, listening to the news of our baby's death, looking pathetic. A surge of hatred welled up inside me. He had his child, our child, who preferred him to me and my stern love; but at that moment, I also thought of her disappointment. She had been as invested in this project as I was, excited to have a sister to protect and guide. One whom she could style, or teach the quiet art of seducing the men in our lives to fight for us tooth and nail. To teach her the code of fierce loyalty instilled in us by Theodore January ever since that fateful day of his arrival in the village on the bend of the Thina River.

Just as Romance had taught me, even after her incident. Thinking of Romance actually made it easier for me to look at that pink mess after they scraped the sac and all the other remnants of my baby out my womb. I didn't find her face in that mess, and I found myself asking the doctors if they were going to flush her down the drain. The doctor was a puffy-faced lady who had no issues with being direct. She replied that the hospital had its own procedures to maintain the dignity of its patients, then told me to lie back so the nurse could administer an injection. I had no choice but to comply.

In the week I had to wait for my "standard procedure", I remember watching Vuyolwethu do her homework one afternoon. She knew by then that Project Sister had failed, but with the resilience of children, she had recovered. When her father and I had told her the news, she had said, "It's okay, you will have another one" and flashed me a toothless grin that had shattered me, but allowed for a rare embrace, the soft bush on her head tied in a messy ponytail brushing so sweetly against my cheek as my tears dripped into her hair. As I watched her write beautifully curved letters on a page, I regarded myself as I might have been. Free to express myself without care, the quality her father protected most valiantly, and which I did my best to repress. For me, it was too dangerous to be without guards.

Vuyolwethu is beautiful because she reminds me so much of Groot Pa Katjie, as we called Theodore January in the family. She has a path charted in her head about who she is to become, and that vision will not be obstructed by anything, which is what makes her a being to be feared. Her determination to be what she wants has no room for permutation or variance, and to me, her mother, the dangers of such thinking are obvious. Was I not the one who had failed Project Sister due to my inability to create more than one child in a family where women birthed children in droves? Did I not just stand there watching Romance suffer, then run away and save myself? Did I not spend all these years away from the sister who needed me? Was I not sent away for this weakness? Did I not marry Mxolisi even after witnessing what he was capable of? I could not allow my only child to fail to understand that beauty and tragedy share destinies like the sides of a coin.

When she finished her task, she snapped her head up, her thick comical brows furrowed, and asked, "What's wrong, Mommy?" I could have replied with the tenderness of a loving mother: "Nothing, my baby, Mommy is just a bit sad about your sister," at which I am sure she would have understood and would have comforted me as best she could. Instead my eyes became dark balls of malice and I snapped: "Did you do all the tasks in the exercise?" She nodded as she slid the open exercise book across the table for me to check. It had to be done, I said as I convinced myself of the necessity of my shortness. Inside me, the dead was leaving my body, and I could not allow space for more weakness.

In the end, it just had to be, as it had been with my mother.

When my father died and the family business fell on her shoulders, she became a parent we could depend upon only for necessities, nothing more. She traded her chalkboard and classrooms for warehouses in Kokstad, where she had to bargain for goods at wholesale prices – and who knows what she had to endure then. The Miya-January magic could only go so far, and men have always had the talent of placing themselves in positions of advantage. She never confided in us about these struggles, but as I grew to be a woman, I realised why the rope of her love was so short.

Romance took over, raising me with no guidance on how to do so. I just knew she would crush me if I wasn't home by a specific time, or was found in a position that compromised the teachings we had received from our deceased father. She spent her life speaking to me in commands, and I never once questioned her wisdom. This is what must have informed Mxolisi's decision to have Romance move in with us after he was unable to shake me out of my melancholic haze.

The last time I had seen her she had been Nobantu January. That was on the day we had unveiled our mother's tombstone. That day had been filled with joy as all the Januarys, Miyas, Miya-Januarys and January-Miyas descended upon Groot Huis in the village. Being one of the eldest girls in the family, Nobantu had led the proceedings, dishing out commands about how money for the event would be spent, and who was responsible for which task. The entire village, though despised by our family, had been invited. In later years, the Royal House no longer had the prominence that it had had when Groot Pa Katjie had first arrived, but an invitation had been extended through one of the royal advisors. It was a massive affair that saw three cows fall to the slaughter, and neither snout nor tail remained when it was concluded. That had been seven years ago, when Vuyolwethu was three years old.

Only Groot Pa Katjie and some cousins had come up to Gauteng when Vuyolwethu was born. Groot Pa Katjie was in the twilight of his life at that point, living just to spoil his grandchildren and impart wisdom to stray members of the family. Nobantu was rumoured to be living in Cape Town working at a shirt factory, which didn't surprise me because Groot Pa Katjie's wife Mam'Bhele, our grandmother, had been an excellent seamstress. Under her tutelage, Romance and some of the older cousins had been taught how to work the Singer that sat in the big hut with the linoleum tiles.

Mxolisi had not told me he had invited Romance to move in with us. I remember her arrival. She barged into my bedroom early one morning with a small plastic bag of groceries, as I lay curled like a baby in the stunned daze that seemed to frighten my husband and daughter. She looked the same, if slightly weathered. "Why are you still asleep after midday?" she asked, thumping the plastic bag down on the nightstand and moving swiftly across the room to open the curtains and windows. She pulled the covers off the bed, and with total disregard for my frailty, placed me on the floor.

I kicked the calf of her left leg and she spun around: "Go take a bath."

"I am not your child, I know where both our parents are buried."

"And I suppose you want to join them? Go take a bath." She continued to make the bed in quick, expert fashion as I crawled into the bathroom and petulantly shut the door.

I was sent away to boarding school when I was ten years old. I didn't want to go; life in the village was idyllic. I moved between the homesteads of all the January-Miyas that surrounded the shop. When Tata was still alive, he would allow me to sit on his lap as he reversed the tractors back into the yard after they were loaned out to various families. After this we would ascend the mountain to our homestead, where our mother would be sitting attending to her school work as we ate dinner. On weekends, he took us further up the river where the strength of its flow was more predictable, and taught us how to skip rocks. Afterwards we would lie on the grass and create creatures and stories out of the slow-moving cumulus clouds that were a constant feature of afternoons in the village, even if they did not produce any rain.

Tata loved to sing. He taught us all the hymns he had learned at the missionary schools in the village before the government had closed them down and he was forced to go far away to study to get a good education. He told us that Anglican hymns were perfection, they didn't need to be tainted by modern remixes, and that the *Agnes Dei* melody was infected by the spirit of God. His chosen hymn was "Praise to the Lord the Almighty". He explained the perfection of the cascading melody, and how when you sang it, the most important thing was how you timed your breathing in order to manage all the notes on key.

When we were allowed to take our first communion at church, I was fast-tracked into catechism class. Most children did theirs at twelve, but I did mine when I was ten. Tata took our first communion with us, impressing upon us the solemnity of the moment and the importance we had to place on the altar when approaching it.

He passed on, through poisoning some said, several weeks after my tenth birthday, an affair he made a fuss over. A whole decade he had said as he threw me up into the air, my face reflecting his, both of us the only small, fair-skinned people in our home. Kleintjie or Teddy, as he was called by his siblings, invited the whole January-Miya clan to my party, which lasted the whole night. We didn't cry at his funeral. Crying is not a common January trait; we endure and we survive, and that was what characterised the following decade.

In the year of my father's death, I was sent away for my weakness. Ou Takkies was to drive me to the train station in Tsolo, a long and silent trip. Romance's broken ankle was still in a cast, and she didn't see me off, but our grandmother Mam'Bhele watched over the loading of my goods, barking instructions to the young cousins who were almost jogging to keep up with her instructions. She had a violent temper with a sharp tongue, and we all feared her except for Tata. My mother stood with balled fists to her waist, barely saying anything to me until all my luggage had been packed into Ou Takkies's van.

Then she knelt in front of me and said: "We are not throwing you away, it just has to be done." She then stood up and disappeared into the hut where Romance was sleeping. Mam'Bhele ushered me into the van and closed the door. From her skirt pocket, she pulled out a sweet and smiled at me. She stood tall even in her old age, her skin mostly still tight except on her neck. "We are Januarys; that means everything, child." I nodded at what I believed then to have been deep wisdom about why I was being sent away.

The younger January cousins, my gang, all ran after the van as it kicked up dust and inched its way from the Thina River that had filled its banks that year. I waved at them until I could no longer see them. The van bounced up and down the gravel road as we made our way to town.

"The ocean, baby girl," Ou Takkies said in his thick Cape accent. Ou Takkies's father, Tat'Zola, was Tata's older brother, number three of the eleven birthed by Mam'Bhele. Ou Takkies was Tat'Zola's first illegitimate son, one of apparent thousands that followed over the years.

"I grew up there until I was exactly your age, then my Ma told me she had found Zola."

He called his father by his name at Tat'Zola's insistence – he said it made him more relatable. "But let me tell you, there is nothing more beautiful than the sea. Respect it, but it is a thing of wonder. You are a lucky angel."

"Will you come visit?"

"Will you cook me fish?"

"I can't cook."

"Then I am not coming."

"Okay, I will learn," I said, chuckling.

"Okay, then I will come." He sang an incoherent song for a few seconds, then he let out a low whistle. "A January by the sea, here comes a thing," he said in Afrikaans to nobody in particular, and smiled to himself. We fell into a comfortable silence for the rest of the journey.

The furthest from home I had ever gone until that day was a small town named Maclear. Tata had wanted to buy wholesale bags of cement, and Romance and I had begged to tag along. We had spent the whole time singing along to the music on the radio, as he pointed out places he had visited, or interesting things he knew about the people who inhabited certain villages.

Maclear was a neat orderly small town but when we came into it Tata appeared visibly worried, so we fell silent. We turned into a small gravel road and he lowered the volume of the music. As we approached a square building made of face brick, we saw a long line of black men waiting outside, chatting quietly. Tata parked and told us to stay in the car. Instead of joining the long line, Tata stood in front of the steps and started his own line. Two white men walked past him, and after a couple of minutes emerged from the building carrying bags of goods. And then for long minutes, nothing happened until another car pulled into the lot and another white man alighted. He walked up to my father and greeted him. They exchanged pleasantries in Afrikaans, and the white man entered the building and came out again with bags of goods. He waved at my father and went to load his goods in his car, when he caught us staring at him.

We ducked out of sight.

"Ek het julle gesien," the white man said jovially, telling us that we had been spotted, so we poked our heads out of the window. Tata was looking at the whole interaction with the same worry on his face that had made him lower the volume of the radio when we turned onto the dusty road.

He asked me in Afrikaans what we were doing in the car. I answered that we were waiting for our father, and he said to me, excluding Romance, "I bet I can guess who your father is." I told him jokingly that he couldn't. The man laughed and asked why my father had chosen to bring a girl as his Johnny. I didn't understand what he meant by this and asked him, "What is a Johnny?" He answered as though he hadn't heard my question: how could he bring a girl to load the cement he was buying? No matter her size, she was still a girl. He gave me a sweet from the packet he had just opened, and hopped into his car. I offered half of it to Romance but she said coldly that he had given the sweet to me.

As we drove home, Tata enquired what the white man had said, and we in turn asked him why the man had called Romance a Johnny. Alarmed, he asked us if we had told the man that we were sisters, and we told him we had not. He nodded his head slowly and kept his eyes on the road. A short while later I saw him bite his wavering lower lip and a solitary tear fell to his lap. We did not speak again until we arrived home. After that, Tata only took Ou Takkies on his work trips, and because we had made him cry, we decided against asking to join him again.

When we hit the tar road, I asked Ou Takkies if Tsolo was close to Maclear or Port St Johns, my final destination. "Tsolo is close to Maclear, baby girl, but St Johns I would say is about four hours away. When did you ever go to Maclear?"

"Once, long ago with Tata. A nice man gave me a sweet before we left."

Now I sat on the bathroom floor indignant at Romance's behaviour. She had been missing for a decade only to arrive and throw me out of bed in my own home. She was vacuuming the room now; I could hear her singing loudly over the din. She could not have just found us; this was Mxolisi's doing, I was sure of it. They must have met in Cape Town and concocted this plan of. But Romance didn't know me as she once had. In Port St Johns, I had grown to be somebody else.

It was a small town right on the ocean. Clean and efficient, blanketed in the sleepiness that was a feature of any of the towns that would disappear if you blinked whilst driving past. The school campus had big beautiful lawns with a cathedral by the road as you entered the premises. The bells of the cathedral tolled every half-hour which annoyed me when I first arrived, but I grew to miss them when I spent weeks back home in the village.

In the first weeks, I learned to enjoy the routine: the tolling bells and impatient nuns calling to rouse us from our slumber. Breakfast was served promptly and classes began on time. Silent meditation was scheduled in the afternoon and there was some free time in the evenings. The latter caused me deep consternation. All the other girls seemed to know what to do with themselves during this time. At any given moment, they were scribbling in diaries or chatting with friends who visited their dormitories.

In the village, having a companion was a given. The Januarys banded together in age groups, not so much in later years, but as children that is how it had been. Romance had her age group, which didn't permit me in their company. They had their own identity and language, and related to each other based on their common experiences of life at the time.

The same was true for Beryl, Tsitsi, Khanya and I. We were more-or-less the same age and by the time I was sent away, we had formed our own cult with its own rules. We played pranks on people we didn't like, and created nicknames for adults who annoyed us. Skhova, for instance, was the boy who lived at Mam'Thembu's homestead. He had the eyes and sharp, bent nose of an owl, hence his name. He decided, one day, to not share the piece of meat Mam'Thembu had set aside for us from the cow that been slaughtered at the function she had attended in Mount Ayliff. We found him hiding behind the latrine sucking the marrow from the thick bone on his lap.

Khanya, who was permanently flared up, smacked the bone out of his hands and slapped him. We thought she was being too heavy-handed, but we were loyal to her, so we just stood back and let the attack happen. She was also the tallest of us, and led our quartet, easily mistaken for differently shaped quadruplets.

"Iphi nyama, Skhova?" Khanya flamed rhetorically, as it was clear who had eaten the meat.

Skhova was our favourite opponent for many reasons. Firstly, he wasn't afraid to fight us because he knew that we thought tattling was shameful. He exploited the fact that we would only tell on him if the harm was irreparable, else we would be accused of weakness for reporting a light skirmish that constituted a material part of childhood. We respected him for this fact. Secondly, Skhova understood that bad blood applied only to a particular specified action; it was never personal. If he defeated us in a fight on Monday, we could still share sweets on Tuesday – much like this meat incident. This was how we had been raised, so the fact that he understood this truly endeared him to us. Lastly, Skhova was always available to be recruited on missions against other boys because he was a tall boy with well-formed muscles, taller than Khanya who was already towering over her father – which wasn't saying much when it came to January men but still.

On this occasion, though, we were enemies. Skhova stood up and shoved Khanya in her budding breasts. She cried out in pain, which gave him a second to escape and run down the mountain towards the steep, rocky staircase. We had fought so many battles against each other that he knew Khanya was afraid of heights and had a heart defect that kept her from vigorous activity. Beryl was too fat to outrun him. I had pace but was too waif-like to ever throw the first punch, and Tsitsi was terrible at both duelling and running – but was at least a monster at saucy comebacks. Our strength was our unity, which he knew he had weakened when he broke into a run and escaped. We let him go that day, but he knew the score would be settled in some other way while the offence still stood.

In the coming days he could not be found anywhere, and we could tell by the pathetic eye signals the boys gave each other when we made enquiries, that they knew of his whereabouts, or were hiding him. Tsitsi suggested cornering Khanda, whom we had named for his big head, as he was the weakest link of their gang. He was poor at comebacks, ugly, and generally an insipid boy whose affection for Tsitsi caused him to make grave indiscretions that had often won us fights. Khanya dismissed this idea for its predictability. We spent the better part of the morning devising a winning strategy as we did our chores. Mam'Bhele asked us to go spring-clean Groot Huis, which is where we overheard Mam'Thembu say that Skhova, whose real name was Vuyisile, had been sent to town earlier that morning and was set to arrive back with the four o'clock bus. She had been requesting Mam'Bhele to send some of the January boys to help him carry the groceries up the mountain to her homestead.

Armed with this knowledge, we then devised a plan to waylay the boys on their way up the mountain.

Tsitsi knew of an abandoned hut on the path up the mountain; the trick was to get there before the older girls, Romance's age group, claimed it for their make-out sessions with the boys from the high school across the valley. Beryl and Tstitsi, being more voluptuous and thus likely to be mistaken as older, were charged with securing the hut. They just needed to pretend they were there to await their sweethearts. Khanya and I would track the boys from a distance to ensure that they really did take the path past the derelict hut, otherwise the mission would have to be left for another day.

The bus arrived on time, and as we watched the passengers disembark, we held our breath waiting to spot Skhova, which we did. Our cousins Lionel and Thembeka were waiting for him, and shook his hand after approaching him. The January boys had brought a wheelbarrow along, and they began to load the groceries into it. Khanya and I watched the boys begin ascending the mountain in the direction we had hoped they would take. It was the least steep part of the mountain, which had a path that had formed as a result of constant use.

The boys were in high spirits, unsuspecting that they were about to be ambushed. In settling scores, the composition of the opposing sides would be determined by what we stood to gain or lose. In this instance, Lionel and Thembeka, even though they were January boys, might be whipped if they delivered damaged goods to Mam'Thembu's house, so they would defend Skhova even though we were family. This must have been at the back of Skhova's mind, which was why he was so relaxed. He didn't think we would want to take on Lionel, an excellent rock thrower, or Thembeka, known for his athleticism.

I told Khanya that I suspected that these two companions had been Skhova's suggestions to Mam'Thembu upon his departure for town early that morning. Khanya agreed and admitted that all she really wanted was to get in a few good punches to teach him a lesson. We both had a feeling that the odds were against us, despite our excellent plan. Khanya decided that we should just enjoy the whole thing. We communicated our fears to Tsitsi and Beryl when we joined them in the derelict hut. Beryl admitted that Thembeka was the biggest threat, and applauded Skhova for being as wise as an owl in selecting our own family members as an escort. We all agreed that we would try to lay a few good punches on him especially. Beryl also highlighted that a hiding was something we could not avoid in this instance, and we offered up names of the adults who would probably administer these. There were a few options. Khanya's mother, Auntie Claudine, was a special form of crazy, and as heavy-handed as her daughter. We definitely didn't want to deal with Tsitisi's father, Malum'Shy, and his switches from the plum trees that grew in his garden. Beryl's father, Tat'Mfundo, always beat the girls less than the boys, so he was our best bet. So we decided that we would park ourselves at Beryl's house in the aftermath and wait for whatever storm would come.

As we waited, the excitement of our imminent ambush was palpable. Khanya kept watch out of the corner of the window as we all crouched behind her. The hut's straw roofing had blown away, and the walls had begun to crack. That Romance and her age mates used this roofless hut to make out with boys was incredible. Anybody's parents might see you as they strolled past or stopped for a break as they ascended the mountain. Soon we heard the loud grinding of the wheelbarrow on the path and fell silent, smiling widely at each other. The boys were talking loudly about the rubbish soccer league they played in at the neighbouring village, and how they had to build up a team of their own. Thembeka was pushing the wheelbarrow. Skhova had a plastic bag with him, and Lionel was strolling along eating an apple. We waited until they got close enough, then Khanya blindly threw a stone over the wall. We heard Thembeka shout, "Nazo! Run, Skhova!" but Skhova hesitated because he didn't know what to do with the plastic bag he was carrying, and when Beryl threw a stone aimed at his face, he grabbed the tray of eggs that had been balancing on the fifty-kilogram bag of flour to protect himself. The eggs fell and smashed on the ground. Khanya rushed straight at him, and punched him in the gut. I tried to join in, but Thembeka had me locked by the neck, with my legs dancing about. Tsitsi had joined Khanya in kicking Skhova, who managed a few slaps of his own. I can't account for Lionel in that moment, but when Thembeka set me down, I recall seeing him pushing the wheelbarrow up the mountain in haste.

The commotion had fuelled the spirits of the dogs at Tat'Sive's homestead, and his wife rushed to the fence and proceeded to shout threats at us: "There go these January rascals again, fighting with each other like dogs! Upon her grave, Ma'Miya would be disappointed! Why are you all like this! Stop this madness! Somebody bring me a belt! Somebody bring me a belt!"

By then we had bolted and were running towards Beryl's homestead, leaving broken eggs and torn sugar and flour packets in our wake. The boys tried to follow us, but when they saw that we were headed to Beryl's homestead, they turned back, and we could see them picking up the groceries that had gone flying in the air when we had pounced on them. We rushed into the yard and ran straight into the hut where Beryl slept, and broke out into crazy laughter. Khanya sat down, saying she felt slightly dizzy after running harder than she was allowed to. I told her she should be more cautious, and she brushed it off and clenched her fist: "We got him!" We broke out again in fresh laughter, and replayed the whole attack.

"We are going to get whooped tonight!" Khanya declared in triumph, and we cheered.

Her words proved to be prophetic, but we got the plum switches.

In Port St Johns, the free time in the evenings at boarding school just didn't offer the same kind of liberty as the village, and the landscape of the town prohibited the kind of mischief that led to reproach with plum switches. The closeness to the ocean was a form of freedom in itself, a metaphor for crashing like the surf onto the beach, and rising or falling like the tides, but the girls at school ran from this invitation to adventure into a performance of coyness. I knew it was performed because I was a girl who had spent a considerable amount of time with other girls growing up. Girls who spent their days conjuring up fantastic schemes of mischief or terror, who had wild ideas about their immediate surrounds, and who challenged any ideas that sought to bind them with limitations.

I had learned this in a short decade of life, but in the free time at boarding school, I learned that girls here spent this time searching for shackles. They held back their laughter and fretted over the size of their thighs. They were not interesting, so I stopped being interested.

I wandered the grounds alone instead, giving myself challenges to read a certain number of books in a week. Then when I met my target, I would revise the goal to read a certain number of books on a specific topic in a week, and so it went on.

The first year was the hardest because I still wanted to play with the gang. I wanted Khanya to shock us with her heated rage, Beryl to astound us with the quantities of food she could consume, and Tsitsi to charm us with her wit as we sat under the shade of the acacia trees at Groot Huis. I still wanted the comfort of being with people who had variations of the same face, so that when I looked at them I saw myself more clearly: fair skin, joined eyebrows, wild hair and spirit. Experiencing it in part during holidays made it hurt more when I returned to boarding school in the sleepy town, and had to learn again the shackles of free time and the performance of coyness. It was a stop-start existence, a reality that was not going to change in the near future, so I chose a side. They were all together in the village, the gang, and I was all alone, so I chose myself. Myself, that was my new adventure. It didn't happen the moment I decided; it was a long uncomfortable road negotiating between the village, Port St Johns, the gang and Romance, teaching them to forget the me they knew. In time, the only wild thing anybody ever saw of me was my hair, even though I told Romance otherwise in my letters.

She wrote to me once a week, and her letters were a source of panic for me who spent all my time reading or studying. I didn't let her know I felt I was missing out. She wrote about when Viri was kicked by a blind donkey and how each person's first reaction, on being told the tale, was to laugh instead of mourn. What was he doing provoking a donkey, and a blind one at that? I told her stories about the girls I spent my days observing, but I inserted myself as a lead character who had a busy social life and a network of friends. And each time she would ask about my friends, and what pranks we had played on the nuns, I would reply with colourful tales of fabrication, names changed and details revved up.

We danced around the incident that had caused it all: the real reason why I was sent away to Port St Johns, to a convent school by the ocean.

I had to repent for that day, and my cowardice.

We knew something was amiss from the moment Mam'Bhele and I opened the gate that led into the homestead. It was too late in the day for the evening fire to not have been lit, and the sheep filled the yard as the gate to the kraal had been left ajar. Mam'Bhele was cursing under her breath, laying the foundations of one of her famous reproaches as she opened a path through the sheep with her cane. She held my hand, but from her staggering gait, I suspected I was propping her up.

In the afternoons, the gang had a tendency to run wild at Groot Huis before we did our homework together and left for our respective homes at dusk. This was how it had always been. Even before Tata passed away, but especially since then, Mam'Bhele had taken to sitting with us until Ma returned from the shop for the evening. It had never been formally decided that our grandmother would jointly parent us with our mother, it was just a rhythm we found ourselves in. When Groot Pa Katjie had no appetite for the administrative duties of the business of which he was in charge, he would also take a turn to stand guard over us until Ma came home. Mam'Bhele often told me she was unhappy about me running amok with my cousins and leaving Romance to tend to the homestead by herself. I couldn't tell her that the older girls had their own after-school timetable that had nothing to do with chores, and everything to do with derelict huts and unloosened shirt buttons.

Then we saw the broken window and the broken door where the intruders had forced their entry. Mam'Bhele let go of my hand and began shouting Romance's name. I stepped into the hut with the broken window. It had been trashed, and the big gold clock that Tat'Mcebisi had bought for my parents on their wedding day was missing. I could hear Mam'Bhele still calling Romance's name in panic, but she seemed to be in the distance. The mischievous girl in me hoped the intruders would still be on the premises. The chances of me recognising them were high.

Due to our relative wealth, January children grew up being cautioned about the rampant jealousy of families in the village who would have no qualms about harming children in order to hurt their parents. It was the litany of our upbringing, to be suspicious of others and guard our own. We were constantly warned to not accept invitations to eat over at any homestead if it wasn't that of a relative, to decline offers of food at huge gatherings, and since Tata's passing after eating mutton gravy to which he was allergic, we had been forbidden from eating anything that we had not seen being prepared. Crime was generally very low in our parts of the world because of the communal nature of our existence, but spite was a vice of many who used it to settle scores. Naturally, we were not a blameless bunch with our fiery dispositions and vicious wit, and on some level we had just cause to be worried about neighbours who wanted to bring us harm.

This knowledge about the village informed my conviction that the gold clock would soon be recovered, and that the identity of the perpetrators of this act, when uncovered, would not surprise us. It was relentless disrespect, I thought, from the way Tata had passed away, to the ransacking of our home, and inside I was ablaze, like Khanya always was. Wasn't taking him away from us enough, had the score not been settled? Now to come into our home and remind us of our wound: it filled me with a flash of anger. But the intruders, who by now must have been sharing their spoils, were long gone.

Mam'Bhele had stopped calling out for Romance, so I went out to find her. I could see that she had dropped her cane outside the burgled hut. I picked it up and climbed the polished steps that led inside the hut. Here I came upon Romance: her limbs twisted and her face bloodied. From her raw knuckles, I could tell she had fought off her attackers by herself.

I don't know why she opened her eyes just as I appeared. I had been ready to take flight, and could have had the story told to me later, with the option of thinking of it as a tale that inspired pity, and not one in which I had partaken. She opened her swollen eyes that had turned purple against her berry-black skin and invited me into the horror. I entered the hut, treading in blood spilt across the floor, and bent down over her. Mam'Bhele was wiping her with the bedspread, and I reached down and pulled at her skirt slightly. This action frightened me so much I bolted out of the hut and ran. I knew I had to call Ma, who had just returned to the shop with the load she had gone to collect in Kokstad with Ou Takkies. I ran so hard that when I burst into the shop, Ma screamed in shock. The only thing I said was "Nobantu", and she gathered up her skirt, breaking into a full sprint, with Ou Takkies hot on her heels. I made it back up to the homestead after them to find Ou Takkies busy chopping wood furiously to boil water over the fire. Romance was still in that hut, and Ma was holding her to her breast, rocking her back and forth in her arms as one would an infant.

The homestead had begun buzzing with relatives who had either been told of the incident or had seen the hubbub and wanted to satisfy their curiosity. Groot Pa Katjie kept them away from Romance, and not knowing what to do, I sat on the couch in the burgled flat, seeing all the people around me, but thinking: why hadn't I run before she opened her eyes? Nobody paid me any mind, they were too busy planning revenge. Most had only scant details of what had occurred: the only person who could bear witness was being nursed like a baby, so it was unclear as to whom the blame was to be allocated. The sensible Januarys lived far away in cities and towns spread across the country, and that evening the ones left in the village made dangerous vows, filling the air with a frenzied mood of retribution.

At last, hours later, Tante Zenariah, Tat' Zola's wife, scolded me for sitting among people while covered in blood. "Uyahlola?" she asked angrily as she commanded me to go take a bath and stop making myself a political statement. Perhaps I had been sitting there wanting to be noticed. I also wanted to be cradled in somebody's arms. All I ever got from people were unwarranted sweets. Nobody held me. Ma walked in as I was scrubbing Romance's blood off my feet. She said nothing, just blinked and left, her body a study in exhaustion. I went to bed that night older than my years, but still feeling like a child needing to be soothed, the same feeling that would be repeated the night I became a woman: but nobody ever came. Then they sent me away. I had blood on my hands. And the next time I was covered in blood, it was at the convent, and Sister Britta said I was a woman now after telling me to wash my sheets. Still nobody held me.

High school was easier to manage. By then I preferred the rhythm of the small town, and had grown to value the autonomy of my existence. All the girls feared me, and most despised me. It wasn't without cause, but not for reasons you might think. Though I was not one of those girls you could describe as sweet, once you got to know me, I did have a different disposition for people I valued. I finished my years at Port St Johns without ever showing this other side to any of the girls there. That was my main offence.

Cwaita, a girl who considered herself my nemesis, bent over backwards to court me in the hopes of understanding what informed my disciplined coldness. I kept no diary that they could steal. I had no confidants or secrets to confide, and displayed no interest in boys or clothes and other adolescent past-times. The only company I kept were my books – those that I read and those that I studied. For me, it was an easy existence, uncluttered and compartmentalised. Port St Johns was not where I felt things. Cwaita wanted me to challenge the consequences of her beauty or the effects of her sensual persuasion for the benefit of the watching girls, who longed desperately for the advantages they believed we had.

I, however, was ordered by a value system that had only true freedom as its goal. Freedom from the weight of the moment when Romance trapped me with her eyes, and when Tata vanished from the earth. I wanted to be set on fire from within. I stood constantly on the precipice of something larger than myself and the voices that lived in my head. The attention of imagined or existing spectators didn't interest me. I fought more sophisticated imaginary duels with Skhova, and Cwaita resented me for this – that I was content with myself, and could not be distracted.

A January by the sea, Ou Takkies had lamented that day he was driving me to Tsolo, or was it a lament? Perhaps I was searching for solace. The first time I saw the ocean it was, as Ou Takkies had said, a great expanse of opportunity. I was drawn by the allure of its infinity. Its function in this instance as a border to the town highlighted the importance of serving out my sentence meaningfully. It was here that I would discover what had made life find me in such a vapid town, having lived out my days until that moment without pause for consideration of the purpose of my existence.

Sister Britta took us on an excursion to the beach that first weekend at the convent. The girls from the big cities played down their excitement; being urban children, they didn't want to feel exposed in front of their rural counterparts by having a novel experience. The wind swirled around us and forced our hands to our skirts. Many of the girls had formed groups, and from these enclaves of security, they chatted and giggled amongst each other.

I sat with Sister Britta, who was preaching about the history of the town to the misfits who had no friends to link arms with, and were forced to be in her company. She and the other nuns were the first white people I had prolonged contact with. A petite woman, she had strong convictions about the importance of heeding the call to save souls in Africa, in spite of her reservations about her chances for success. In my time at St John's, she provided us with ample evidence to corroborate this, when she referred to us as "your kind" or when she would wipe vigorously with a cloth any cutlery we had touched when serving her food. She told us to not smile for the annual photograph accompanying the letter to the sponsors of the mission, who were based in England. I didn't begrudge her these conflicts in her spirit; I recognised them.

"More often than not, girls are stupid; but you, you have potential," she remarked one day, handing me back my English paper. She was the first person to tell me such a thing; it was close to an embrace.

Sister Britta had a gift for speaking in ambiguities, but in this instance she was clear, and this strengthened my own belief in my potential. I knew she meant it in a general sense, not just in terms of my academic performance. There was no need to highlight my academic potential; three other girls in class matched and sometimes even beat my scores.

Sister Britta's compassion made her want to mould me. She saw herself as a saviour, and in my soul she saw a pain that she thought she could heal. In Religious Studies classes, she spent a considerable amount of time ensuring that we understood the significance of Jesus's parables. She called them the backbone of the Christian faith. Under her tutelage, we came to know all one hundred and forty-four replies to the questions of the catechism, the order of the books of the Old and New Testament, and also the order of the books of the Gospel. The parables returned repeatedly.

Until my arrival at the convent, I hadn't ever referred to myself as a Christian. We attended church on Sundays like all other families who wanted to raise wholesome children. In all the January homesteads there was only one bible, which was kept by Mam'Bhele in her trunk full of fancy plates. She only bought it out at Christmas to commemorate the holy day.

At the school in St John's, Sister Britta attended mainly to religious education, while the other nuns, Sisters Anne, Elizabeth and Mary supervised the vestry duties and Christ-like behaviour classes, which in modern education would be called sex education. We hypnotised ourselves with all the recitals of the Eucharist, the lessons for Advent, the allegiances of the Nicene Creed, and the solemnity of confession. We spent an hour each day meditating on the Lord, and three times a week we had thirty-minute Religious Study classes. Some of the girls joined the choir, which met on Saturday mornings for an hour-long practice, and the rest of us were on a roster for vestry duty, which entailed cleaning the apparatus used for the Eucharist. It also involved ensuring that the altar was set in accordance with the season of the church, tolling the bells every thirty minutes, checking if there were sufficient stocks of wafers and wine for the Eucharist, and laundering the altar cloths and vestments for Father Benedict. I understood when I left St Johns why people thought the church was too much work, and ran away from the countless committees required to run its operations.

Those words – *you have potential* – changed who I could have become: the girl I told Romance about in my letters, the one with friends from Johannesburg who snuck out on Fridays to meet the boys from St. Albert's down the road dolled up in glove-like dresses. Having potential meant that I had a purpose; I could be something other than a January lost at sea.

Now, after countless hours in the bath, I emerged and found my bedroom empty. Romance was downstairs clanging pots. I opened the plastic bag she had placed on my nightstand. Apricot jam, a toothbrush, and some batteries. Seeing that these were her supplies, or maybe how she thought she could heal me, a faint smile lit me up.

Nobantu January, the sister I had known before the blood, was the apple of my father's eye. The two of them were joined at the hip to the detriment of anybody who tried to split them. Such love gave her easy confidence and a generous spirit which she showered on me from the moment of my birth. The four years before my arrival meant she could allow him to learn to have equal devotion for me. I had no thoughts of my own, nor did I make decisions that she didn't approve. A day without her was too long and too quiet. Her presence was my strength and it was from under the shield of her love that I fortified myself. Imagine running from that person when they needed you most. I didn't know it was guilt that had kept me from her all these years. I had convinced myself that she had let me down.

It was the whole business with Mxolisi.

When I first met my husband, it was like exhaling after having held my breath for a long time. He was as kind in real life as he was in my dreams, and the dimensions of his face held my gaze for so long on our first encounter that it was obvious to us both that something divine had occurred; that we would be struck out of heaven if we did not pursue a relationship, or at least speak to each other to test the truth of this feeling. I was struck by how similar he looked to my father; but for his eyes, he was the same man in shape, height and manners. The only real difference was that my father adored the fire of Romance, whereas Mxolisi preferred the moon shades I used to veil my emotions. He knew how to find me in my head and when to leave me alone to brood. He knew the tides of my furrowed thick brows.

In my family, Mxolisi came with peace, like the meaning of his name. He mostly remained out of frays that did not concern him, and protected Vuyo and me fiercely against those who would harm the tranquillity of our lives. Those who chastised me for bearing only one child and who on the side-lines encouraged him to shack up with other women to bear him children – as if our relationship had no other dynamics other than the production of offspring – faced a man whose words were so scathing they kept the searing effect of his retaliation to themselves. These whisperings were never made by Januarys, as we protected our own, but came from his sisters, who felt they had the right to mould me into a Fani woman. Of course, I was not a favourite in his family. Aloof is what I was commonly called, even though they treated me outwardly with reverence, often remarking on my beauty and hardly ever denying my requests.

Mxolisi despised the provincial nature of his upbringing just as I did not always enjoy the close-knit nature of our community. It was oppressive when you wanted to be singular, not to be held to account for decisions that would not impact anybody other than yourself. So we ran off to the city, to Johannesburg, the one thing my grandfather held against Mxolisi until his death.

Nobody trusted Johannesburg in the parts of the world where we had grown up. A city famed for stealing souls and for leaving people so bereft that the shame of returning, even as a prodigal child, often left people trapped until their deaths, rather returning in a coffin to avoid the grapes of wrath that awaited them.

But we had a plan. It was a common belief amongst the people in the village that Mxolisi and I lived in a shack or some small rented room in a city of strangers, leaving behind the rolling hills and open land that had been hard won by Theodore January on the day of his trial as a potential trouble-maker.

There were difficulties, naturally, finding our way in a city famed for diversity when all I had ever known was the singularity of identity framed by the measured flow of the Thina river. I clung onto my husband because my bond with Romance had finally snapped. It had not frayed over time, as one might expect with ropes tugging apart like our lives. She rejected Mxolisi, without telling me why. I exposed him to her, hoping for an ally, never expecting that I wouldn't find one. I had stood in her blood and had been sent away. I had repented. I had received absolution, but she wanted me to be bound to that moment.

Until Mxolisi, Romance was the only person I had truly loved; I thought only of how to please and protect her. She was my whole universe, from her rich dark skin and wide shoulders, to the strength in her arms when she swung an axe and split the firewood for cooking the evening meals, from her straight teeth that had a gap in the middle and her round, full breasts that the boys in the village tried to avoid looking at when they spoke to her. She was a force that drew you in, and engulfed you in the charge that swirled around her very existence. My love for her made me feel unworthy and incapable of such power.

Me loving Mxolisi, I'm sure, made her feel less like a deity when perhaps that is how she wanted to remain in my mind. Mxolisi represented a distance too far for us to meet each other halfway. When you are young, you don't know what words to use to fill the space of tension, and a man often has the power to elevate your understanding of yourself simply by gazing at you.

Romance did not understand this. She had never loved anyone that deeply. Her feelings were warranted, and I did not begrudge her them. I just was unwilling to spend yet more years bound to a painful moment, banished from the joys of my childhood for something neither of us had been able to control. When we were children, I didn't see the limitations of Romance's world view; I could not have predicted that she wasn't brave. How she clung onto my arm when I introduced her and Mxolisi, how cagey the conversation that we suffered as we walked home. The distance she put between us the next and every other day after that revealed her disapproval to me – and my indifference to it.

On our wedding day, I looked out onto the crowds of people who had come to celebrate with us, and I saw my sister – tall, dark, fearsome and alone – and that is how she remained in my head over the years.

It didn't help that years later, Vuyo would come to adore Romance, creating a further gap between the two of us, my daughter and I. They had similar dispositions, save that Vuyo had a steady shyness to her that I attributed to her having spent most of her time by herself. They took to each other as though they were old companions who had been waiting on a platform for something to come along, as one would a train. Nothing could separate them unless they willed it. This was a particular talent my daughter possessed, the ability to wrap herself up in people. I envied this quality in her, because everybody wanted to be close to her because they felt themselves to be better people for it.

They tried to draw closer to me, only to be disappointed by how little I could or wanted to do for them. I had spent too many years in my head to be able to climb out. I could have been a better mother if I had allowed myself this one indulgence, but I could not, not even for the only child I would ever be given in this life. I wanted to teach her strength and protect her from all that I had seen, knowing it was the only true duty to which I was bound until the end of my time on earth. But something stopped me.

The child I had to have scraped out of me was the third one I had lost in a couple of years, and after her, I told Mxolisi I didn't want to try anymore. I rolled over one night, some months after Romance had come to "deal with me", and her presence had given me space to grieve without attending to my other responsibilities. I told him I didn't want another child. I felt revived by the decision, but still shrouded in residual melancholy. He pulled me closer to him, and I laid my head on his chest. That was the only answer he ever gave me, and we never spoke of it again.

Much like how we never spoke of the time I saw him some minutes before the transformer exploded, running away dressed inconspicuously, nothing like the suave gentlemen with whom I had conversed on the train some days previously. The gentleness that had enveloped him then had vanished, and his face was cold and shut-off with calculated intention, an urgency that didn't match the calmness of the surrounds. He didn't see me as he ran past the fence outside school that was the boundary enclosing the cathedral from the veld and the main road that led into town.

I had been on vestry duty, and Sister Britta had asked me to fetch the prayer books from her classroom when I heard a loud hissing sound. The black plume of smoke caught my attention first. From behind the church tower, a black ball of smoke was growing. Curious, I walked towards the fence to see if perhaps there had been a vehicle accident on the main road, a fairly common occurrence as the road fed into a national route, and the mission school was the only point of interest before getting into town. Drivers would speed past in reckless abandon without catering for the bend that dipped into the valley as the land began sloping down into the ocean.

But I saw nothing but him leaping into the great expanse of the veld, running from what I saw now was one of the electricity poles opposite the entrance to the mission school. Father Benedict was waving his hands at me in the distance. I couldn't hear a word, but I sensed his urgency. He had been on his way to give a class, and like me, had been caught by the sight of the smoke. It was a clear day with no distinction between the sky and ocean, and a pleasant breeze was blowing intermittently to displace the heat. I looked again out across the veld to see if I had imagined the figure dressed in a black top with grey jeans. Confused, I convinced myself that it hadn't been him, or in fact anybody, and I urgently turned on my heel to alert Sister Britta to the fire when there was a loud boom, followed by a flash and a fireball.

When I next opened my eyes, I was enveloped in ash, with the heat of fire burning all around me, warming my skin. I placed my hand on broken glass as I tried to lift myself out from under the rubble and a piece from the shattered cathedral window cut into me. Wincing, I sucked the blood from my hand as I kicked away some of the bricks that had landed on and around me. Standing up slowly, I stumbled towards the classrooms. Here I found the two Standard Six girls I had caught sight running to class seconds before the blast. They were two sweet girls who held hands all the time like children, and who spent countless hours giggling at the ridiculous anecdotes they conjured up, or the pranks they played on their peers. Because of this, they were constantly an eighth of a second late for every class, which at the mission school was sufficient offence to earn detention. They were now lying on the ground with their bodies twisted, far apart from one another. I stared at their frail frames lying in the dirt. The one no longer had one arm, and her white underwear was exposed between her splayed legs. Her friend had been crushed to death by a wall that had collapsed. The bell of the cathedral tower now lay sideways on the lawn outside the front entrance of the church.

I wanted to find Sister Britta. The only thing I could think of was to give her the prayer books she had instructed me to fetch. I wasn't even carrying them; I just wanted to find her. She had been in the vestry marking our Creative Writing essays as I was wiping the chalices in preparation for Sunday Mass. In a rare chatty mood, she had been complaining about how heavy the rains had been of late, and how the works of nature often disturbed her peace; it was one weakness in her faith she had yet to conquer. In our exchanges, which she called conversation, I would often wait for a moment where I could make one slight comment. Depending on her mood, she would either respond or scoff, and we would continue in silence.

We were nevertheless comfortable in each other's presence, especially now that I was in my last year here at the mission, and considering attending teachers' college in Natal. It was a decision I had been mulling over; whether to return to the homestead to run the business with Mama and wait for a suitor, or to continue my studies. I had no guidance on this matter except from Sister Britta, who supported the idea of my being out in the world on my own.

She had recently been recounting to me her early days in the country, after she first arrived from her village in northern England. "It's a difficult thing for girls to know themselves outside of duty; much of our lives are tied up in obligation. Those few years when you can be without that burden – take them and make the most of them. Nobody will ever tell you that because they think that the inevitability of the situation makes it futile to explore other options," she said as she sat marking papers in her office, where the windows had an enthralling view of the ocean.

She stopped and placed her pen down on the stack of papers in front of her with a distant look on her face. "I left home with a man far older than my father in years to pursue the work of the Lord. Who knows how my name lives back home? But I know myself."

I had sat opposite her, watching this monologue play itself out as I polished the chalices, readying them for the evening services that Father Benedict gave during the Lenten weeks.

Now as I moved through the rubble, I kept hoping I wouldn't see her crumpled like those sweet girls I saw outside. As I picked my way through the now open-sky church, I could hear groggy moans from somewhere in the haze of ash and smoke. Some girls crawled out into the light and lay facing upwards, coughing, then covering their faces with their forearms. Other were weeping, and I just kept searching for Sister Britta. She was found in the vestry by a rescue party, her leg broken from the thick wooden table having fallen on her thigh.

A few days afterwards, the police confirmed that the transformers had been tampered with. They informed us at an assembly called by Sister Mary as Acting Principal, as Father Benedict had been found dead close to where the bell of the church had fallen. The school was still swarming with police and clergymen from various dioceses in surrounding towns. Helicopters flew overhead constantly and all manner of vehicles lined up along the perimeter of the mission school. None of the pupils were permitted to leave without an escort or unless they had formal permission to be taken away. Parents had come from far and wide to take their children home. Members of the local media camped opposite the school. Local villagers stood as interested onlookers.

It was considered a sign of the times that churches could be attacked, that innocent young girls could be killed. Something had changed radically; up until this point we at the school had been sheltered from the reality of the country we were about to step into as young black women; in which were we going to raise our daughters.

When Mxolisi and I first met, when he sat next to me, he had been, to my mind, a handsome gentleman on the train. I had immediately wanted to be close to him, and throughout the decades we spent together this never changed, but the feeling wasn't significant until I saw him later, running away from a fire he had started.

It was him. That was my secret thought as the police "politely" requested for anybody with information to come forward. I don't know if anyone else who survived saw him running into the brush of the veld, but I had no intention of saying anything. When I had first seen him, he had been in a tailored grey jacket, and looked to be in town for business or on some official matter, not some sort of renegade. Unknown to me and unknown to the teachings of our institution, which valued so much the texts and orders of old that it ignored the shifting landscape in front of it, he symbolised a call to a new adventure. Frightening, but exciting. So I said nothing, waiting to be exposed or discovered. The man I saw in nondescript clothing that afternoon had layers of faces, a feeling I understood well. He had to be different things in order to survive. His faces had characters – the gentleman, the renegade, the activist – and the possibilities excited me. He was somebody I could peel a thousand times and still be no closer to understanding. January men were linear and predictable: that was their charm. Mxolisi was a wrecking ball swinging in all directions.

I wrote to him once the dust had settled down, but didn't send the letter. If he had been involved in such mayhem, I doubted that he would have been genuinely interested in me that day on the train; it might have been part of his plot, and I still had my pride. Maybe I hoped for a confession or to be his confidante, I don't know, but I prayed hard that he would write to me. To prove to me that what I had felt that afternoon on the train had been reciprocated. I hankered for this attention.

    For weeks afterwards, I dreamt of his changing faces. I missed those of my peers whose lives had ended so unexpectedly, but something about losing them felt part of the design of life.

    I found out something I didn't know about myself and this country until that explosion. I grieved deeply and privately for the loss of my former perspective and naivety. I realised that somebody else was moving in to live in my body, as had happened the moment after I stepped in Romance's blood. I would always be a conduit, and that epiphany was almost a relief. As I grieved the last shreds of my naivety, I realised that I could do nothing about the world except to exist in such a way that nobody could attach their labels to me. Black women are always being lauded for their strength, our strength, and it's a deeply unfair way in which the world justifies its poor treatment of the black female body. It's a manipulation of the ability to understand who has the advantage, and how to survive in spite of the imbalance. This was the only way I would be able gain my freedom. The only way nobody could walk into a building and blow up the walls of my false security. It might take a lifetime, but that is who I would be.

    I could be his revolution, and he wouldn't have to reach for the man who burnt things in order to survive. We could help each other carve the way. Nobody else would search to understand him. Nobody else would defend the parts of him that were kind and gentle. I wanted his arms around me. I was certain I could soothe the bitterness he had learned, and in the future, together, we could hope to be happy.

I fell so deeply in love with the idea of loving him back to himself by being myself, it gave me joy at the time when all there was in that graveyard school was sadness and grief. It felt so exciting to know what I was going to do after school, the question that had been looming over our heads long before explosions came to interrupt our mundane existence.

The days after the fire I spent mostly with Sister Britta at the hospital, getting instructions as I assisted her with the administration that now fell to her and Sister Mary following the death of Father Benedict. We had to remove the names of those pupils who had died from the register, and return their belongings to their families. This work entailed posting several letters and ascertaining the addresses of the rest. Eulogies had to be written for the deceased pupils, and posted along with notes of condolences to the affected families.

The police visited the school daily, and spent hours pulling in girls for questioning at random. The day the police questioned me, it mostly revolved around my love life: did I have one, and if the other girls did, what were the names of their lovers, and which girls showed anger towards the school authorities. The questioning continued for weeks, and made many of the girls skittish. All the letters we wrote and received had to be read first by the constable now permanently stationed at the school. This new development was primarily why I had refrained from sending Mxolisi the letter I had written him; I had destroyed the letter and address the moment it was announced that we would be monitored in this way. It was humiliating to submit a letter for public scrutiny to a white man requesting your parents to replenish your sanitary towels, or giving accounts of the personal tragedies we had suffered. How much more embarrassing or mortifying would a rambling confession of undying love for a man you met only once on a train and seen later running into the wild be?

Constable De Witt paid no mind to these sensitivities; he carelessly tore our letters open and read their contents, making notes as he went along. He used Sister Britta's vestry as his office. Upon her release from hospital, hobbling around with a cane, she would often find herself turning the handle of the door only to find it locked; or walking towards it with stacks of papers before remembering it had a new occupant.

Our rooms were searched at a moment's notice sporadically during the week, making it difficult to concentrate on our studies, even in the hours designated for the preparation of our final exams.

The nuns protected us as much as they could, but even they could not hide the grotesqueness of the ruined cathedral. It stood at the head of our school, and the windows that had no glass sang eerie wind songs from the breath of the ocean sweeping into the classes where there should have been young enlivened girls.

The number of students meanwhile dwindled, as most who had survived the fire were pulled out of the school by their parents. The matrics were in the majority of those who remained, as we wanted to complete the syllabus and exit from the education system with a solid foundation, even if it was in uncertain times.

Nobody knew how long the school would last after our class graduated at the end of the semester. Sister Britta confessed that it was perhaps time to sail to other shores, and it hurt me to think that her good deeds would be remembered as having come to a disappointing and violent end. I wanted to tell her I was proud of her and that she had raised a woman in me, but I kept these sentiments to myself. I didn't want to embarrass her or have her deny that she too valued me deeply. It was best to take from each other what was left to give in a world now shifting at a disconcerting speed.

The truth of her insinuations was later announced via a letter from the bishop, and by the end of the school semester, the only remaining students were the matrics who milled about waiting to write their finals before the school closed its doors forever. Not even the church would be rebuilt, as the diocese in that region felt that it had suffered irreparable harm from the fire and explosion, and the possible connection to terrorist acts. Much of the administration focused on tying up loose ends, which resulted in the mood of the school being clouded with a precarious energy.

In the midst of this sadness, the thing I longed for most was a letter from Mxolisi. At this late stage in my high school years, I had finally become the ridiculous infatuated teenager who whiled away her hours longing for a boy. And somewhere in these solemn days, I received his letter. Constable De Witt, who was fluent in Xhosa, praised the letter, saying how well written it was, and teased me, saying I had chosen well, which made my stomach churn in anger. Before handing me the letter, he questioned me for a long while about having not disclosed my lover, at which I denied having a lover; rather an interested party who wrote to me so intermittently that I had misplaced the few letters I had previously received. He asked if the letters were always from the same address, and I replied that I had never paid attention to where the letters came from because, and I restated, the letters were intermittent. He regarded me suspiciously, then warned me about obstructing justice and the dangers of acting "too big for one's boots".

I nodded and he handed me the letter. It was a long one, detailing some of his travels in the past few months – which I knew was mostly fiction. He wrote to me in high Xhosa, idiomatic and full of poetry which made my heart dance. He begged for a reply as proof of life, having read of the tragedy of the explosion – and at this omission, I smiled wryly.

When I finished the letter, I folded it and felt the wind run through my hair and blow it in all directions. That first day when I had gazed out into the ocean upon my arrival, this small town had represented endless disappointment and guilt for actions I had not yet atoned for, but as Mxolisi's words rang in my ears, I was overwhelmed by how little else I felt. I had locked myself up within the confines of whom I might have become had the road taken other turns, but just then I felt balanced. I felt again as though I were standing at the edge of all I could become, and again the tingling excitement of life after school rushed through me.

The ocean roared around me and crystallised my thoughts – I had to release the moment when Romance bound me up in her pain in order to love the man who had penned this letter. I could not love him otherwise. I had hoped Romance could love him, but if she couldn't, I felt convicted that severance was imminent. Unfortunately, I was ultimately right, and I stood by the decision I made alone with a graveyard school behind me. Distance came to govern the nature of the relationship between Romance and me following years after their initial introduction.

Vuyolwethu loved Christopher in the same way. Her rebellion was sweet to witness; if only she knew how alike we were in this regard, no matter how different the men. Closing Mxolisi's eyes when he finally passed made me smile. Only death had done us apart; we had kept our vows. He had cherished me until his dying days, and loosed me from all I had left undone that day Ou Takkies drove me off in a cloud of dust to a small town by the sea.

When I pulled Christopher out of the pool that morning and saw his ice-blue eyes pierce lifelessly through me, I thought it a mother's grace to allow only Vuyolwethu close his eyes. To allow her the space to free him from the vows he had made to her, and to let him go to his resting place. She thought I was cruel for doing this. She asked me why I had left him lying outside in the sun. She thought I didn't understand. Mxolisi had wasted away slowly prior to his death, his illness making him somebody else each time he survived a further deterioration.

Perhaps Vuyolwethu was the one who didn't understand.

On my first day out by myself when I left high school, I ventured to town. I was wearing a dress Sister Britta had bought me as a parting gift, and after hours of amusing myself in various ways, I had sought a place to eat. I saw a café across the road from the post office where I had just posted a letter, the main reason I had come to town in the first place. Crossing the silent street to sit outside at the small round turquoise table while I waited for service, I casually placed my handbag on the table and felt the beating of my feet in the pumps I was wearing. It was a welcome relief from the humidity trapped in the grey clouds hanging so close it felt as if you could reach them.

I sat for long minutes in quiet hope that the waitresses inside would come out and take my order, but they didn't. Instead, an elderly lady eventually approached me. She appeared tired and nervous, her straggled hair tied carelessly at the base of her neck, her light-blue wrap dress fluttering in the lazy breeze that sought to displace the thick warm air that was forming beads of sweat down the glide of my back. She stood in front of me, shifty-eyed.

"You can't sit here."

I didn't understand so I waited for her to finish or to clarify what she meant, which she did: "You are not allowed to sit here."

"What do you mean, are these tables for display, I am sorry–" I stood up in an apologetic flutter.

"No, these tables are just not meant *for you.*" She looked down in embarrassment as she said these last words.

I knew of these rules before I came to town, and had, throughout the day, adhered to all the limitations placed on my presence in town by the law, but this café was in a predominantly black area, from what I could perceive, and I had not seen a sign prohibiting me from entering the establishment.

Taken aback I asked, "Why?"

The lady was equally puzzled, and she turned on her heel and left me outside. Nobody ever came to serve me. In all my life I had never experienced this. For some it may have been humiliating, but growing up a January in our village meant that condescension was your birth right, and at this moment what overwhelmed me was a pity for that woman, who had not known to whom she was talking. In our family, we didn't follow rules, nor were we threatened by the mechanisms of authority because more often than not, we owned them. I was a January; she was a poor white woman in a threadbare dress.

So I pitied the woman because her only victory in this life would be denying me a service that she was providing, which in and of itself made no sense. We had served the vilest of the village at the shop we owned because it was a going concern, and in that space who cared where the hands that exchanged money for goods came from? What mattered is that they did. I had more wealth than she ever would amass in her small corner café in a sleepy town in a forgotten part of the world. Incensed, I walked back to the bus stop, silently awakening to how much my presence was regulated, and how easy it was to accept this as the norm. Nobody fought it – nobody but people like Mxolisi. He changed my politics. I graduated from high school just in time to catch the revolution, both inside me and out on the streets.

When Mxolisi was arrested, I punished him because if I hadn't done so, he would have lost respect for me, and might have grown suspicious of our relationship. I knew what he was; I had seen it on the day I had watched him running into the veld. I wanted to prove to him that I could stomach the revolution; that I was no longer blind, willing to participate in the malaise of oppressed contentment in which our people were drowning; at least in the countryside, that was what was real. Of course, we didn't know that in later years children would be shot openly in the street by their neighbours, or that girls could be necklaced for failing to attend a funeral. We didn't know just how much we would lose in the fire; we were just determined to be free.

The man whose eyes I closed that fateful morning in the hospital had given me a life I could never have dreamed of. His love was total and pure; yet he was equally conflicted and imperfect. He went to his grave never having spoken to me about that morning I saw him running from the church. I lived with the unspoken knowledge that the man who put our daughter in my belly was probably responsible for the deaths of young girls quietly going about their day – and I loved him anyway. He helped me traverse my politics, moving from indifference to defiance. I did not know of the violence that was attached to having dreams. Men have other worries that are placed on their shoulders by the structures of this world; you cannot rely on them, no matter how much you love them.

I loved him until his last moment. Why then would I have closed Christopher's eyes when I knew how hard it was to fulfil the promises of a lover? Christopher had promised never to leave Vuyolwethu, and yet he did. Only she then had the right to release him back to where he came from in order to absorb, in all its intensity, the mystery of our faith – that those leave, awake in us to live eternally.

Vuyolwethu says I hated Christopher. There was some truth in that, but not for the reasons that you might think. It wasn't his skin that held me up; it was how much she needed him. A seasoned woman can see the idealistic stars that dance in the eyes of a young woman who has imbibed the promises of her beloved. In my limited conferences with other women it has occurred to me that other women would have made different decisions after the explosion; but I am a January woman. The world for us is carved from the flesh of weathered skin; we are built to withstand the controversies of the day.

And Vuyolwethu is a January woman. Her whole life I tried to rear her in this tradition, to protect her from being too easily enthralled by romantic delusions, and mould her into a woman who could bear the tides that were sure to come. For her, they came at too young an age when she lost her father, but he had been too gentle with her. Now she had to consider herself without his protective gaze on her. Her growth from that moment on was seismic.

By the time she tied herself to Christopher, I felt my prayers for her at birth had been heeded, but only just. I respected Christopher, but it didn't escape me that there was a part of their history that they covered up. They often tripped over themselves regarding the timelines of their meeting and their decision to be together. I suspected him of being encumbered when he first courted my daughter. But this wasn't something I condemned. There was poetry in their struggle that endeared him to me ever so slightly, but I also wanted my daughter to know she could do just as well without him.

This prophecy has now come to pass. For weeks after his drowning, I sat on the balcony outside my bedroom and observed the savannah grass bend to the invisible force that breathed into it. It seemed my life had been spent witnessing the tragedies inflicted on those closest to me. It no longer broke me when such things occurred; surrendering to them cleared my mind and strengthened my resolve.

God has always been unfair in the execution of His divine will – that is the meaning of this life – but he is forever justified, and on that score, His wisdom has to be acknowledged. As I watched Vuyolwethu's stomach swell each day, she was moving further and further away from the time when Christopher had lived towards the days when she would speak of him as a memory. It made it clear to me what my new revolution would be; to help preserve him for the babies who would never know him. To raise them to be at peace with their conflicted history. To protect them from the violent history that had preceded their parents' union in a different time, one now dressed up to align with conventional morality. My prayers for more children had been answered in the form of the twins we would soon meet, and my shame at my prematurely barren womb would be cured by watching the child I had neglected for years double her takings from the Lord.

What an insult to throw at a woman.

Black black black black girls,
A commodity.
An oddity.
A curiosity.
A fetish.
Black black black girls,
The invisible.
The neglected.
The molested.
Black black girls.
We want to be loved.
We want to be respected.
We want to birth what is in our minds.
Black girls,
Beautiful.

Nobantu "Romance" January

There is no value in being a beautiful woman where I am from. It will not mend the fences or keep the monkeys from being a nuisance. It will not even endear a lover to you. Beautiful girls are stupid, flighty things that go out into the world only to cause messes that they either cannot afford or cannot live with. They are awful tiresome things.

In our world, January men gave no attention to women with slight arms and slim waists. They warranted being overlooked, and nobody wanted to be overlooked by a January man. Small but fiercely loyal men. The kind of lovers women feared to love because they were difficult to replace with a man of equal measure, but whose attention one longed to hold – for what often came with that adoration was a life of peace in a family that truly built each other up. From Groot Pa Katjie's Groot Huis, doctors, lawyers, entrepreneurs, renowned academics, teachers and priests were birthed. So proud were these men that it was often said by Groot Pa Katjie that a January man never keels over and dies; he is called by his ancestors to hand over the baton when his time has come to an end. This call is known by him and heeded in a manner so dignified that both the living and the dead honour him. That is how a January man dies.

A beautiful woman could not slay a man with one swing of her arm, as Mam'Bhele did when she met Groot Pa Katjie. She was a girl from a distant village, a Hlubi village just before the Bhaca villages, and she had come to visit one of her relatives over the summer season. Groot Pa Katjie had been living in the village for two years, having buried Ma Miya not too long after that business with the chief. He had assimilated into the village, kept to himself, and when he did venture out he spoke mostly to his elderly neighbours who, on account of their age, still treated him with suspicion. This distance suited Groot Pa Katjie, who preferred that fences between neighbours remained erect. It was a January inheritance to mind one's business; and the punishment for meddling was often far more severe than the consequences of disobedience.

Due to the chief's mercy, Groot Pa Katjie had remained quite close to the Royal House, often donating the fruits of his harvest to the household and offering his services to mend the perimeter fences if bulls had destroyed them or they had deteriorated over time. When Nonti and I were children, we often accompanied Groot Pa Katjie to the Royal House. He would sit us on Tsiba, Phelandaba's predecessor, who as his name told, was an excellent jumper. We would ride without a saddle all the way to the Royal House, and on the way, Groot Pa Katjie would tell us stories about the village.

Down in the valley, he would say, where the road runs parallel to the Thina, there used to be a beautiful girl who lived alone in her grandfather's hut, which she had inherited upon his death. Of course her living this way was considered a travesty by all and sundry: why would a woman of birthing age not want the protection of family and children on whom to dote? was the common cry amongst the people in the village. Then, as it would be in any place, a certain young man fancied his chances and decided to make a man of himself by acquiring her affection. Like a veld fire, his intentions spread throughout the village and reached the girl's ears. It was hard for anybody to discern what she made of the news because she kept to herself and spent most of her time indoors.

The boy made his way to her home one morning, and like a man confident of his success, he skipped across the river and knocked on the door of the small hut. The banks of the Thina were quite low that year as the rains were late, and the large boulders of clay sand that were normally hidden under the fast-flowing waters now baked openly in the sun. The boy knocked for what must have been a half hour without any reply from the girl. Refusing to be deterred, he decided to serenade the girl with the songs boys sang to woo girls after they returned from the mountain ceremony that initiated them into manhood. He had a lovely singing voice, and kept repeating the part of the chorus that he thought would weaken her resolve: "Beautiful girl of the forest, you need hide no more." He sang until he became hoarse. Fresh out of ideas, the boy decided to sit resolute on her front step until she had no choice but to emerge.

He sat there dozing until nightfall, when he was jolted awake by a clanging sound. Alarmed, he jumped to his feet and cast a glance at his surrounds, but saw nothing. Again, he heard the clanging sound, and realised that the girl inside was moving around. The boy ran around the hut only to realise that it had no windows, which caused shivers to run down his spine. In the very next moment, the door was flung open and the girl stood barefoot in a rag of a dress before him. Gossip of her beauty was not without truth. A short girl with arms toned by hard work, and a small pinched nose that ran the length of her face, from her almond-shaped eyes down to curved full lips that pouted slightly. She was holding an enamel bowl to her hip and a dishcloth in her other hand. The boy stood paralysed as she approached him and placed at his feet the bowl, which was filled with the clay mud of the Thina. The girl knelt down and began smearing the clay all over the boy's body, and as the clay dried, it turned an ochre colour.

After this, the girl said the only words she had ever been heard to say: "Lean over forward until your hands touch the floor."

Fully terrified, the boy did as instructed. The girl walked back into the hut and closed the door. The boy vanished, never to be seen again by the village, and after him, nobody ever dared to recommend themselves to the girl. It is said that the mountain that runs parallel to the river, the one arched like a bent back where the trees at night sing songs into the morning, is what the boy became. That is why you are not allowed to point at it. If you do, the pointing finger will bend permanently into position, much like the boy. It's a cursed mountain.

At the end of his tales, Groot Pa Katjie would point out exactly which part of the village whichever story he told us pertained to. In this instance, we asked him how come he could point at the mountain, and he said he couldn't be cursed because he was a January man – such things didn't apply to January men – but he still cautioned us against pointing at the mountain. Nonti and I loved these stories, but they let us know of Groot Pa Katjie's inherent mistrust of beautiful women.

When Mam'Bhele choke-slammed Groot Pa Katjie by the water well, they had been arguing over who had the right to use the well. At that time he hadn't been governed by this mistrust. In fact, this was what had emboldened him to fight her, because he had no patience for this supposed preference he was birthed to gift to women. The custom of the land was that the young girls were to collect water at dawn when the silt was undisturbed and contained the fewest potential threats. After that, the well had to be covered, often with corrugated iron, to keep it clean and protected from wandering animals. During the day, young boys who herded the livestock of various homesteads were permitted to drink from the wells, if they so wished.

Mam'Bhele was unfamiliar with this latter part of the custom, as in her village herd boys had no business at the drinking wells, and it was for them to find sources to quench their thirst. It was this confusion that stirred up the temper of the usually reserved young Theodore, who found himself obstructed by a tall fearsome creature with skin the colour of liquorice and black balls of rage. Fired up by his disregard for custom, Mam'Bhele gripped Theodore by the front of his shirt and threw him to the ground. He fought back hard all the while threatening what he would do to her as soon as he gained some advantage, as he had with Nyathi that fateful day at the Royal House. But that moment never came. As she choked him down on the ground, his small frame was lost under the boulder that was her body, his flailing arms weakening as she crushed him.

Eventually, he stopped struggling, and she glared down at him to ascertain if this meant that he had conceded, which he indicated with long slow blinks. She stood up from him, grabbed the bucket she had filled with water, placed it on her head, and ascended the mountain to her relative's homestead. She apparently told all who could hear of the offence of "Katana", the small cat-eyed man, which name morphed into Katjie, the same diminutive in Afrikaans. Until the grandchildren were born, only Mam'Bhele referred to him as Katjie.

When Groot Pa Katjie used to gloat to men with women trouble, he would describe in detail the prize he had won in a wife who could easily kill him with her bare hands. It kept him honest. She didn't fear him or care if he left. She was his because she had chosen him. Most women hardly ever went against the grain, so that when you found one who did, you guarded her like a nest of eggs. The decades that followed were filled with nothing but the highest respect for each other. Together they were a model of balance between loyalty, mutual reverence and forthrightness, which earned them the respect and the envy of their neighbours.

Groot Huis was where we sat without men and passed to each other the pearls of how to navigate the world's curveballs. Mam'Bhele sat at our centre, almost always behind her Singer with a pin in her mouth and rolls of cloth on her lap, listening to whatever event had unfolded amidst her children or their relatives. We had high regard for her intelligence and her dedication to cleanliness and order, and her general pedantic nature.

Mielie, the daughter of one of Mam'Bhele's middle sons, had married a man from the Bhaca villages. This was always referred to as a shame – imagine willingly submitting yourself to a nation of backward clans that had no care for education or progress. This was the kind of discrimination that was passed around as easily as the tape measure in Groot Huis. Each time Mielie ascended the mountain after having fled her husband for the umpteenth time, the women who frequented Groot Huis could be heard clapping their hands and covering their mouths in shock.

Mam'Bhele would say in her deep jazzy voice: "You should all be ashamed. That fool over there is our fool. Same threaded eyebrows as all you yellow idiots. *We* failed her when we let her marry that brute. Shame on you all. You, Nellisiwe, where is *your* husband since you are so fond of pointing out to your peers how to hold the attention of a man? And you, Khayakazi, where is the money to feed the flock of children that you make additions to every other year? Are we to be surprised that your increased appetite and bulging stomach are signs of yet another lamb born to the slaughter? That child out there is your kin – a stupid fool like you all – but our fool nonetheless, and we do not laugh at that. We acknowledge it for the travesty that it is; a shortness of sight. Whoever here is free from that, I dare you to be so bold as to put forward your name."

Mam'Bhele darted her eyes about the room of young women, and nobody spoke to rebut her words. Only the Singer rattled on, pricking straight lines in cloth to form a dress for one of the girls or curtains for the home of some relative. When Mielie entered the Groot Huis to share her distress as though it were a surprise to her audience, she was also meted out the savage words of love that were the hallmark of Mam'Bhele's rearing. She carried the varied afflictions and fortes of all eleven children she had birthed, even if she wasn't sentimental. From her Singer, she dictated how the world should shape itself. Her neighbours she drew close, making strong allies with which to battle the decades.

Mam'Thembu would often descend from her homestead to have afternoon tea along with Mam'Bhele and Mam'Fusi. They would lay out their straw mats, and with legs outstretched, would pour tea from their cups into their saucers and sip it as they traded tales of how they had turned the day. It was a tradition that lasted until their deaths. Groot Pa Katjie entered Groot Huis only when it needed repairs. He often inspected it in the evenings when the three women had quit the room and returned to their homes, and Mam'Bhele was attending to some or other activity on the homestead.

Tata shared an intense bond with her. As her last-born, he was the only one who rarely faced her wrath, as the responsibility of raising him fell mostly on the shoulders of his elder siblings. He treated her not like a mother, but like his favourite grandmother, and because of this, he saw more varied shades of her personality. To him, she was a person with a past, dimensions denied to most of the other siblings. It wasn't a situation that lent itself to jealousy, but a natural order of things that was wholly accepted and even admired within the January clan.

Tata built the family business from a modest means of sustaining the family to a thriving enterprise that serviced many of the surrounding villages and the chief's relatives in lands further afield. He was the only man who ventured freely into Groot Huis, where he kept the teacups of the women filled and the roof raised in hilarity, blessed as he was with the refined quick wit of old Theodore. It was fitting that Tata was his namesake even though everybody called him Teddy. Groot Pa Katjie and Teddy had their own separate rituals and these endeared him to his father as well. Teddy was the one trusted with any renovations needed inside Groot Huis. It was their most favoured annoyance, pleasing Mam'Bhele, and they were the only two, I believe, with whose work she rarely found fault.

The heartbreak of his death unravelled both parents. The witch hunt for who had fed Tata mutton gravy, causing the allergic reaction that had brought about his death, was as extensive as it was brutal. A couple unafraid of unleashing all kinds of hell to protect their children, they became so unbearable that Tat'Mcebisi, their firstborn, was called from Port Elizabeth to intervene. Groot Pa Katjie was slow to release his bitterness, but Mam'Bhele, after having stormed through those she suspected of murdering her beloved son, found ways to live in the village with those she detested. She brooded behind her Singer inside Groot Huis, her fortress from which she sent out her battalions. Tata's death was made palatable only by the competency of Ma, who proved herself to be more than the widow for the jealous neighbours; one who could not only comfort her grieving mother-in-law, but pick up where her husband had left off and do even better.

Mam'Bhele grew to value her daughter-in-law so much that she took it upon herself to be the mother our mother could no longer be when she had to be the husband of provision to all. The type of resilience Ma showed Mam'Bhele revived her energy a lot sooner than most had bargained for. In a few short months, she was once again the woman who busied herself with the countless activities that filled up her days. In all the years of my life, her linoleum floors were kept bright and shining even by great-grandchildren who had been cheated of her brand of love by her death.

She lived long enough to witness some of our tragedies, though.

An old woman by that time, still dedicated to the family, she found me after they had left me twisted in my broken bones. That is how they had overpowered me. They broke the bones in my ankle so that I fell to the ground; two of them held down my other leg as the third one climbed on top of me. He kept his eyes on me the whole time, and in defiance, I didn't look away. If he was going to take what didn't belong to him, then he would have to remember every line on my face, and count all the tears that poured out of my eyes. The next one couldn't let his eyes meet mine. He took the shortest time, and was the first to run away when they were finished. The last one will remain with me all the days I am given to wandering the earth. He was my love. At least, he had said those words. A boy with the lazy eyes of a thirsty animal, the arms of a warrior and legs as thick as trunks, pressing his whole weight into my pelvis, tearing into me and breaking all the promises he had made.

He made the others watch, long minutes until my body convulsed in an orgasm, and then he said to them: "That's how you do it."

In the minutes after they had left me exposed, all alone in the hut, it dawned on me that this moment alone was the last time I was going to exist without being shaped by what had just happened. I wanted to remember it. I could hear their footsteps disappearing down the mountain as they raced each other in childlike joy after their conquest. They had not yet shared notes or lived to regret the moment. They were still driven by the reckless abandon that had made them brave enough to execute this idea to begin with. I was still myself. Nobody had seen my bleeding violated parts. Nobody pitied me yet. I could still walk into any room and be feared by the wasp-like girls who could not understand how I walked into a space and filled it. Those girls had yet to learn that I was not as infallible as they believed. I was still a giant of possibilities, who wore the best dresses, made by myself.

I began to take notes of everything around me. The dark burnt straw that was the roof of the hut. The soothing clucking of the chicken sitting on its eggs in the corner. The bed from where I had been pulled onto the floor that smelt of cow dung. The painful pulsing of my split lip. The small windows of the hut let in weak sunlight, and I wondered if I should pray; it was so quiet, I felt alone. God felt so far from the clutches of my thoughts that inviting Him in would be an admission of a need that I had not had before; an admission of change, when all I wanted to do was remain the same. I mattered in this old version of myself. The one of tomorrow faced less favourable odds. As I concentrated harder on being as I was before they had entered me, I smelt the sweet scent of the fallen fruit outside, the trampled apricots. That was the last thought I had as myself: a longing for apricot jam. I lay there watching it all vanish and slip away from me.

> *Tata, where are you now? Deep under the ground where I wish also to be. In your sun, we basked; when we entered the room, your eyes shone so bright, it was as though a vision had just appeared to you. Now, alone in this red pool, I lie without your loving eyes to erase this moment from my life. He said your words like you did, but then he cracked my bones, and here I lie a broken mass of a thing longing*

for when I had nothing but hours with you. Kiss me again and toss me in the air so I can recall only the sound of your voice and the charge of your smile as the measures of my happiness.

Mam'Bhele had made it her duty to check on us each evening before my mother returned from Kokstad with her load of material for the shop. My father had operated a building warehouse business, which Ma took over after his passing. Nonti preferred to spend the afternoons with Mam'Bhele at Groot Huis and would come home in the evenings when Ma returned. After school, I would attend to the chores around the homestead, assist Ou Takkies in rounding up the cattle and putting them in the kraal. That day, Ou Takkies had gone with Ma to Kokstad to help load the cement delivery onto the lorry which Ma had to drive, as Tat'Mzamo was in East London that week.

I heard Mam'Bhele's call of panic as she stood over me asking for an explanation of the obvious. She could not lift me; I was as heavy as she was. Nonti had the build of the men in our family, not our mothers; small and slight. She stood at the door taking in the scene. I wanted to shield her from it, I wanted her to stay the same and not be scarred by my violation, but she came to me, to the side of the unknown, and became an ally. She stood in my pool of blood and pulled my skirt down before running out to call my mother, her small feet leaving a trail of blood prints out the door.

Later, Mam'Bhele and my mother bathed me in that very room and fed me. That night, Ou Takkies, in an uncharacteristically pensive mood, accompanied me to Groot Huis where Groot Pa Katjie led me to the room not too far from their bedroom. He too had that grave appearance when he stared at me.

In the morning, Mam'Bhele came to my room and asked one question: "Who?"

She was not a forgiving woman when it came to her children, especially since the death of my father, and if she had still possessed the strength she had the day she had choke-slammed Groot Pa Katjie by the water well, she would have gone herself to find those boys.

I offered their names, and how I had come to know them. They were local boys and not hard to find; later, when the January-Miya uncles had brutalised their bodies, not a single one of their families reported this to the chief or the police. It had been settled in the old way. The boy who could not look at me when he climbed me committed suicide the following year. He hanged himself, and even then his family levelled no accusations against our family.

Their hatred was passed along instead in muted voices on Sunday afternoons after church, or in haughty laughter as they made loud deliberate conversation in the shop when I worked the till. No boy from a good home would be found near me; even if they could marry a deflowered girl, it was the January-Miya mafia that was feared. A man was easily emasculated in our family, according to the legend. Even the children birthed by women from this family took their features, it was said. There was no chance to be anything but a slave to the machinery of the wealth of the family, either as a shop manager or by accepting favours in the form of further studies and moving on to even more lucrative careers.

The incident, as it was often called in hushed tones, split the village, and yet again the culprits belonged to the blood of old Theodore. Some said they rued the day the chief had ever allowed the stranger to steal the land and name of the Miya family. The Miya family had lived amongst them for three generations without scandal, but since the entrance of this young upstart, there had never been peace. The women of the family were particularly vile, it was often said, uncouth wild beings who saw it fit to govern themselves even under the cover of marriage. Others would throw in, *well, if you are married into a family descended from a rascal, it was bound to be this way.*

I heard all this commentary in my days working behind the till in the shop. I did not return to school after the incident. Each morning when I tried to, I thought of those three boys. I could smell each one of them, and I saw clearly the shape of their bodies and the looks on their faces when they were on top of me, save for the one who had kept his face turned away from me. Ma, as a former educator, threatened me with all manner of poverty if I refused to get an education, but Mam'Bhele was more flexible, and under the cover of her porous views on education, I was left to run the shop with Ou Takkies.

My lover, the one who had told the other boys "That's how you do it", took his beating by my uncles as a provocation and a challenge to exhibit his menace. The beating had left him with a glass eye, which made him appear more dangerous than he was, but once the ankle he had broken had healed, he couldn't beat me in a fight, so that didn't scare me. What wounded me most was the way he reminded me of the sounds I made when he made me climax. He reminded me of the contours of my body which he had let two other boys examine, even though he was the only one I had invited that afternoon; and he reminded me often how it was by invitation that they had come. I had made myself available for an examination. He told me that my father was a weak man who had died like a dog, and derided him for having none of the January magic that Groot Pa Katjie rubbed people's noses in. Nobody could prohibit him from herding cattle in open fields, even if those fields were close to where we collected water each morning. Even beating him to a pulp again one afternoon after he had followed me home did not give him the incentive to cease taunting me.

Nonti had been moved to a boarding school in Port St Johns after the incident, and I only ever saw her during the school holidays, where we spent countless evenings with Mam'Bhele, who sewed us the dresses of our desires. By then I had picked up her skills from watching and assisting her with the orders she got from our relatives and neighbours.

Mam'Bhele was the only person who never called what happened "the incident". One day we were sitting alone in Groot Huis, studying a pattern for pants that Nonti had requested for a disco she was attending the following Friday, when Mam'Bhele suddenly said to me: "Were we wrong to keep you here after those boys violated you?"

I didn't know what to say, so she got impatient: "Speak, no point in dithering about in the shadows. Your mother won't do the mending work, she is too busy and rightfully so, so speak."

My hand shook as I tried to stick the thread through the eye of the needle: "Where would I have gone?"

"We have family everywhere. Nonti is away. You could also go."

"Is this what you think is best?"

"I moved here from a very far place when I married Katjie and it was good for me. A new place has the opportunity for renewal. What's the point of being an old maid locked in by one moment of your life?

A moment that was not of your doing."

"It was of my doing," I said meekly.

"What is of your doing is this church mouse thing you have going on right now. The world will never be kind to girls like us. Black as night and thick as bulls, that's back of the line material, but we can be ourselves without their frightful glare. I didn't set out to get married; it was never in the cards for me. Katjie married me for himself, who knows what I have done for him beyond carrying on his lineage. If he dropped down and died tomorrow, I would still see through the years living as I do now. I have never had this feeling of wanting to be with a man. It has never driven me as it seems to drive other women. Maybe that makes me queer."

I chuckled involuntarily at this.

"Yes," she carried on, "this godforsaken need to be assisted to be the creature you already know yourself to be – I don't have this problem, and perhaps sometimes it informs my problem-solving in a bad way. We went out to exact the same level of brutality those boys inflicted on you, but it solved nothing, did it? Because the pain wasn't in the brutality. It was the deception that hurt ,and that cannot be whipped with a cane."

I wiped the tears from my face as they spotted the tissue paper on which the pattern was drawn.

"I have never known such deception, and that was my blind spot – it was our blind spot. So you have to leave then," she said decisively. "You have to find again that stone in your gut that terrifies them and makes them think three times before they run their mouths like dogs to you." She took the pattern from my lap and sent me to go boil the water as Mam'Thembu was almost about to arrive for afternoon tea.

So it happened that when I turned eighteen, I left for Cape Town. My lover had married a girl from a neighbouring village and everyone but the January-Miyas had attended, which is why the wedding was recorded in history as a flop; we were a difficult family to disregard in the village. I hadn't believed that such a thing could have a powerful impact on me. I didn't know the girl, and she was marrying a man known for violence, which claims he had rubbished to the girl's family, who had been poisoned against the January-Miya name. There was no reason for me to have envied her.

Yet when I saw the procession pass in front of the homestead, with him holding her hand to welcome her into his family, I had a severe anxiety attack. Ou Takkies fanned me with a piece of cardboard and turned me onto my side after I collapsed. Mam'Bhele had few kind words to say about the affair, having warned me to stay away from the event. To this day I cannot say what broke me about that moment; but I knew then that if I didn't leave, I would die sooner rather than later, and my lover would have won.

The whole way to Cape Town I kept seeing his hands holding hers, locked in the promise he had once made to me. A promise he had kept to her. For weeks, even as I was busy at my work station in the factory, I would see those hands locked into each other, and my lungs would constrict in pain. I would have to focus intensely on my breathing to avoid having a panic attack on the factory floor, which would surely have resulted in my termination.

The city was a place of strange existences, and I found that in many ways I grew even more silent in my first years there. I rented a small backroom at the friend of a relative who had been contacted when I announced my departure to the family. Groot Pa Katjie was forever saddened by my decision and spent years hoping I would return to the fold of the family business, or at least marry a decent man. He felt that the incident had robbed me of my best years, and that stirred in him such hatred for the perpetrators that he refused to tender his services to any of their families, but the rest of the family still did.

Mam'Bhele was proud of me, though she never said so. I saw it in the trunk full of new dresses she gave me on my departure. Ma accepted it silently; she had seen us through the years as best she could, and her parting words were simply for me to not fill up the earth with fatherless children like her cousin. But I knew I couldn't have children after what my lover and his friends had done to me. In a moment, they had given me the same amount of lovers most women accumulated in a lifetime. No other man would ever touch my body, or even be allowed to see it again. I had retired it for life, and my luck was that no man was ever in a hurry to see me naked.

The women at the factory were flighty girls who spent their lunchtimes building their bonds over the harrowing tales they told about their respective varieties of domestic strife. Even in my grief, I found their stories entertaining. For most of my life, Nonti had been my only friend, and in our family, we didn't have cliques that operated like gangs. When you walked into a room, you could sit with anybody and join any conversation you wished, depending on what mood you were in. The boys were treated the same as the girls, and we carried on without ever noting the difference because our combined skills kept Mam'Bhele satisfied. She didn't discriminate when she dished out her savage hidings for failure to complete chores around the homestead.

The women at the factory subscribed to a different code; some were more important than others in their group. It was interesting to observe a person allowing a stranger whom they had just met to have dominion over them purely because they thought she was prettier or had a more suitable spouse. I couldn't see the benefit of banding together only to tear one another down, but I longed for their company regardless. It was a lonesome thing to not have anybody to trade tales with, like I had grown up doing.

In my first month in Cape Town, the only time I spoke was to the cashiers when I was shopping for groceries, and possibly when strangers asked me questions. My loneliness sprung in me a new habit of watching people live their lives. I created narratives for them. If I saw a young family, I would create for myself a short sketch of how the young lovers must have met. Perhaps the baby they were carrying had been a miracle that they had been unsure they were going to be granted. I would try to decide what their combined income was, and what they did for a living. I took care to not be found doing this, but even after the subjects of my observations had left, I would still wonder what they were doing at that moment – sleeping perhaps, or playing with their infant. Perhaps the young mother had taken a bath, and finding her in her natural state, her husband might have thought of making love to her. I did this so often that one day in the taxi home, the women I was riding with were in such hysterics over a story that one of them told about a date she had been on, that I felt jealous of their bond. The woman relayed how she had spent an evening with a man she had fancied for months, but whom she had thought was uninterested. The man had handled the date so well that the woman was considering heading back to his flat to consummate the relationship. Just as she was about to make the suggestion to be intimate, he asked her if she had ever received a butterfly kiss. Naturally, the woman said, you don't want to be a prude – if there are new things to be tried, you have to remain open. The women listening to this story all made scandalous sounds, and others clapped each other's hands in anticipation of the sexy soundbite that was coming. The woman then told how the man had leaned in close and fluttered his long lashes against her cheek for a few seconds, and then pulled back. She said that dried up her panties in a minute. The hilarity that broke out made even the taxi driver laugh; he commented on the wretchedness of women who would humiliate a man so publicly in his absence. The women laughed so hard that even I found myself smiling. Their community reminded me of home and my aunt Khayakazi, who was constantly pregnant with every good-for-nothing who could be found, and how the January cousins used to laugh about this in Groot Huis under Mam'Bhele's watch, knowing she would pull us back with terse reproaches if we got too out of line.

At the factory, Karlien Nortje, who fancied herself the team captain of these women, came to me one day during lunch and asked me if I was a dark coloured. I had no idea how to answer the question on the basis of not understanding it. In the village, there had been no segregation, and the fair skin of most of my relatives had just been a genetic fact, with no political or other consequences. What I learned quickly in the city is that there were always consequences to the texture of hair and the lightness of skin, but I stayed away from such things. To be fair to her, my surname did add strength to her summations, and the fact that I went by an Afrikaans nickname – a language I spoke very well – could have given rise to suspicions of a heritage muddled by racial ambiguity.

I had left the village to escape those newlyweds who had flaunted their promises to each other in my face. I had run away from my lover; the politics that charged the air in this part of the world didn't interest me. Most of the women who worked in the factory as seamstresses were coloured women, with the black staff relegated to the cleaning duties. I had been given the job because Ou Takkies had a girl in Cape Town to whom he had passed himself off as coloured in order to get her to sleep with him. She had remained devoted to him. She assumed from my surname that I was a coloured woman, and when I arrived, the supervisor turned a blind eye to the tar of my skin when he saw the quality of the hems that I sewed. My arrival had caused a rise in political consciousness that I had been unaware of until that snide question. My disappointment at understanding that the women staring at me were not trying to figure out how to approach me out of friendship, their stares were laced with suspicion, even hatred instead. So I told Karlien I had no idea what she was talking about, after which she quipped that I was a Johnny-off-the-boat, and proceeded to walk away from me. Angered by what had led her to believe I deserved her disdain, I grabbed her by the loose hair of her ponytail and spun her around. The women in the canteen all stood to attention to watch the ensuing fight.

"Where I am from, you say what you mean," I said, my hand twisted around the loose hair of her ponytail and her neck bent to one side. I was triple her size and could have severely harmed her. "The boat of my naivety sailed a long time ago; don't test me."

I pushed her away from me and returned to my workstation angry that I had exposed myself. I was once again the black slab of a woman who, when faced with making acquaintance with people, found herself with clenched fists ready to throw jabs. After that, the women kept their distance from me until the day I resigned a year later.

By then there was a fever in the air, and when the police shot those men they called activists, one of whom lived not too far from the room I was renting, all the people in my circles went berserk. They showed the dead activists they had shot on the news that evening, their limp bodies covered in red sand. The police were turning them over onto their backs with sticks as the newsreader referred to them as "black terrorists", and at that you didn't want to exclaim too loudly; perhaps the man had indeed been a terrorist or a criminal, or an innocent man who taught at the primary school down the road. It was just so hard to know. I had never known anybody who ended up on the news.

It was such a different space to the village. In the village, our anger centred on family issues, and our common enemy was a named person with an address where we could go to exchange blows. In this space, collective anger centred on the operations of the state, an intangible thing. It felt like none of my business to be involved with whom the police did and didn't shoot. Groot Pa Katjie had taught us well the art of never finding your nose in another's pot, so I watched the violence like a spectator would a soccer match. If we were told not to take the trains, I complied; and if there was a mass funeral (as there always were in those days), I attended so not as to appear to be making a statement. I maintained a few strategic friends, those who could corroborate my life story in full should the revolutionaries come to ask if I was a spy – and anybody who irritated the comrades was at risk of being named a spy.

So for a while after I resigned from the factory, I made a living making curtains and whatever else in the township for my immediate neighbours, mostly to stay away from the violence, until having to chase people down for money owed made me quit the business altogether. A tough few months passed by without anything formal, and then one day Phelisa from my days at the factory bumped into me at the grocery store and told me that one of the fancy hotels by the Company Gardens had vacancies. I applied and was hired as a cleaner. The pay was good enough for me to put some savings away and send some money back to Mam'Bhele, who didn't need it. I nevertheless felt it was a rite of passage to be able to do such a thing for your elders.

In the first few weeks of working there, I witnessed the kind of wealth that put our January dynasty to shame. Mam'Bhele would have loved that hotel. From the crisp white bedding to the high shine of the heavy oak furniture, it was immaculate. I loved cleaning those rooms. When all was in order, it gave me such peace to walk about the room examining the expensive furnishings. I replicated the layout in my rented backroom. The clothes the guests wore were of such high quality that I would find myself examining the seam line of a dress that I was supposed to be folding and putting away, or taking down to the laundry. Other times I would sketch the pattern so I could later make myself a copy of the dress. It was work I enjoyed; it kept me away from the ceaseless humming noise of the township and its impoverished surrounds. In the hotel, music was played at a decent pitch and people spoke calmly and quietly.

Arriving each morning was transformative and even cathartic for me. Changing into the white uniform and moving about as a shadow amongst the guests whom I greeted politely as they made their way to their meetings or fancy dinners was an art form I came to perfect.

Although I never learned to speak English fluently beyond murmured courtesies, I soon learned to understand much of what I heard spoken, certainly enough to pick up commands and instructions.

I was soon distinguished from my colleagues and promoted to a supervisory post. This turned out to be a mockery as I had a supervisor to supervise my super-vision, and the pay didn't change that much. It didn't bother me as much as it seemed to harass the nerves of my colleagues, who called it out for the condescension that it was. That was none of my business. My business was to ensure that the standards I had found remained high. With my new position came a name tag, a better uniform, and an opportunity to gift new staff with the spirit of attention to detail that was required to maintain such perfection.

One afternoon at the end of a shift not too long after my promotion was announced, I was called into the floor manager's office. Ms Raath was a woman I had modelled myself upon when I first started working at the hotel. When you thought of her, you thought of a box of precise dimensions that left you feeling as though you had seen something of perfection. From shoes to hair, nothing was ever out of place. Even her smile, put on mostly for the benefit of guests, was perfect in its form as pretence. She was heavy-handed if work did not meet her standard, but overall a fair woman who was equally respected and loathed by the staff. Mam'Bhele had similarly exacting standards, so Ms Raath and I worked well together. Fairly early on she had noticed and complimented me several times on my dedication to perfection.

When I stepped into her office, she was sitting inspecting the new stationery the hotel had ordered, checking that the spelling and branding of the hotel had been captured correctly by the suppliers. "Please sit," she said, distracted by the folders in front of her.

I sat down and folded my hands into my lap, casting my eyes around the room. Behind her desk were large bay windows that gave an amazing view of The Mountain and the ever-present scarf of cloud wrapped around it. The room was tidy and well furnished.

Eventually, she looked up and laced her fingers together. "Right, I called you here to check up on your paperwork. I see that you have not yet submitted a copy of your identification records. Now this is an irregularity that we cannot allow, especially in this new position.

I know that some of you have issues with documentation, and don't quite know when or where you were born since we no longer have proper regulation in that regard, so I advise you to go to Home Affairs to apply for an identity document as soon as you are able. In the interim, I will need a name to submit so we can order your name tag. There is just a small issue, you see: Nobantu – 'Bantu' – the politics of it all can get in the way," she said, opening her palms as though the explanation was obvious. "Do you happen to have another name?"

I didn't. Nobantu was the name of crazy old Ma'Miya whose land Groot Pa Katjie had supposedly stolen the day he arrived in the village. I was proud of the name, of being named after the original rebel who had refused to smother her baby on account of it being custom. She had seen right through the stupidity of ageing men and useless cruel rituals. Ma'Miya had set our family on the trajectory it now enjoyed; she repudiated the conventions of her time and took against the important lie girls were and are taught to believe: that they don't have choices. Many of the January children had only one name, either Xhosa or Afrikaans as a testament to our heritage. I thought of the nickname my father had given me as a child, but didn't know its English version or how to spell it, so I told it to Ms Raath, hoping she would write it down so I could put it in my identity book: Romance. The English version of Room-ys. She wrote it down on a form and handed it to me to sign. I saw the spelling and memorised it, scribbling it down on a piece of paper after I left her office.

I had a new name in a new city with a fancy job. If my love could have seen me now. I had left him in the dust with his sweet newlywed in that village on the bend of the Thina River. In my job, I met people who were said to be presidents or ministers. I led them to their rooms and ensured that their requests were timeously met. It was an honour to serve them and have them say my new name: thank you Romance, how did you come about such a fascinating name. In my one perfect sentence of English, I would say it was the name my father gave me, and they would say that he was a good man. In my heart I would agree: he was a good man. Tata would have been proud to see his Room-ys, his sweet ice cream, rubbing shoulders with the rich and famous. So I came to the city, and didn't bring shame on my family's name. I became someone. The Januarys were on the rise again, Groot

Pa Katjie's tenacious spirit had slain yet another dragon. Mam'Bhele had been right all those years ago about how a new place offers renewal. My lover had a glass eye and a not-so-new bride in the same place where he took from me the only agency women are given in this world. He did it to remind me that even that agency was trite, even my body could be owned. But I had a new name now. He didn't know this woman. He hadn't violated her. He hadn't placed her in the shadows of her own life as he strolled into matrimonial bliss, never blamed for the methodical execution of his menace. Romance, NomaRoma, Rom-Rom was a bird who had taken flight, and nobody was ever going to cage her again. In my small rented room, which I furnished with a single bed, a small bar fridge, and a small reading table on top of which sat a small radio, I rolled out the years.

Occasionally I would go home to visit Groot Huis, where I observed the changes, younger generations growing up together forming their own bonds, connecting with old faces – Khayakazi whose womb had thankfully finally stopped working, and Ou Takkies, whose name was now warranted.

Nonti married a sensible man the spitting image of our father, and a year later, gave birth to a female Groot Pa Katjie. When Vuyolwethu was born, the family was in a buzz because she had brought back the hazel eyes that we were seeing less and less of in the younger generations of the January-Miya clan. She was a sweet baby who, when I saw her three years later at the unveiling of Ma's tombstone, followed me around like the ball of a chain. She loved to climb into my lap and trace on my face the same joined eyebrows she had. She would say in her perfect English accent: "Same like mine." I didn't see her again until she about ten years old, when her father came to Cape Town to enlist my help.

Nonti had hidden Mxolisi from everybody for a while. I don't blame her: family matters precluded outsiders, but between each other, there was an expected compulsion to share every detail of one's life as it unfolded. In our adolescent years, Nonti and I had kept close by writing incessant letters. I told her about the village happenings – from Thando spewing his sperm all over Namhla's face because he couldn't keep it up for more than a minute, to Viri being kicked by a blind donkey. She wrote back to me about the girls at her boarding school who were from Johannesburg and wore the latest fashions found in magazines, dated men who were fighting in the struggle and sometimes ended up in prison. She said the nuns at the school were batshit crazy, and the girls had to wear white underwear to assembly on Monday mornings or they would get detention. Other times we would talk about how we missed Tata, and try to remember the ingredients to the sticky toffee treat he used to make for us at the end of the school term. Sugar and buttermilk, I said to her in a letter – those were the ingredients. No, came her reply, has to be something else – I'm sure you are forgetting something. It's sugar, butter and milk.

During the school holidays, she would help me out at the shop by doing the stock-taking. The traffic of herd boys who came to enquire about the price of cement or thinners naturally increased during this time, but she never gave one person the time of day. I wanted to tell her to not be afraid to have a sweetheart, but I couldn't say that and mean it. We were tied by that moment when she bloodied her feet to pull down my skirt, and we both knew we couldn't move past it. It was the Great Silence between us even though we spent the holidays in careless reverie. All the cousins from Port Elizabeth and as far as Newcastle found themselves at Groot Pa Katjie's homestead, and then there would be no time for the Great Silence.

Once she left again, we would go back to letters about Sqibo falling asleep in his sedan only to wake during the night and punch and smash his windscreen because he thought he was bewitched, and she would tell me how the nuns had found the girls stealing condiments from the kitchen as part of a midnight dare, and made them kneel in the courtyard in the burning sun.

"That's him," she said to me one afternoon as we were cashing up.

I looked up to see a man with the slim arms, full beard and yellow skin of our father. He even had thick eyebrows, although his were not as much of a feature as ours were. He was a good-looking man whose confidence was grounded in more than his good looks. He also had kindness in his eyes that I didn't relate to.

"Who is that?"

"Mxolisi," she said in cool resignation that I could tell hid the depths of her excitement.

I felt their easy affinity for each other as he kept glancing at her. In her early adult years, having grown accustomed to the pestering that was due to her beauty, she had grown distant to anybody who was a stranger to her. That he had managed to cut through this and the Great Silence proved to me the strength of her feelings for him.

Later that afternoon the three of us took the longest route home so she could afford me the opportunity to approve him. He had our father's cheery disposition, and held a conversation well. I tried to like him, but found that I wanted to protect Nonti from what it might mean for her if he was too good to be true. She already had my blood on her feet; I didn't want hers on my hands. I was intentionally distant and unkind, which hurt her deeply and placed between us a boulder that could not be dislodged. I could not access her happiness, much as I tried. For me, love was a space of constant disappoint-ment and a moment of unimaginable violence. If it wasn't Tata, it wasn't love.

That afternoon with Mxolisi set Nonti and I on diverging paths that I could not have foreseen in our younger years. Mxolisi "that's him" Fani had stolen my sister's heart, and I resented him for it. He was as good as I had wanted my lover to be, perhaps even better. It wasn't that I begrudged Nonti the happiness she deserved; it was that with Mxolisi's arrival, the Great Silence had to be buried. Loving him meant that Nonti was unburdening herself of being complicit in my tragedy, handing it back to me to do with it what I saw fit. I didn't know how to tell her that I needed her; that without her to pull down my skirt, I would forever be exposed. But "that's him" had told me I was already alone – and being forced to acknowledge this to myself made me want to hurt her.

By the time I was summoned from Cape Town for the occasion of her wedding, I was merely a function and relation: maid of honour and older sister. The joy that should have accompanied sisters celebrating a watershed moment became an occasion clouded by stiff conversation and unusual diffidence that prompted Mam'Bhele to investigate its origins. If she ever found out the truth of it she kept it well hidden from me, because the wedding went ahead. Afterwards, we barely spoke or saw each other unless it was in a crowd full of people.

When I ran into Mxolisi in the foyer of my place of employ, it was easy to spot him because he had not aged since the time I had last seen him. He looked so much like Tata. He had gained weight slightly, which suited him. He was sitting with a group of white men speaking with seriousness etched all over their faces as I approached them. I had just finished my shift and was dressed in regular clothing, so it wouldn't be deemed odd to approach him; any onlookers would most likely assume that I was also a guest at the hotel. I ignored the floor manager whose eyes were already piercing me for using the main entrance to exit, and remained locked on me as I broke protocol by approaching a guest. But Mxolisi was family, and his joy at spotting me approach was my relief. He excused himself from his colleagues and walked me outside.

Here he relayed that Nonti was in bad shape, and asked for my help. "The child has nightmares every night, even now that I am gone, I worry that Nonti isn't capable of taking care of things by herself," he told me when I enquired after the health of his family. "You have been missing for years." He stated this last part as a matter of fact.

"It was needed. I have a life here."

"You are missed."

"You just said that."

"Anyway, I will tell Nonti you are well, last we heard you were working at the factory. It's good to see that you have carved out a place for yourself here." Everything he said felt like an accusation.

It was obvious that I would agree to help. It had been a long time, and I had denied for too long how much I missed my sister. It was my turn to guide her out of what could easily become a state of permanent stagnation. I understood the ghosts in her head; nobody knows better than me what it is to kill a dream. I did it the moment after my lover and his friends left me there with nothing but apricot jam.

I watched Mxolisi skip up the short flight of stairs back into the hotel, then walked down the long drive and over the road to take a turn about the Company Gardens. I did not often walk here; it was hard not to feel repulsed by the homeless people and drug addicts who made their beds over the open drains. I had been in this city too long; it had changed so much that I had not realised how much I had changed with it as well.

This was clear from my altercation with Karlien Nortje, who felt the changing winds and was threatened by what they might mean for her livelihood, to the jittery existence we led in the township during the height of political violence, right through to the release of the imprisoned leader of the liberation movement from prison. I had been knocking off on a shift that afternoon at a cooking position I had taken up after resigning from the factory, and when I came upon the square known as the Grand Parade opposite the old bank to join the queues for the taxis, I came upon packed crowds of people jostling each other for an inch of space. The city and its teeming streets had never endeared itself to me, who had grown up watching the rise and fall of the Thina River, sleeping for hours under age-old acacia trees that were also perfect places to sit perched on a sturdy branch and observe the world below. Being in that excited crowd, irrespective of the occasion, made me feel ill, and I recall turning back to where I had come from to find an unused table, where I sat impatiently for the fever to pass. Mam'Bhele would have hated the city too; there was too much filth, and even in a relatively clean state, you could still find the wretched of the earth poking out from its drains, reminding us of the debt owed to them by nobody, but still compelling us to feel indebted.

The Company Gardens was full of sunlight. It was one of those rare days in Cape Town where the weather was predictable for more than an hour, and the sickly wind hushed long enough for me to hear my thoughts. I passed a group of tourists who tried to lure me into taking a photograph of them or with them, I couldn't quite make out – either way, I declined. I sat down on a bench to enjoy the sun beating down without the constant obstruction of clouds.

In the years when I first arrived in the city, such a moment was an impossible dream; being found in the Gardens enjoying the shade of protected trees was as political as throwing a rock at a police van. It felt strange not to know how I had been afforded the duplicity of being born into rural wealth and yet being considered a poor urban black. I had spent my early years in this city hearing countless stories on the train to work of people who had left their villages after battling such abject poverty that the city held all the promise of a sprouting harvest after good rains. In our family, we had been loved, deeply so, and money had hardly ever featured as a challenge or problem. I had only left because my lover had clasped the hand of another, and told all by doing so how little he thought of me.

They had not been present when he had courted me by the water well in the mornings. He was a vision of a man, so different from the men of my family, who were so small in size. In his embrace, I could disappear and not feel so much wider and thicker than other girls my age, fourteen-year-old girls who had only just bled for the first time. I had been bleeding since I was twelve, and my breasts at fourteen were already full round melons to accompany my fully formed thighs.

Tata insisted that I looked like Ma, whom he said he had spotted at the bus stop one afternoon in a nautical striped dress and white high heels, falling in love at once with her wild hair and full figure. The truth was that I bore no similarity to our mother save for my dark skin. Nobody ever saw my mother without commenting on how pretty she was for a dark woman, an evaluation they never extended to me, but it didn't matter to me because such nonsense was just not part of our world view. We were Januarys; we were graded a notch higher. That's why the other girls didn't like me and despised Nonti. While I was riding purely on the propaganda of Groot Pa Katjie, Nonti had the kind of beauty that created enemies of women and made men reckless. In sorting through the pain of what my lover did to me, it had crossed my mind that perhaps they had meant to harm her as well that afternoon, and for that, I punished myself for having let my lover access me so easily. If they had harmed her, it would have all been my fault. And she still stepped in my blood and was sent away because of my naivety.

I found myself on the steps of the famous St George's Cathedral and I walked in, finding the reverend of the church alone cleaning the altar.

"Molo Mfundisi," I greeted him in Xhosa, unsure of the quality of my English.

His portly figure was bent over the altar dressed in the classic black gown and white collar of religious robed men. He looked up, panting. "Welcome." He moved towards me and offered me a hand-clasp: "Confession is tomorrow," he said in Xhosa.

I explained that I was just in the Gardens, but being led by curiosity, I had decided to enter to see for myself the famed church. I sat down in the front pew and he followed, wiping his forehead with the sleeve of his cassock. "Interesting. And? Is it amazing?"

I ignored his question and continued to speak. "I am about to leave this city, Mfundisi. When I first moved here, I thought it was a place of freedom, but now when I walk about, I find that I have not seen much of what is so famous about this city. It makes me wonder what it is then that I have learned. A decade spent not needing anybody has left me without true memories to savour. I have only learned how to survive."

"This bothers you, I gather?"

"Is this God's intended plan for us, to be alive in this way?"

"Well, I'm not at the altar right now, so perhaps I can answer you as a man finding his way in this life. When I was a child, my parents were shot in front of me by a neighbour who, in his inebriated state, accused my father of owing him a debt my father knew nothing about. In his rage, the man raced into his house, fetched his rifle, and fired rounds in the direction of my parents, who perished, leaving my sisters and me as orphans. This was in Kimberly, where the shifting slopes of the desert sand were the only change you ever saw. Imagine then spending the rest of your childhood affected by such a tragedy. Years later, as I was doing my prayer rounds in a prison as a young priest, I found myself having to pray over my parents' murderer. This is how God works, I have learned. You can take from that story what you will. They say a good priest should never be prescriptive, but I spent my early years in the ministry missing the point. You will be met by God at the place of your needs, and what you do when the decision lies before you to depart for your destined place will define you."

Between us, for a moment, there was a celestial silence. The years were flitting by in my head. So many years I had spent running, but also standing still. I had never been born for convention; I had accepted this about myself even before my lover raped me.

"What if the places you are sent to are meant to prepare you to heal others? Is that an operation of God?"

The priest chuckled. "Well, seeing that He is the CEO of the company, He has His own discretion."

I didn't join in his laughter because I didn't under-stand what he had just said. Seeing this, he immediately became serious: "What led you here today will be there for you, wherever you are going. There is nothing else to do but to trust that. I can tell that you have faced this moment before. Whatever makes this time different does not invalidate your ability to make the best of the experience and to harness the wisdom that it holds for you. Nobody else was called but you. And that is the source of your consternation."

I glanced up at the stained-glass image of Jesus crucified on the cross, His followers' hands outstretched towards him. Januarys didn't go to church to find God; it was simply what decent families in the village did. I had not attended church in ten years, but at that moment I knew that if I was renewed, I could be Romance anywhere. I could leave this life behind and still make friends, build a life, and be near to those who could build me up from within.

Many of them had already gone from this life. Mam'Bhele had died after refusing to undergo an operation to drain water from her lungs. She said she didn't see the need to cut up an old body, it would be foolishness. Nobody talked her out of it because we all respected and recognised the singleness of mind of a January woman. Groot Pa Katjie had died of old age, having endured a long life of hard work that had started the moment he famously arrived in the village one fateful afternoon to build up a family whose name was about to disappear with the dementia of my namesake. Ma died in a crash as she was driving the delivery van back from Kokstad. The van was pushed off a cliff by an oil truck that lost its brakes coming down the hill. She was by then too old to still be making the trip, but habit had motivated her to be hard-headed. Tata I always missed, and it was strange to think that I was older now than he had ever lived to be. Ou Takkies had succumbed to Aids, which nobody called Aids or HIV but the "sickness out there", and had looked far older than his forty years in the end.

The more I lived alone and apart, the more strange the world was going to seem when I emerged from my solitude. I didn't want to die alone like a person who had not been loved or who had not fought back when I had been dealt a hand meant to crush me.

My lover had lived in me all these years, and our marriage was far older than the one he had with the woman he had married. Our feelings had mutated over the years from hatred and resentment to pity and depression. These days I mostly felt nothing when that incident replayed itself in my head, because in this place it had no power. I had to leave him in this city because I had come here to hide from him; and although I could hardly be recognised, I knew that if I saw his face it would erase all my hard work and shift the ground from under my feet. So many people around me were poor, and it occurred to me that his poverty was in his spirit.

I grew up with everything, and it hid from me that other people come out the womb only to be fed ashes – and it's only these ashes that they know how to spread. We heard all the time about what the police did to those who fought against them for liberation, but I worried about those whose struggles were not documented. Those who inherited the spirit of violence because of their proximity to it, who inhaled it like the fumes of a fire. They were the ones like my lover; men who become husbands and fathers even though they were broken things that hurt everything they touched and were vindicated by a society overloaded with so many challenges it could not even reprimand the ill behaviour of a wayward child.

I saw these broken boys on the trains, gangs of them held together by bravado that could be smashed to pieces if it was hurled against a wall. When violence took hold over our neighbourhoods, and young boys skipped over fences, much like athletes, running from the police who had no qualms about dragging them by any limb into those big yellow vans, nobody had time to coddle the ones like my lover; and so they fell off the radar. They were either too cowardly to fight or too afraid of what would happen if they did. So they remained safe while the cities burned, and preyed on those that they could, never having known a single day without a cry from someone they had crushed. This city helped me understand my lover more than I think he understood himself. He was safe in the village, but even there boys were summarily whipped for all sorts of indiscretions, and scores were settled with public duels like the one Groot Pa Katjie fought with Nyathi long ago for the right to claim his ancestral home.

In the villages, the violence was nuanced; men ate first, bathed first, spoke first at public gatherings with no reasons provided for such privilege save those that they created themselves; and the exception and reverence with which the men in my family treated their spouses was seen as something that needed correction, not as the mutual coexistence of loving partners.

I did not have many friends, but I could not be the only woman who had suffered at the hands of a man who came from places like this. Every women who stood with me on the platform to catch a train must have had hundreds of moments when they tried to erase a grip similar to the one my lover had over my thoughts and my body. Moments when they had hoped that *their* lover would revel at the mundane activities of domestic life as they watched the years roll out from the safety of their homes. Many of these women who were proud wives in public were surely weary of dealing with the things of men daily, and handing over the credit, and telling nobody of the brutal disappointment at finding out that men were just flesh and bones. Juvenile, cruel men are nobody's dream come true. Even kind, generous men can struggle to place their needs above yours. Angry, violent men can have deep but misdirected compassion. Joyful, caring men can be insensitive and distant. Sweet, honest men can covet a life you could never have imagined them living. They are just men.

To this day no man has ever seen me naked, and I am certain that I would never want to be naked for anybody else but him. I am loosed but tied to him for life. These are my vows. I will keep them until I draw my last breath, but now I was leaving this city. I had a sister to love and a niece who needed protection. It was exciting to know that there would be a life for me after my internal turmoil. I would embrace a different truth, one that would redeem and strengthen me throughout the coming years. I didn't know if he would ever find such peace for himself; it was no longer my problem. I had only one thing left to do, and that was to forgive him.

The church was quiet, with a few other people coming in to sit in meditation. The reverend was seated beside me, anticipating how I might respond to the advice he had given me.

"I'm leaving this city. Father. Please pray for me."

"The prayer of Saint Christopher, the patron saint of travellers goes like this; repeat after me: Dear Saint Christopher, Protect me today in all my travels along the road's way. Give your warning sign if danger is near so that I may stop while the path is clear. Be at my side and direct me through when the vision blurs. Carry me safely to my destined place, like you carried Christ in your close embrace. Amen."

Saturday

Mxolisi Singatha Fani

The man lying in the bed next to me was losing his mind. He called the police and said that he had been kidnapped and was being held against his will. This, after having enquired sweetly from the nurse the address of the hospital, and her obliging out of pure exasperation as he was whined about one thing or another. The nurse was kind; I am the one who is unkind in my retelling of the moment. Later on in the day, two young constables were led by the same nurse to the bed of the man as he lay asleep. The nurse explained that the man had early onset dementia and was currently waiting to be transferred to a more suitable facility by his children. The constables were friendly, taking time to engage me briefly about the behaviour of the man, and even joking that I appeared in good health to be in the company of the demented. I laughed at the comment, but it grazed my nerves. I was dying and I knew it. I was in the right company, but one can never know that one day you might be the youngest on the boatman's ride across the River Styx.

I had no opinions of my life. It wasn't a great one worthy of a memoir. I was just writing to stave off the boredom that nobody knows but those patients who lie facing the ceiling, thinking of their bodies breaking the bonds of life signed with their occupants at birth. Was it even an oath, I wondered, or do souls force bodies to accompany them on their missions? It was immaterial now; I knew I was dying.

When I was young, I never thought about death, although spending much of my time in my father's church, I heard about its terrors from the more aged congregants. I would listen to them giving gloriously vivid accounts of their days, only to end with lamentations at their loss of virility. Comparing stories like these to my life, I should easily have had another three decades. I had the will to live. I wanted to see the changing world that I read about in the papers: the return of the Cold War under more uncertain and less bureaucratic leaders; the benefits of technology in a globalised world; how to make money last in a world where people lived longer. I wanted to sit with my grandchildren and describe, to their incredulity, the operation of some outdated technology that they were now using in its evolved form. I had tried to keep up with the times and be fashionable where it mattered, but my wiring was in conflict with my will to see out the years as I had imagined.

My first stroke caused me to rebel. I felt the limitations of my body powerfully during the healing process, often masking my frustration to cry alone at night once my family had left after their visits. I was not prepared to wind down, even as the nurses and doctors were shoving disability forms down my throat. I couldn't accept that a long active life would end with me rendered an invalid. I had been brutalised in jail, and had spent years carelessly dancing with criminality in the confusion of my youth, and a part of me was proud of this. I was content with the light and shade of my life; it meant I could call it my own.

The next day the man lost his temper at being trapped at the hospital and refused to co-operate with the nurses when they tried to bathe him or feed him breakfast. He was seething and gnashing his teeth like a wild animal. His tantrum lasted for hours, and the nurses asked if I wanted to move to the other side of the ward until the commotion had subsided. I declined. I wanted to see what the end looked like so I could prepare myself before I had to prepare my wife and my baby girl, who was a woman now – as she kept reminding me. I wanted to audit my sins and account for them.

Sometimes I spoke to the man from behind the curtain that separated us. He told me about the times when he thought he might have loved men. He said he knew early on that he was a bit eccentric, and in the sixties in England, society accommodated subcultures that would once have been considered a disgrace. He wasn't an artist by any stretch of the imagination, but he was friends with artists and their fluid lifestyles influenced him greatly in his early twenties. He had never known before that men could love each other, but for him, it felt natural to be fondled by a man, or to hold hands with a man in the darkness of the cinema – what he called "'the pictures". I think he liked being controversial; at least, that was what I told him. This made him laugh uncontrollably. I didn't know if I believed him: can one believe the confessions of a crazy man? He could have been telling me a story he had once heard, or expressing his deepest cravings. I had met his children and his wife; she visited him often, and she was as sweet as any woman who had tolerated a man for decades, quiet, unassuming, and elegant. She sat at his bedside, coaxing him gently to sit up or to eat. They could be the couple you saw at church waylaying the vicar to trap him into coming over for dinner, as their children didn't come around as often as they wished. The kind of couple newlyweds modelled themselves after, certain that death was the only thing that could remove them from each other.

It was hard to believe that Geoffrey was a man who had engaged in the 'subculture' of British society of the Swinging Sixties, or had any sort of eccentricities besides the ones his now damaged mind was gifting him. But I was in no position to judge. I wanted somebody to witness my end days, and the sense of humour of God is such that a man like Geoffrey was that witness.

"You are an artist, aren't you?" he asked me one night.

It was deep in the night, and the only sounds to be heard were those of the machines to which we were attached. He coughed a guttural cough and I felt something thump against the metal railing of the bed. "I see you writing all time, or are those sketches of my shrivelled arse?"

We both laughed. "I am married to an artist. I met her on a train. She was staring out the window, and then she suddenly turned her head and looked directly into my eyes. I found myself seated beside her in the next moment. I had to be close to her – you know that feeling, right?"

"It might be faint now," he said in a distant voice.

"I didn't even know what I was looking at." I cleared my throat, "I didn't know what I would say when I reached the seat next to her. Anyway, she writes poetry, books, essays – she just writes, much better than me anyway. I gave up my writing after reading hers."

"So what are you always scribbling in that small book of yours, then?"

"Tales for my daughter. Wisdom I have gleaned. Confessions."

"Of an affair?"

"I have never cheated on my wife."

"That is the answer we give, even at the end. We never admit to it. I am glad to see that it's a code."

I didn't suppose I could convince him of the truth of my statement, so I continued, "It has occurred to me that I won't be there for the pivotal moments of my daughter's life and she might need me." I paused. "She *will* need me, so I am telling her things I hope will help her."

He kept quiet for a long while. I was drifting back to sleep when he said in a low voice: "It might be a burden to know the truth of your father instead of keeping him as the great figure of your dreams."

"Maybe you should read it; you can tell me if I am wrong."

"My brain is wasting away," he confessed. Quietly he added, "I won't remember reading it, I won't remember you."

"Can I at least write about tonight? I feel as though this is who you really are. Tomorrow I might wake up next to somebody else."

Again he waited before he responded. "Love bound me to things that never belonged to me, but I grew to accept. I weep now as the noose with which I tied myself unravels on its own. I see at last how futile my efforts to cling to control have been. I am all alone."

That was the last thing Geoffrey ever said to me.

The next morning he woke up in a panic and kicked the sliding door beside his bed, trying to escape from his kidnappers. The nurses wrestled him for over an hour until they managed to sedate him, and later that morning he was moved. I never found out where.

Cradock

Let me tell you of a patriot.
He waylays men in the dark,
Four men, unsuspecting, unarmed,
And upon them he inflicts horrors
Not to be repeated with our mouths.
He is vindicated by this violence,
And hopeful for the demise of what he does not know is good and true.

Before this, you might have seen him
Under the cover of night,
Stewing in all his convictions,
As he waited, biding his time
Nothing able to deter him.
His impending actions, covered by instruction,
His menace, a condition of war,
His hatred, a birthright
Until at last, he sees, moving through the night,
The tempests,
The beasts vivid in his dreams,
Those who would live as he does,
Love this land as he does,
Cherish their lives as he does.
And towards them he runs,
His lungs burning with murderous conviction.
After that, they lived no more.
They were gone from this life.
They were burnt back to ashes.
They became the past.
And he lives: the patriot lives.

I wrote these words and so many others in the days after my father was murdered.

My father was a reverend of the church: who would harm a holy man? My mother's screams had subsided, and she had now become a whimpering fool. It was harsh of me to think that of her. She was at least sitting upright, rocking herself back and forth.

Perhaps it had been wisdom, or the sweet dance he had secretly had with death that had made my father decide against taking me with him to Mthatha that night. He had received a call about a man who had been missing for several years. He was a relative of some distant cousin who had found himself in a mess with the authorities on account of his involvement with the politics of the day. Being in a town as remote as Cradock, and given the attention of the police to some of our community members, my father had spent some days turning the matter over in his mind. A very precise man, I often saw him during that time looking into the distance, mumbling to himself. When the letter was slid under our kitchen door in the dead of night, and finally uttered some words, they made no sense. Its very method of delivery was an indication of the dangers associated with the sender.

On weekends, I worked with my father in his church. Every day he woke up at five for an hour of private morning prayer. Thereafter he would move to the vestry and begin poring over all the administrative business required to run a church, holding various meetings with the committees set up to ease the load, but who were often additional burdens. By then I would be in the church cleaning the altar, polishing the floors and placing the wooden pews in equally spaced lines along the red carpet that flowed all the way to the main entrance. The altar had behind it a large stained-glass window picturing Christ being crucified and his followers lifting their hands up to the dying man.

I had lived here for all fourteen years of my life. I knew all the families of this neighbourhood, and they, in turn, held our family in high esteem. The Fani family, so loved by the early settlers in Cradock that they took our great-grandfather under their wings and gifted our family with a plethora of theologians and black academics, a novelty in that region. This history was subsequently erased by the politics and realities of oppression – that obsession with how the black man spent his time being black.

I didn't become political until the night my father was murdered, but my kind of politics was very different from the organised activities with which the liberation movement became synonymous. Cleaning that church on the weekends of my adolescent years, and staying away from all the silent whispers I heard exchanged in between the hymns, had kept me safe. I had no business running about with revolutionaries; they had been fighting this war for decades. They seemed like hedonistic degenerates at the time, and although having a six p.m. curfew did stir in us bitter resentment, for me it was just how things had always been. The missionaries had patronised us, but educated us; now the government was monitoring us, but giving us our "independence". Each system had its benefits. Under apartheid, we could run our own affairs in accordance with our customs, far more than the missionaries ever allowed; and we had the discretion to educate ourselves in preparation for the working world. Most people

I knew had professions; my father was a clergyman and my mother a teacher. They had both benefitted from Presbyterian teachings, but had found a home in the Anglican Church. Likewise, I had the option of becoming a teacher or a theologian. These options never struck me as limitations. My noted brilliance in the field of mathematics could only ever lead me to becoming a maths teacher. That was the squared nature of my thinking then. Until they gave us back the charred bones of my father, and actually referred to him as my father. Then there was not a thing I did not burn.

I stepped out of the church that had been my fortress and into a burning country. We were all angry. We are still angry.

They killed a holy man. Reverend Fani, my father, a man who had thin fingers like spiders' legs and the grace of a dancer in mid-air. The only politics my father knew were those of the church. He believed himself chosen to cure the ills of the wretched and to comfort those in their time of need, to reprimand the more loose-lipped congregants, and to pray for better times. The church had been burnt down once, but that was on account of one of the congregants – being a misfit who had been summarily arrested more than once for various crimes. It took four years to rebuild the church, through donations from the diocese, the cathedral in a neighbouring town and the community's goodwill. But my father forgave the boy who set the fire, and even convinced the congregation to treat him with some measure of decency.

We would sit with our family and neighbours who had come to comfort my mother, listening to the news report of my father as a terrorist working undercover as a priest, who had used his church to hide "operatives" that threatened the nation. At this, my mother would burst into frightful tears that often resulted in her having fits that resembled epilepsy. People would have to pin her down until she regained her calm.

I often excused myself at these moments. The thought of pulling at my mother's skirts as she threw herself around led me to feign an indifference that equally made me feel guilty. I would leave the room calmly, but as soon as I swung open the front gate, I would break into a sprint to nowhere, anywhere, as long as it just was away from there. I had to block out the newsreader calling my father a terrorist.

We didn't even know that word until they started flinging it around like a hot potato. They made a mockery of his education, which he had received from some of the most outstanding missionaries of his time. They referred to it as a front. A covert front. What did all these words mean? we kept thinking. We knew with whom we lived, whom we loved, whom we revered as an upstanding member of the community. They wanted us to doubt not only him, but our reality. At the height of my rage, I found myself incarcerated in prison as a detainee. Rage is an emotion with a voracious appetite, and to be an angry young black man wasn't an original concept, or even one derived from the chaos of our neighbourhoods. I inherited it as a legacy of the compounded limitations on my being. I was bound to be angered by the circumstances of my life even if they had not intruded to pull me into the fire. If it hadn't been the cramped houses stacked next to each other amidst the free rolling hills around us, it would have been the eventual discovery of how, amidst the same free rolling hills as ours, white people lived in such excess of comfort.

In those cells, rage was a political statement. It gave you allies and fed you when you longed for a world still under construction. The guard who shoved us into a packed cell would tremble as he locked the door. The jeers coming from myriad black voices whirled around him; he must have known that while they taunted him, they wanted to pry the doors open and attack him. He knew they could. He knew his ilk would lose this war, but he couldn't tell his young wife that. Instead, when he went home he probably made furious love to her and called it passion. Then, as she slept, he would drink cold beers until they warmed his blood and filled his stomach, silencing the repeated sounds of metal gates slamming shut and multiple black eyes behind the bars, enraged and emboldened by the burning furnaces they called their homes.

In prison, I felt I had met the men I wanted to emulate. They knew things, things I thought mattered. They had committed atrocities that had hardened them, but this shell ensured their survival, and so they were admired. Some knew comrades across borders or in hiding, but those were never public conversations. The real comrades knew how to find each other. Other prisoners had tattooed faces and bodies, and sat in groups with sharp eyes watching everything. They had codes and systems quite separate from the political prisoners; for them, the prison was part of the culture of their brotherhood, a rite of passage, a means of showing strength. Though mistrust was high between the various groups, the common goal of terrifying the enemy formed strong bonds amongst us.

This camaraderie covered the foul smell of unwashed bodies and the thick air of yesterday, not yet ventilated by the new day of which we knew only because of the bleak sun shining through the small windows of our cells, stinging our eyes.

I felt so far from the life that I had expected to live while growing up. When I closed my eyes, I could see my mother as she was before my father had been killed, humming as she peeled vegetables after church, the heady smell of roast chicken blistering in the oven, and the tiled floor smelling of lavender polish. Everything was clean and in its place on the counter, and a cold jug of water stood covered with a doily. The dusty street was always empty on Sundays, or so it seemed in the humid air rising from the ground and blurring images of far objects or people. After lunch, my father loved to listen to the choral radio programme as he read the newspaper or wrote meditations for his sermons. Between these two individuals, I had balanced my life for close to fourteen years. Years that had been swallowed in these cells. Years that our gaolers could not imagine, as they decided should be the life of those people they reviled and condemned – for fighting for the inalienable rights ascribed to us at birth.

I think about being black every moment of my life. Even in my later years, now that I have given expression to my deepest ambitions. I am black: it's an admission that is a monitor and a measure. In those days, I was proud of it, but with no ideology behind it. Yet where I was from, it was common thing to hear that "a black man running is a black man sinning." Running towards his dreams, towards his children, towards his wife, in the street – he had to be stopped at all costs, three bullets put in his back, or new permutations of slavery found to suppress him. He had to be contained.

We died in numbers in those cells, and nobody has ever recorded the truth of that time. If you were in there and heard that your friend had "slipped in the shower and cracked his skull", it clogged whatever air you had to breathe because you wondered when your fall was coming. Even in the deepest of sleep, you would hear the rail of the metal door sliding open, and your heart would beat fast as you placed a wager on life and, equally, almost fervently, prayed for the finality of death. Night after night, oscillating between the two feelings upon hearing hard unkind voices, doors opening and others slamming shut. The pervasive darkness of our cramped cells, praying that someday we would once again look upon those we held dear in our hearts. Each morning waking to find yet another person gone from this life. The closeness to death was chilling, and when I finally walked out of prison, I was glad to be free, but I wanted to tell somebody what I lived through. I wanted to be celebrated for surviving, but I also wanted somebody to suffer. They, our enemy, were so far from suffering. They had their hands on the wheel and were spinning us in all directions with the arrogance of those who know they own you.

I was questioned during sessions of solitary confinement and whipping, gagging and starvation. Questions repeated in varied ways in efforts to tire the mind so that I would make a mistake and confirm or colour whatever information they had already obtained. My torture sessions often felt relaxed, with police officials casually walking about the room, trading sport updates with each other as though what was about to occur was normal procedure. The atmosphere put me at ease; I preferred that to being in the cells feeding off the fear that reached its climax daily, only to be breathed back in by those who stirred it up. It was the constant anticipation of death that caused the breakdowns – no matter how fortified the heart, the mind cannot survive that. In the interrogation rooms, seeing people doing normal things allowed for some release of our fear. It allowed access to a modicum of peace, so that even if it was your last day, it would not be in a dimly lit shithole. When the torture began, the fortified heart and the will to survive granted you the endurance to suffer the pains inflicted for information.

I knew nothing. That was my truth. I told Nonti nothing. All she knew about was the poetry I longed to write. She was protected from this side of me, and all the police could glean, from what I could tell, was that I had been writing letters to a girl who had attended the school that they suspected had been bombed or suffered the crime of arson. They had no leads to follow, and all I had to be was an infatuated lover with no connection to Port St Johns. Their suspicions arose mainly from the inferences they drew from their experience. I had motive because my father was Reverend Fani, which they pieced together quickly – but they thought I had died too. The second fact kept me detained for a long time because I had to account for my whereabouts in the past decade. There were no records of me attending any school, but I also knew that I was not attached to any sort of political or underground movement, which gave me the confidence to maintain my story about being a high school dropout who worked as a lackey in various small towns following the planting seasons for work. I had met Nonti in Maclear while she was on holiday, and she gave me the address of her school. I had never been to Port St Johns. All my letters spoke of the places my seasonal work had taken me. I used post offices to send her letters and my mother money when I had the chance. All of these things were the truth.

At times the investigating officers accepted these truths, and on other days they fed me variations of the actual truth of that day and my real whereabouts, but I never confessed. Their only satisfaction came from humiliating me during their torture sessions. What worked in my favour is that I had actually worked on the farms I had named. I had been friendly enough to be remembered, and in other towns I had kept mostly to myself, or had stayed for only a night or so to execute what I had set out to do. I could not be trapped by any lie, so I told only the truths that would keep me alive. When the pains they inflicted on me became severe, I held on to a simple dream in my heart: to drive down the highway with the windows down. That is what it was all worth – to feel a cool breeze created by the vehicle's motion through the tight, stiff air of a summer's day. To feel a force on my skin whose grace refreshed me. Nothing that was done to my body could take that away from me. No questions posed, regardless of how viciously they were posed, could reach through the whizzing in my ear of cool fresh air blowing through a fast-moving car on an open road to nowhere.

The worst memories came from when they placed us younger inmates in cells with small boys, barely in their teens, breastmilk still fresh on their tongues. They did this in order to be able to easily identify their torture victims. Boys were dragged out daily, taken away for hours, to return brutalised and maimed. For those who remained behind, what began as bravado for facing the enemy reluctantly turned into alarm and fear that robbed you of sleep and made you convulse in the night, imagining what might befall you. The boys who returned from these long periods of truancy lay whimpering next to us on the cold floor, sprawled across thin blankets that soaked up the blood from welts that would never be attended to. Some died. After battling a long cold night, we would wake to find a rigid body beside us. The guards would take their time clearing it out of the cell. When they did come, they not only collected the dead, but would make a fresh picking from the trembling souls whose gallant entry into struggle politics began with their naivety about what it meant to fight for a cause until the death. Nobody would sing songs or name roads after these boys. They would only ever be the shivering bleeding bodies who died in the middle of the night that some president, decades later, would cite as the "thousands upon thousands" who perished under the brutality of oppression. I witnessed this in prison as I waged my own private struggle. Others among us were true knights of valour, but I was a criminal with a father to avenge and a penchant for burning things that belonged to the state because the state had burnt my father to ashes. My actions were bound to land me in police custody sooner or later; but I cannot account here or ever for the horrors I saw in prison.

Of course, prison is also a state of mind. This is a truth I learnt seeing so many men my age traumatised by torture; how, long after release, they relived daily what had been inflicted on them. In each moment of their day, from when they climbed into their cars to when the backs of their skulls ached as they listened to their children's juvenile squabbles, to the hurt they felt when coveted sweethearts left them for better men – men who weren't involved in the politics, as though they themselves had chosen to be oppressed or enraged by it.

I remember being let out of prison with only the clothes on my back and the five cents I had in my pocket when I was marched in. My version of the truth had at last set me free. I walked out into the road and, unsure of where to go, I sat down and tied the laces of my shoes. There was nothing to see but a long road lined with thornbush trees framed by mountains in the distance, an idyllic picture set against the horrors that lay behind the walls at my back. I sat on the pavement leaning against the wall for close to an hour. I wanted to make sure I was breathing, slowly, certainly, and that my breathing was providing life to the parts of me that had not been damaged inside those cells. Sleep crept up on me, but as soon as I was settling in to enjoy it, I heard a rattle of a car on the weathered asphalt, and leapt to my feet, afraid I might be arrested again.

I marched along the road until I found a shopping centre, where I convinced the taxi operator to let me work to earn my taxi fare back to Cradock. In the taxi back home, I slept deeply for the first time in a year. I opened my eyes just as the taxi approached the town hall. It had weathered, and the town had a tense mood that showed in the shifty eyes of the locals. When I had left Cradock, I had not meant to return. There was too much of my father in all the corners of the town, but now, as I looked around, I saw that it had all weathered away. The fever of the search for freedom had gripped the inhabitants, and what used to be a charming small farming town was now a dangerous place to live; any sudden movement could set the place alight. Friendly chatter and mindless buzz had dissipated, and scowls etched themselves on the faces of what would be, on any other day, a beautiful girl.

My mother had refused to come to see me in prison. I had received a letter spelling out her profound disappointment that I had read repeatedly, if only from a longing for something familiar. I treasured it even though it held little kindness. She thought I was reckless for putting the family in such danger; but in truth, I knew she hadn't come to see me because she only wanted to make the trip once: to collect my body under the cover of the many stories the police told mothers about what happened to their sons while in custody.

When I left Cradock, there had been no parting words; we were drifting in our own worlds after my father's death, so there was nothing to explain. I had no idea where I was going, just a sense of not being able to remain in Cradock. Something was coming, and I had to choose a side, and I couldn't make that decision in Cradock.

On the day I decided to leave, I met a group of boys my age walking past our gate. I joined them, and that evening found myself at a meeting where in coded words a short man with midnight-black skin and shockingly white pupils spoke softly but clearly about it being time to render the country ungovernable. He described the careless way people were being killed in our neighbourhoods – good people who were shot at from anonymous cars that sped off into the night, murdered while doing something as mundane as going to buy bread. He gave many other examples, and ended by asking us to think deeply about what we thought our lives were worth – given that nobody else was considering this. I didn't care that much about his philosophy, but about being in a community of vagabonds, even if they operated autonomously. Working in tandem seemed far more appealing than waiting for justice. We were being conscripted into an army of rage, of which I had an alarming amount.. We were anarchists, our manifesto being chaos. We had no role but to ensure that buildings blew up with no one to claim the honours. None of the boys present left the gathering; all of us inched closer to the fire that blazed in the middle of us, illuminating the face of the speaker. At the conclusion of that meeting, I took a bend in the road that led to the national highway and left Cradock, to return only a decade later.

I lived under bridges and in farmhouses built for seasonal workers. I lived in squalor with the wretched of the earth who shat on themselves in their sleep as infants did. Sometimes I found an empty backroom that a family would rent to me in a township I didn't know, where I would hear from locals about the struggle heroes in that particular part of the country, or learnt about impending revolts. Everybody had a different idea about what needed to be done to reach freedom.

I thought I was free just by being away from the forlorn look on my mother's face. I would sit in small tin taverns drinking warm beers with music blaring overhead. Other men around me were wetting the sorrows that made their bones brittle ahead of the weight of the years they had amassed. The owner of one particular tavern was a burly woman dressed in a sarong clumsily wrapped around her waist while viciously stamping out the life of the chewing gum in her mouth. The yellow T-shirt she wore was stretched to capacity, which paled the colour of it. She trotted over with the warm beers and smiled mischievously at me as she set them down. I watched her sashay away seductively, catching the cues of her lust. I was a handsome stranger and the night was young. Later that evening in the backroom where she resided, I fucked her. Afterwards, we shared a cigarette. She had many questions, like any business owner interested in her patrons, she said, but I smoked in silence while she warned me about some activity planned for the following day. I nodded and thanked her for the information, which is what she thought I had wanted from her. We drifted into sleep, and early the next morning I was on the road again, not interested in getting entangled in the politics of that place.

Other places I stayed longer because I had seen a pretty girl I longed to court, or made a friend who eased the loneliness that followed me everywhere. When the time came for me set things alight, it was often in a town where I made no connections, and from which I moved on as soon as I could, not ever remembered or traced by anybody.

This existence, being near then far from the fire now ablaze across the streets of the land, never made me choose a side. All sides of violence are still violence: people die and they never return. Other people struggled for the civil liberties that are our birth right, and if I were to tell this story to my grandchild, I would say I was on the right side of violence. But when you watch a man die, something inside you snaps from the proximity to depravity, and it's a brokenness that will remain until you are loosed from it at death. I saw many men die. In prison. I also lit the fires that sometimes killed them. I placed obstacles that derailed trains, burned railways carriages and buildings, never thinking of the innocent people going about their days in spite of all the chaos, whose lives I was disrupting.

This is what I did. It is who I will always be. Even now when I walk the streets in what we call a free country, I see myself still as a shadow, a man who comes to the light only because it is part of his treachery. I am forever on a mission. I have never been able to relax into this freedom. A large part of me still wants to fight. There is still so much we have to fight for.

This vagrant anarchist is the man that Nonti met. I had just finished working on a cattle farm, and longed to see the ocean for a few days. I donned my only decent jacket, and started the journey. The taxi operator told me that the closest place was Port St Johns, and I could take a train which departed from Maclear. In that train, she was sitting by herself staring out the window. I had not seen her until that very moment: I blinked, and she appeared. Nonti, throughout the decades, has maintained her ability to pull me towards her just by being near me or by denying me her presence.

On that day of our first meeting, we fell into an easy conversation. I will never be able to account for what was going on in her head, but I knew even then that I needed to find a way to be with her. My life as a vagabond came to an end the moment I sat beside her. It was a decision I made long before I ended up in the pits of hell, fighting for my life each night as metal doors clanged open and shut, missing her, praying that she would not take up with another man.

When the train reached Port St Johns, I walked her to the bus stop where stern-faced nuns stood watching me in perennial disapproval. She got into the bus and waved shyly at me as she found her seat. In my hand, I had a square of paper wrinkled by how tightly I was holding onto it. She had written down her school address for me. I had promised her I would write, terrified that she would resent the necessary long silences between the letters, but I had told her that I was a travelling man, and that didn't seem to bother her. She came from a family that had built its wealth on, amongst other things, the equivocations that came with regulating races and the ambiguities attached to her complexion. The crushing weight of my unworthiness sat in my chest as I made my way to anywhere, no longer needing the salt ocean air much as I thought I did.

I sat on the beach until dusk, not sure of what I was thinking about. When the wind began to swirl in an uncomfortable way, I buried my jacket in the sand and walked back to the road, where I hitch-hiked until I caught a ride with a man who decided to put me up in his house for the night. He knew of my clan because his sister had married a man from one of those villages. Everything I told him about myself was a lie.

When we reached his homestead, a young girl led me to a hut set a bit further away from the others. It smelled of fresh polish, and the linoleum floors gleamed, even at dusk. The room was cool inside and from the small window, I looked out onto rolling hills with grass green from the spring rains. The land stretched out for miles with no cultivated fields or buildings in sight. The young girl slinked out of the room, and I heard the door creak close.

I stood looking out into the vista with nothing and everything on my mind. I recognised my unworthiness, but the desperation that came with oppression was one I could not easily name. I felt so distant from the boy my father had raised; who had not lived to see me become a man. I wanted to be like him, but he was gone from this life, and I didn't know how to emulate a ghost. As soon as I laid eyes on Nonti, I felt his absence sharply. He would have known what to say to me in these moments; even just to have him tease me would have been enough. I longed for his counsel. I longed just to be near him.

Tears dripped down onto my chest, and I let them fall with my fists locked in the pockets of my pants. I had led myself down a road he would not be proud of, but I didn't see options for black men in the life we lived. That was never a matter of self pity, but rather a hard fact backed up by the numbers dying on the streets; in overalls watering gardens; in homes lifting heavy furniture. Workhorses not recognised for their talents, but only for the strength in their limbs. Blank clay to be moulded into the desires and fetishes of any man of means. Blackness coloured every area of my life so darkly there was no escape but the narrow one we created for ourselves; and that truth I will hold onto until my death. In all occupations of servitude, if a black man decides to loosen himself from his shackles, I give him credit, no matter what method he uses to rise. After all, nobody seems to have hands when we need help, even to be good men.

I have spent my life contemplating and challenging these matters, but now, in the dark night as my body fails me, I realise this one thought has directed me through-out my life: the permutations of a life lived in second class, at the back of the bus. Things got better in my later years. I mellowed and made peace with the colour of my skin, its trappings, the stereotypes associated with it, the pain borne from the history of its oppression, the legacy we pass down to our children, who will forever be burdened by how their race will be manipulated for personal gain of others, or how the cultures associated with it are appropriated for profit.

When the young girl returned, she had a plate of food that she placed on the small rickety table next to the door before slinking out as silently as before. The aroma of the food filled the room, and it was then I realised that I had last eaten at dawn. Settling on the bed as I held the hot plate of food, my thoughts turned dark. At the time, I had no way of knowing that Nonti might get hurt. I had not looked at the address she had given me at the bus stop. It was only later that I discovered that I had nearly killed the woman I had fallen in love with. Only when the smoke was high, and I was hiding in plain sight preparing to pen a letter to her, did I realise in horror that I might be writing to ash.

I had waited for the transformer to start blowing out smoke, a signal that it was overcharging and ripe for a spark caused by the pressure of not being able to cool itself down. I had little time, but the open field in front of the school was safe enough for escape and even cover from the impending rupture. I ignored the chatter of young school girls wafting in the air.

I had spotted the school yesterday from the van of the man who had given me accommodation for the night. He had said that the priest who was principal of the school used the villagers' fields to grow food for the girls who attended the school. Black girls who lived in the lap of luxury, eating the harvest of locals who ploughed the fields with their own tools, with no assistance from the church. The chief allowed this because his daughter attended the school free of charge, and he received a stipend from the government in Pretoria to administer the region, and keep his villagers preoccupied at home rather than flocking to the cities for work. The mission school had no pupils from the surrounding villages. The man driving me was full of scorn as he spoke, and in my mind another sort of flame began to burn.

The day I set the school alight, I ignored the cheerful voices of the young girls coming from the premises. I decided to view them as entitled blacks intent on benefitting from the woes of the masses. Even if the scornful man ever thought to blame me for the incident, I knew his happiness at the desecration of such an establishment would buy me his allegiance – we were of the same politics, and I was passing by never to return.

I think of those girls a lot these days. Young girls with their skirts blown back, some still sitting in class, and some crushed by fallen mortar from the crumbled building.

When I realised that the school was where Nonti had been headed the day I met her, my stomach heaved. I walked out of the tavern where I had stopped to take refreshments and vomited in the street. I stood as lost in the street as I was when I walked out of prison two years later; dazed, and with no clear idea of what to do next. My legs wanted to carry me back to where Nonti might have died, but that meant certain arrest and possibly death.

Love was for peaceful times and for people who could afford folly. We were in a time of war; love would have to wait. It could find no place inside me. I strolled aimlessly around the town for hours. I passed two stray dogs in heat furiously pounding into each other. They filled me with disgust, and an unknown rage welled in me, filling up my lungs so much I thought I would pass out. I wanted to believe that this was the life I had chosen, but it wasn't. The years that had passed could have been spent differently had the boot not been so tightly pressed against our necks, had we not been born trying to understand what we did to be despised in the country of our birth. The country of our ancestors. The country that held all our dreams. It was ours: we were here first and we had every right to own and even destroy it. I was a freedom fighter. But this was a lie – freedom fighters have no time for weakness. Running back to find a woman I had only met once was a weakness. So I continued on to nowhere, and when I found lodgings, I lay in bed for a week, gripped by a fever that made me convulse and feel acutely all that had passed and all that I had lost.

Cradock then, after my release from prison, seemed to feel the tension of the country, but not to be affected by it. I made my way down the dusty street that had marked my exit from this small rural town. It had been the backdrop of my childhood, but now it felt stifling and unfamiliar. I saw the small face-brick house with the red stoep that still shone from its polishing, probably from just that morning. The grass was cut and the unpaved driveway had been swept. The only change I noted was the burglar proofing in front of the lace curtains, that the bars creating a black painted barrier separating the indoors from the world.

The door was answered by a man with a tinge of grey in his hair and small eyes. He appeared alarmed at me being at the door. "Mxolisi?" he said slowly. My mother broke out into screams in the background, and I heard a child crying, then a young girl who was the spitting image of my mother pulled me by the hand into the house and closed the door. The man was fanning my mother who was hysterical, and the young girl picked up the wailing toddler and placed her on her small hip, bouncing the child up and down. Everyone, besides my mother, who was still in shock, was staring at me.

"What are you doing here?" my mother finally asked through her tears. "After all these years.... Who did you bring with you? Are we to have no sleep for the pounding of police on our doors at night from here on out? This is who you are, isn't it? A criminal? And now you bring the curse of prison here into—" she caught her breath, "—into my house! With my children!"

I wanted to endure her reproach silently, as I had been the cause of so much of her distress, but I had lost somebody too, so I rebuked her: "This is also my home that is now filled with strangers." The man shot me a glare. "It was my father's house, he was also…" My words caught in my throat, and tears ran freely down my face. My lips quivered and my body shook with rage. I didn't understand how for her, life had moved on after my father's death. She had replaced all that I had known with new people – people who seemed unperturbed by those in prisons and in various townships all across the country. Innocent, good men blessed with varied gifts, whose long black shadows haunted them when they weren't being hounded by the police like dogs; and she here was, living with a man who was wholly outside of the fire and drank afternoon tea like a white man with no problems.

The trouble with moving on is that often those who are left behind are not notified. They find themselves outside of love or a home that they once had easy access to, with no explanation for the restriction. Those left behind drown in lament for a time gone by without ever rationalising why the change that has occurred might have been necessary. This was the moment at which my mother and I found ourselves upon my return. The love between us chilled as a frosted window. I did not know now what I had expected to find. I had hoped that she would think I was a hero since nobody else would – the prodigal son who had avenged the slaying of a father and whose sins could be washed clean by a mother's approval.

It sounds trite now, but I regretted killing those innocent schoolgirls as they were bettering their lives. I really did. They caused nobody harm, and were circumventing the limitations placed on them by the state-sponsored education. The threat they posed, however, was that they risked becoming indebted to the cushioning provided by the mission. Foreign aid always has ulterior motives. By liberating a few in the creation of an intellectual elite, they were countering the efforts to liberate all while the state continued to make slaves out of the masses.

I had no way of knowing that I would meet somebody who would send me spiralling down a different path, and make me question my commitment to vagrancy and rage.

Nonti made me question liberating myself, which I since came to see was the nub of the whole revolution. The best of all those who led people through the dark places we went to during the times of oppression knew that how we lived was not acceptable for those born into a country rich not only with heritage but abundant resources. Their dreams were simple. They wanted to kiss any girl they desired who wanted to kiss them. They wanted to drive really fast down the highway in a car they couldn't afford, but that the bank agreed to pay for on account of them showing a letter of employment. They wanted to be free to think that their education could buy them entrance into a company alongside those who had employed the generations before them, and to bring worthwhile contributions before an open-minded audience. Or just think freely. They wanted to dance in any hall around town to the latest hits, in the coolest clothes, and come home as the sun was kissing the sky, inebriated from a night celebrating their youth simply because it still coursed through their bones. They wanted to excel and be loved. Simple dreams.

Coming home, I expected to walk back into the skin I had left behind a decade before, without accounting for what it means when you leave, and time lapses in a space without your presence to affect it. This is why my mother refused to acknowledge me. It wasn't easy to be reconciled to this on that first day; it was only much later, when my mother had grown kinder to me and could trust that my presence wouldn't mean continued police harassment, that she could share with me why she had moved on.

There was nothing special about the day, like most days when significant moments occur. She had just come from a church meeting, and was wearing the brooch my father had bought for her early in their marriage.

"You still wear it." I fingered it as I sat down next to her. It was raining outside, the first of the October rains, which were late that year. She was watching television, some lifestyle programme with women twirling around in high-shine candy-coloured dresses.

She smiled. "It goes well with this top." She smoothed her blouse: "How was work?"

I had been working as a mechanic in the auto spares shop Shamus ran at the back of his yard.

"It's been quiet, I think it's the rain."

"The girls cooked earlier."

I waved my hand to decline the offer of food, and broke out in a chuckle as a fresh bevy of girls stepped out onto the stage on screen, also in high-shine candy-coloured dresses and twirling about. "What are you watching?"

Amused, she replied, "This is the kind of girl your father liked."

"Really?"

"Yes, he liked silly girls. He got into the ministry quite early in his life, and for all his shyness, he was an archetypal man."

"Doesn't being a man of the cloth require it?"

"Maybe, but I just think he thought he was more handsome than he actually was. Luckily you take after my family," she laughed. "Your father used to be surrounded by girls like this. There was an allure back in those days to being married to a reverend. All the privileges and duties made you quite an important woman on the social scene." She pursed her lips and was lost in thought for a second. "We were so silly." Then she added quietly, "It was such a long time ago. I lost you both."

This last statement hurt me. "I came back."

"You won't stay here long; whatever you are hiding from will come to find you. At least I know now it's not the police. I know what it's like when they are looking for somebody. The boy who left isn't coming back."

"You have so little faith in me, Ma."

"My faith is what bought you back, but when I search your face I see things in you that terrify me. What you saw when you stepped out of those gates is alive in you, and it sits between us now. You will follow its call again. Tell me I'm wrong and I will apologise."

Unsure if this was a blessing or a curse, I said nothing.

Years later, we were at the town hall in Port Elizabeth, my mother and I. I was standing outside searching my pockets for a cigarette. A man in aviator shades, his jacket hanging over the bend of his arm, offered me one of his, and we struck up a conversation. He was a nervous fellow with eyes that would lead women to make up all sorts of outrageous truths about him.

"Gert," he offered his hand. I told him my name. He nodded, took a long drag of his cigarette, and pushed the smoke out his nostrils. It was a gesture he had seen somewhere else, I was sure, and he had longed to perfect it for the moment when he had an audience. "Your first time by the ocean?"

My Afrikaans was without flaws, but I spoke to him in English: "No, I have spent many years here."

He then switched to poor English. "I used to live here, and it's not like how it used to be." His hands were shaking. His uneasiness made me wary. He had the perpetual shrug of an insecure adolescent boy, and kept darting his head about as though he were expecting someone to appear from around the corner. We smoked in silence looking out towards the ocean together.

Later on that morning, he took the stand as the main accused in the amnesty hearing of the murder of my father. Sitting there watching him unveil the depths of the depravity he had enacted under the guise of duty, I felt nothing for him, not even pity. He was a man who had let his uniform dictate to him to whom to ascribe humanity. I had flashes of the young warder in prison who always seemed unsure when he led yet another enraged black boy into the cell.

The very church on which Gert based his beliefs had done nothing to dissuade him from meting out the violence he described that day to a holy man. A man who found violence a poor replacement for God. I thought about the workings of God, and how he came to us when we least expected it. That was my father's favourite teaching: God will meet you at your place of need, he used to say.

Before that day at the town hall, I had left Cradock, as my mother had foreseen, but to seek Nonti out, praying that she had forgiven me for my year of silence. I needed to somehow explain that I was trying to protect her from the man that I could be sometimes, unsure of whether I had completely left anarchy behind.

When we settled into a rhythm, I found a job as the apprentice of an electric engineer in Mthatha, so I could be close to Nonti's teacher's college – in the end she had chosen to study closer to home. The local technikon accepted my application to be an artisan because the retired engineer, Alf, who did odd jobs to supplement his pension and perhaps to get fresh air, taught me his trade. He was a second-generation German migrant, who had no profound beliefs beyond the flow of electricity and the cleanliness of his tools. He was estranged from his children, but pictures of happier times hung up on the walls. He had no wife and if she had ever existed, we didn't venture to speak of her. All he ever spoke of was electricity.

In the evenings, after I had gained some respite from the day's work, he would knock at the cottage at the back of his house where I lived, with two plates of whatever he had rustled up for dinner. We would sit in silence eating our food. Some days we ate in his dining room with the sliding doors open overlooking the pool. The house held traces of a long-gone woman, but had a cavernous feeling as though she had taken all her warmth with her. He kept the place clean, but it lacked the sentimentality often attached to home. Some nights he would try scrape together a conversation, and in those moments I learned of a crippling shyness that locked all manner of expression inside him, so I would cut the conversation short, and never ventured into any laboured discourse.

One night, however, he had a whiskey, and as we listened to Herbie Hancock's *Maiden Voyage* record spinning on the record player, he said, "You know more than you tell me."

I was jolted out of the dream-filled haze the music had induced, and nervously ran my forefinger around the rim of my glass. "What do you mean?"

"I won't ask any more questions. I am an old man and fighting doesn't interest me now but at your age.... You are hiding, but you are capable."

My heart was beating wildly. I stared at him, my breath held, feeling as though I was on the verge of a dangerous moment. In the shadows, you learn to rely solely on your instincts, and until this night, Alf had seemed to be exactly who he said he was. Almost immediately the thought came to me that all my misdemeanours had finally caught up with me, and this moment was the atonement for the young girls who had perished because of my rage.

His life had never made sense to me, but now as I considered his wiry frame with leathery old muscles I realised that I knew nothing about this man. I had just answered an advert for an electrician stuck up at the post office. I wasn't even an electrician; I was a young man who wanted an escape from the fires killing my peers. Fires I had grown tired of starting. But you can't contract out of anarchy. It's a debt that is paid only with information or death, and during those times, it was usually both. So it occurred to me as we sat in that long pause that I had been trapped this whole time, and all along I should have been fearing for my life. As fear tingled in my fingers I asked, "What do you mean?"

"I know what is going on out there. I have always known. My grandparents left Europe because they wanted a place to accommodate their advantage which they had lost after the war. As things stand now, it appears that advantage has come to an end here."

"But what does that have to do with me?"

"Why would you hide when your time has come if you didn't already know something of it?"

I could hear my breathing and my heart beating in my ears, like a flat hand repeatedly thumping on a board. He stood up and I wanted to reach over and snap his neck. My kind of treachery had up until now excluded combat and overt murder, but I had flashes of prison and metal doors slamming shut and shivering welt-covered boys whimpering in the nights, and a ferocious fear overtook me. Alf stood by the sliding door with one fist jammed into his beige pants and a white vest that exposed his biceps tucked into them.

"You have to prepare for the worst times. Everything is a fight, all the time, until the end." His last words were ambiguous, so I sat waiting for the certainty of danger in order to decide my next action.

Normally by now, I would be winding down the conversation between us to alleviate the discomfort of his having to accommodate me in his home, even if I was there by invitation. That night I surrendered to what I thought would imminently befall me.

"I—" My throat was constricted so I cleared it with a cough as I clasped my glass. "I am tired of fighting."

"Then you are tired of living." He turned to face me. "Why am I wasting my time?"

"I am not your cause." I tried to mask the anger in my words.

"No, you are not." Then he said sarcastically, "I am an old man, what do I know?"

Recognising that neither one of us were willing to move away from the veiled conversation we were having, I reclined slightly in my chair.

"What do you want to know?" I asked, my voice low.

He shook his head and the ice in his drink clinked against the glass. "Is that an admission?"

"Tell me the accusation and I will let you know what it is."

"I know enough and I won't say anything of it. I just wanted to know if I was right because we all have to make new wagers now; nothing is certain."

He turned back to look out into the garden and continued to drink his whiskey, the reflection of the water in the pool outside marbling his face. Then he said, "Hiding won't heal you. You will die by yourself."

Later that night when I returned to the cottage at the back of his house I thought of my father, and I cried so heavily into the night I woke up with a headache. The years had been long and unkind, and still there was no reprieve in sight.

So years later, as I sat in that town hall listening to the man with whom I had shared a cigarette, I thought, if I had known of this man's evils a moment ago, I might have killed him and been content with the direction my life would have then taken, despite the tragedies of prison. I would have felt justified. I would not have cared. I know that now as I knew it then. Despite Alf having supported me by helping fund my studies and finding in him a father for the second half of my life. Despite being newly married to Nonti and content with the mundane trials of everyday life. Despite peace having come at last to all my people in the land of our birth. I would have risked it all to render to his family the hopelessness their son gifted us that night he killed my father like a dog.

Not many of my peers were like me. So many of them were bonded by the very real nothingness that came with having half of themselves missing. I had a father, both as an institution and as a personal albatross against which to weigh myself. His death only heightened this burden; it immortalised him and made him an unblemished hero, one that militant cadres fashioned themselves upon. It was often strange to hear the qualities attached to the symbol my father had become. The man they spoke of was a figure I had never known. He had none of the bravery they ascribed to him. He often cried at funerals, publicly, in front of other men. He wasn't a martyr, he was murdered.

Everybody speaks about fathers, but rarely about who becomes a father. Hurt boys in gangs or rage-filled children spend years standing at the gate in anticipation of this glorious figure called Father, egged on by mothers too ashamed to admit either their indiscretions or the violence that produced conception. Often, these are places the men I know come from. Then a lover tells such a man she's carrying his child, and the hope of his presence in their lives burns in her eyes, betraying her pose of indifference. There being no template for this task, he runs away. A good man, or so his friends say of him, one for whom they would be willing to die, and who is counted amongst the few listed friends. But a father he is not. A father he cannot be; it is too much to ask from a child raised in the black plumes of smoke rising from the chaos of protest, the humiliation of poverty, segregation, blackness.

I would have liked to kill Gert, but instead, I watched him tell tall tales of how my father had become violent upon his arrest and then a struggle ensued; to subdue him, he had hit him over the head with a metal rod, and he fell and died. He had not intended to kill him: he had found the metal rod at the scene; he had not bought it along as a means to torture my father or inflict harm. He said he burnt his body because he was scared that he had exceeded the scope of his mandate, which was to bring him in alive. His panic caused him to create an alternative plan, to make the death appear an accident. He poured petrol over my father's corpse and set it alight. He watched it burn. He could not explain why he had not placed the corpse back in the car to make the staged motor accident appear real, or why the body was found so far from the car from which they had alighted. He said he could not explain the deep cuts on his arms; that he was sure he had not bound my father and made him walk into the night. He said my father had long been suspected of being a terrorist who was aiding the youth in trying to overthrow the government. He said he didn't know any better then, and that now he was reformed and believed all black people deserved the same quality of life as white people. He said it was the church, it was his upbringing, it was the training of the police, it was the law at the time, it was his youth that made him unable to speak out against the instruction he was given to eliminate Reverend Fani. It was everything but him.

When the history of our country is told, it's surprising how the politicians of oppression don't often feature. It's the proverbial "white people" and their police that are the faces to which we attach our hatred. The former silently profited from an unfair advantage, and the latter were complacently and continuously exceeding the mandate of their operation to maintain that advantage. The politicians of apartheid retired to their expensive homes in the country, and remained there pontificating about the righteousness of their cause until they dropped down and died of natural causes. Meanwhile all the Gerts of the world sat shameful in front of their victims, exposing their horrid acts in a system they were told to maintain, but never thought to question, to look outside the lines for an alternative. Those who were sentenced for their crimes never thought to put the guns and the metal rods and the petrol in the hands of their suited commanders – the same commanders who never deigned to visit them as they served their prison sentences.

Forgiveness is only understood by an enriched soul; the rest of us would much rather be singed by the flames of anger than release from our spirits the misguided who have hurt us. We want to carry them with the mounting load of the passing years. Hatred doesn't tire me because I have lived with it so long that it has now married into my logic; it informs the lens I use to look out on the world.

But when I watched my daughter learning how to take her first steps into this vicious world, I contemplated the fences in our hearts more seriously. It would be so easy to take them down, but then who would we be to our lovers, our community, even ourselves? Would we walk in a public space and recognise ourselves in the reflection in the glass, or would we be terrified of our nakedness after being loosed from the revulsion of whiteness? I cannot say even as I lie here at the end of my life that I know myself outside of what a white person says about me. They erased all the empirical evidence that we come from the kings of men, and left only their voices in our heads. The generations who have unscripted centuries stretched out before them have to build their history and identity up again for those who will be blessed enough to live in that dream world. The blight of my life has been my preoccupation with an evil system that robbed everyone encased in a brown skin of a decent life; and for those whose skins were white of the opportunity to be decent. I am not equipped to build the country of my skull when lucid dreams of screaming girls caught off guard wake me in the depths of the night; or I see a flash of the face of a boy with whom I used to play soccer, dead in a packed prison cell.

These days there is no public space for lament, as the rhetoric is one of impatience towards the poor who suffered under unfavourable political times, and who now see no difference in times of peace. We are all moving in our own directions. The young speak recklessly about the sacrifices of their fathers and bathe in a freedom they didn't earn, but treat it with such disdain that one wonders what they will do with the mantle once it's in their hands. I spent all my youth in anger. It is a useless emotion if not directed, and a dangerous emotion if not explored.

The irony of it is that Gert's testimony saved my life.

I had come to Port Elizabeth to accompany my mother, who wished to hear the account of my father's death for herself from its perpetrators. I wasn't interested because the motive for his murderer coming forward for amnesty was selfish; it ultimately resulted in a doctored truth that was legally sound but morally void of atonement.

I didn't and have never told Nonti about this other side of my rage. She knew the sadness of my loss, and how I had survived it. I told her the hero's tale, because she might have left me otherwise. She almost did after my year in prison, but I had told her that was a case of mistaken identity. I had gone to collect her accumulated letters from the numbered post box I had given her the day we met, and as I turned to leave the small white building between towns in the middle of nowhere, I was met by two men who arrested me on suspicion of arson. They had kept track of all the girls who had attended the mission school run by Father Benedict, and the steady flow of letters to this insignificant town were all the clues they had needed.

At that moment, I feared I had killed her. I found out that she was alive only after I was released. So I lied to keep her. She might not have wanted to be attached to an arsonist and criminal, a murderer, a man who had spent a year surviving detention without trial and torture in prison. My release was also a test, a way to trap me into serving the police; they hoped I would lead them to a wider network of operations, or that my commanders would come to eliminate me for fear of me having exposed the movement. But I wasn't attached to any movement, and I had told them the truths which would allow me to begin again with a new slate. I tried to do that in Cradock. I tried to love my stepfather and his daughters, but in truth, the relationships moved up a notch only from diffidence to duty. I constantly lived on edge, even as I sought out and found Nonti again, and trained with Alf, until one day I realised that I was lagging behind the revolution. It had mutated to open rebellion, and oddly, that is when I began to relax.

This gave me the freedom to marry Nonti, to start a family and try to move forward from all that I had seen and done.

I knew I wanted to be a good man but my father was a good man, and he died at the hands of men who claimed they were doing God's work, fighting against blackness and purifying the land. At the amnesty hearings, the commissioners projected a picture of my father in his cassock standing next to his church. My mother broke into tears and I placed my hand on her shoulder. I didn't even remember what my father had looked like before he was placed before us in a canvas sheet, a charred mass of flesh. I had forgotten that he enjoyed polishing his shoes and ironing his clothes; that nobody in the world appreciated more the clean straight lines of things constructed by men. I had forgotten that he loved jazz music and the melancholy crooning of Brooke Benton. I had forgotten what his laugh sounded like, and the fresh smell of incense that followed him after Mass on Sundays, as he strutted into the house to enjoy the Sabbath as he had commanded his congregants to do. I had forgotten how thin his fingers were, that he kept his beard unkempt so that he could tug at it as he read scriptures that placed him in deep thought. His strength, masked by his fragile air, had disappeared from me; and so too had our quiet moments together, watching a television series we didn't care for but latched onto so that the contented nature of our home would keep us safe from all the ways we were being oppressed outside. His killer knew nothing about my father save that he was black; and for a while, that is all that I remembered too.

Floating in the ocean, in his expansive arms, so much of our love here.
I rest in it.
Shadows of birds hiding behind the clouds as the sun lightened the sky.
The smell of the morning soothes my body and the salt of the water feeds me the first meal of the day.
The moment lingers and sadness grips with its long tentacles.
He doesn't live here anymore, like Jesus on the cross.
He doesn't love here anymore, like a bereaved spouse dishing up for herself; opposite her an empty plate.
He doesn't laugh here anymore; nothing can be heard from his heaving chest.
Way past noon his body lay wrapped in linens that thirsted for the last signs of his life, which they soaked up as his soul parted from him.
That day shattered the world I had known.
Though we had seen him, we had yet to know him.
I only had his one last breath to live by.
"Love me, come to me this way."

Christopher, my love

I had an affair with Christopher.

For years we lived in a space where we would clutch each other in the dark in hotel rooms, and walk past each other in the day as though we were strangers. He had a world I asked nothing about, but accepted that he had to attend to. I had to close the doors in my mind that tried to open to my ambitions of being with him exclusively. I could do it when I concentrated really hard; I lived in the moment when we were together, and filled up my days with trivial activities I convinced myself made me happy. Thanks to these distractions, I met so many people who made my loss bearable.

It was not rebellion that attracted me to Christopher. He was an attractive man, yes; physically, he was tall, lean and muscled with striking eyes, but it was the magnetism with which he charged his immediate environment that tipped the scales. He was aware of this pull; the clues lay in his immaculate and well-tailored clothing, and the debonair swing of his slow long gait. He had delightful manners, and his wit held you in his company long after he had left. So naturally I wanted to be near him; but then everybody did.

Christopher approached me one day after a lecture as I was strolling out the hall, answering a text on my phone. Our conversation had been brief and pleasant, hardly memorable, but I thought about it later that night. If I had been older, I would have been able to read the desire in his eyes, I might have been able to see he was positioning himself to be someone of importance in my life, but I ignored the obvious and labelled his interest as insignificant; a chatty lecturer conversing with an engaged student.

Our interactions escalated incrementally; from walks after lectures to conversations with clues hidden in carefully crafted innuendos and sophisticated puns. Eventually he had to spell it out for me.

I knew his charm had an effect on me, but his feelings were all a figment of my imagination until the words of his desire hung in the air between us, and I had no place to run. I had to confront my fears of having feelings for a white man. White men existed as lovers only in my teenage daydreams. They could not be multidimensional, let alone want to share my bed. In my head the celebrity I adored was a white man who fitted into my black world without question or change. He spoke my language and somehow had a handle on all the cultural cues he had soaked in when he emerged from fantasy into reality – which was all still pure fantasy.

Christopher's azure gaze made me uncomfortable, but the novelty of his attention thrilled me. I felt chosen; I admit that I even felt vindicated – my upper-class schooling had gifted me the subliminal dream to be white, albeit by association. I could be the girl who was stared at in public spaces as she went about her life with her lover in hand. Later I would complain of the narrow-mindedness of our country to anybody who would listen at upmarket establishments where we quaffed over-priced Champagne.

I would have heated debates with my girlfriends over the afflictions that were men, making contrived claims like "this is why I only date white guys" before going on to list all the celestial characteristics of a white lover as opposed to his wretched black equal. I would feign disdain when asked private questions about our lovemaking and how he compared to black men; I would insist that there was no difference, even though I secretly pretended there was.

In my least favourite memories now, I would claim to feel culturally out of touch with black people, given that few of them had the opportunity to travel abroad for school excursions, or to attend finishing school as part of their education to prepare them for office and wifely decorum. Compounded with Christopher's lavish dinners and his intellectual achievements, he buttered me up so easily that by the time I was playing hard to get, it was merely to appear virtuous to an invisible yet omnipresent society that he considered a surmountable obstruction. He pursued me with such cunning that some might have found it predatory. In fact, if my father had ever known that Christopher had lured me to his bed while he was still my professor, he would have cursed him from the grave.

Christopher introduced me to sensations in my body I hadn't even dreamt of, and challenged the laziness of my thinking. That is what he termed it, anyway. I accepted his feelings as real. What is real and what are feelings? This is how he wanted me to approach any subject I decided to have an opinion on. To me, this was cumbersome. I was content with understanding him as someone who altered my moods, and about whom I was terribly possessive without any actual right to be. There are few things more shallow than having feelings as your only claim for being enamoured with another person, because the risk of delusion is high. But I still fed my appetite with each rendezvous, convinced I was able to manage my raging need to be a priority in his life.

The realisation of this goal was always so close. He came back to me over and over. He remembered the things I said. He found me irresistible.

I fancied myself better than his wife. She, to my mind, was a culmination of all the mundane things to abhor in a spouse. Opposed to her, I was young and confident, virile even. I had a body that had not weathered storms, ripe with taut skin. I thrilled him, reminding him of the days before he had her as a responsibility. I failed to take into consideration that a love that has taken years to build is rarely shaken by a superficial trapping such as beauty. This is a common assumption made by an ambitious third party who fancies that their brand of love will keep their embattled beloved from any woes. I imagined he was unhappy, although he never told me this, and when he went away for periods of time, I fancied it was because of her. He was trapped in their relationship, and each time he came back to me, he was mine – briefly.

Our conversations always became intense intellectual exchanges over wine under crumpled sheets, our naked bodies pressed against each other, and his free hand absent-mindedly tracing the curves of my body. At intervals, he would plant kisses all over my bare shoulders without my being certain of what he was adoring, and what consequences such adoration might yield.

He was careful to manage the expectations between us without ever committing himself as to when he would next see me, or letting me know if our continuing interactions were signalling a possible change in his marital status.

When he spent weeks without needing to see me, the bile of hatred would cloud my thoughts and the days lacked joy. His absence eroded my confidence and stirred frightful pangs of doubt in my ability to be desirable to anybody, particularly him. I came to need his validation, elevating this to love even though the evidence was scant. Then, in a bid to reclaim a measure of peace, I would decide that he was insignificant. A surge of strength flowed through me in these moments, and I found a way to turn the days so that they featured him less, to the point where I believed that his disappearances could not hurt me anymore.

Where I once had a burning passion for the subject he taught, having to attend this class twice a week became a cross I could no longer bear. I had to endure his indifference as he provided in-depth analysis of readings he had prescribed the week before. He behaved as though I was not sitting in the midst of the other students, and I braved it as though I wasn't battling to sit upright and placid-faced. I hated him most in those moments; his self-control in the face of my confusion cut me in the deepest way.

Then he would return to me, and I would forget all the desperate vows I had made to myself during the nights of loneliness. I knew when a period of absentia was about to end. He would arrive to give his lecture in an irate mood, and distance himself from the class, as though the students' capacities to reason were an affront to his superior intellect. Since his students adored him, they would sit quietly, suffering his mood without understanding its genesis.

I knew, though. I knew he would call me later that evening, and speak to me as though weeks had not passed. He'd be jovial and joking, playing up the inflection of his Scottish accent – which he knew had an effect on me. It was a silly thing to risk my self-respect for, a Scottish accent, but tell me when logic and love were ever used in the same recipe. Even when I put up a token resistance, he knew he could walk all over it, as my need to see him and feel him inside me overwhelmed my need to feel respected.

In time, we gained a rhythm based on my counting on his returning to me. This allowed me to accept his disappearances without killing myself wondering where he was. It was not an ideal situation; but then nothing about our situation was ever ideal, not even when it appeared that way.

Never having been a girl with many friends, I had no confidante with whom to dissect my woes, and I would sit brooding at night. The obvious and boring conclusion – that I lacked self-esteem – did cross my mind, but I was learning that we all do frightful things in the name of love, and that is how I came to forgive myself. If I was having an affair, somebody else was healing from unrequited love, or piecing themselves together after tying themselves to someone only for it to end in divorce.

I was overwhelmed. And not by his charm alone, but by the politics of his skin.

White skin.

I loved Christopher; I could not say his skin meant nothing to me. Its politics weighed me down. My ideas were not clearly formed enough for me to conclude sufficiently where I stood on the matter. That it should confront me in this area of my life clouded the judgements that seemed so easy to make elsewhere in life. After all, intimacy required surrender, and that meant, at least to some extent, relinquishing ideas that might have informed who you were and who you aspired to be.

In the families I knew, the white body was a symbol, a place and a structure. It wasn't a person. In the case of most people I knew, I wondered whether they had actually ever wanted it to be a person. It seemed better to scream the word "white people" without ever getting close enough to determine if there were truths to be confirmed in the hatred held. I called it hatred to bounce about invectives and criticisms of the invisible guest who dined with us each night, but was never allowed to speak. Admittedly, the flaw in my argument was that I came to call it that only after I had gained sympathy for another perspective. Prior to that, no part of me had ever questioned it. I had challenged it structurally because of how significantly it had affected my childhood, but beyond that, I believed myself to be immune to its effects. In more sophisticated parts of the world such a conversion – even such a thought – would seem dated, but in this country we loved the white body, a national obsession that turned the day quicker than the orbit of the sun.

It is a profound thing, a name. Christopher told me he was named after the patron saint of travellers, a man who carried the Christ-child across a turbulent river and was thereafter blessed by him. When I think of how our country is named for its direction, perhaps the significance is that its people have an open canvas on which to create that which we seek. It's an opportunity.

Back in primary school, I wrote this in my creative essay, for which I received a gold star. Andreas – a boy in my class – and I were tied for the prize in our written prayers for our new country. It had been birthed a few months prior in the Great Election, but as we stood in front of the class to be handed our respective merit awards, he said "k-----" to my face when I turned to smile at him.

Ms Wolffe, having overheard what she thought was a silent curse, smacked him on the bottom right in front of the whole class, whose hum of excitement died down at the violence of the action.

"Andreas has used a bad word, and for bad words, we eat soap to clean our tongues," she explained to the children, who were wondering how a morning spent clapping for each other's successes had turned into a lesson on bad and good words. Andreas was then pointed to the glass jar that sat on the window-sill of the classroom, and made to pull out a small green bar and rub it on his tongue. Of course the whole interaction was fascinating for me, who had no idea of the harm he had been trying to inflict on me. "K-----" is a word for white people and used by white people. The disgust they attach to it is solely in their heads. Before Andreas, I had never heard the word used, not even when my father watched the cricket and a wicket was taken. My mother wrote anthologies and presented papers on language, and when she let me sit beside her reading her discarded ideas, not once did I see the word used. The dictionaries in our study didn't contain the word, and in our neighbourhood, when the young boys played rugby outside, or I could hear the neighbours screaming when their team lost a game, nowhere did anyone ever use this word. How then did Andreas believe it had the power to hurt me? What was in his heart that he had to reach for such a sacred word to undermine the achievement we had jointly attained?

"What is "k-----"?" I asked my father when he picked me up from school that day.

My father stiffened: "Who called you that?"

"Some boy in class. The teacher made him eat soap."

"Why did he call you that?"

"I don't know, he just said it. Is it a bad word?"

"It can be, for us." For a while, the only sound in the car was the tick of the indicator.

My father was frowning, his white shirt loosened at the collar, and his tie on the backseat next to me. He kept checking the road even though the movement of cars was controlled by the traffic light, which had us paused on red. The mood inside the car was tight, and I distracted myself with the changing shapes of the clouds. Eventually the car moved again, and he said: "The boy who called you that hates you, and his parents taught him that word."

"What does it mean?"

"I will tell you another time."

Another time for me meant I would ask my mother. She never treated me like a child. Sure enough, "The history of that word is attached to a history of people who were being persecuted and who felt threatened, as they still do now. It should have the same force as 'nigger' in America, but in that country it had time to prove – to gain a subculture in the minds of the black people there. In our country, most of us could go our whole lives never being called that," was what my mother said.

My father replied, "For you who grew up insulated from the woes of blackness."

"And of course you were a farmworker or deep in the mines, where such words lived not as words, but in pay and accommodations."

"Don't minimise its offensiveness."

"Don't heighten its importance. White people love that word, but how is it supposed to demean us? You have a higher chance of offending me by calling me poor and stupid than by calling me a k-----. We already have so many damn problems, if we add a word we might just break our backs trying to stand straight." Then she turned to me and winked: "Now *damn* is a bad word."

My affair with Christopher wasn't a question of morality or lack thereof on my part. It was a question between us that needed an answer, or better yet, expression. We needed to be close to each other because we recognised each other, and that needed no explanation. There was no life I could have lived that would not have had him as a chapter. Yet our affair meant questioning how relationships operated. It was confusing. My parents had a solid love, or so I wanted to believe. When I looked at my father, I would wonder if he had a woman somewhere else. A woman who knew him in a different way, and who occupied his heart in a manner my mother could never mould herself to occupy. If so, would I love my father the same way if I knew such a thing? Would it invalidate his love for and commitment to me? I wondered why my mother deserved the protection and status of a married woman more than this other imaginary woman. Was it my mother's behaviour during their courtship that had made her stand out from the rest? Or was it the inexplicable magic that is given the name of "soulmates" that made my father give her his name? Was this magic between married people hereditary, or did it spring from strength of personality?

Were some women destined, due to their inability to command respect from men, to be mistresses or side chicks, as they were colloquially referred to? Was it my destiny to be a side chick? Did I have "daddy issues" even though my father had been full and present in all the important moments of my life? I knew his name and that of his father's. I had seen my great-grandfather's grave; I came from a long line of men who prided themselves in loving their children and their spouses. All around me were examples of the relative happiness of couples who had built lives together from nothing, and who remained married for decades, and here I was – a side chick.

The other side of this confusion lay in my intimate moments with Christopher, when he shared deep parts of himself with me. He told me about growing up poor in rural Scotland, a land I had never visited; but his accounts of the shape of the land, its constant wetness, and the shame of having nothing were part of what made me fall in love with him and his sad blue eyes. In his younger years, when he attended Cambridge University, he was crippled by his obsessive need to accumulate wealth. Universities with ancient traditions often oppress their students with their remarkable histories. These are absorbed in the dining halls where huge banners hang down with dates from centuries past of feats of greater men. Men who were born into the aristocracy and could therefore mandate explorers to voyage the earth, collecting desires dreamt of in order to stave off boredom. From such travels, ideas of enlightenment poured onto the pages archived in their great libraries.

A student with a delinquent, poverty-stricken father and an illiterate mother couldn't lay claim to such a history. Nobody he knew understood his need to get as far away from the backwaters of Scotland as possible. At home, they held their breath for his return because his non-return signified that life was possible elsewhere. Though they could tolerate others judging them for being what they were, an insult from one of their own would be revealing.

Christopher wouldn't relinquish the ambition born from lack. He couldn't see the impediments of excessive wealth on the souls of those who had it until he sat in a college dining hall as a student, and realised that he had come to a place that had never intended to accommodate him. A place where, in order to inculcate the culture of being a gentleman, it was required that lavish dinners be hosted with requisite dress codes, no matter how exclusionary. This reinforced the poverty of his upbringing: even if he looked like his peers, those like him who couldn't afford formal jackets or didn't hail from a long line of gentlemen were quietly shut out. It formed the roots of his revolution.

Poverty is humiliating because according to covertly defined standards, you find that you are unacceptable and come to question the validity of your contributions, let alone your existence. Christopher said being poor was like seeing your mother naked; worse, the whole world seeing her naked. No matter how hard you tried to hide how little you had, the world already knew your poverty. To this, money was the only answer; having it, not having it, wanting it, keeping it, saving it. It had a language you couldn't quite latch onto, each time exposing your standing in the world. Your standing might be summed up only by those acquisitions that could be visibly seen; and not by systems you created or owned, systems that could sit quite apart from you and generate streams of income while you slept peacefully on the opposite side of the earth.

But Christopher couldn't win the war, despite his good intentions.

It took too much energy to write papers for both himself and his future self, and even when he came top of his class, nobody respected it because he alone was playing the game. The others, from long lines of gentlemen families and significant surnames, must have smelt the holes in his shirts and never extended invitations to join their clubs.

For Christopher, to be one of the elite meant money; it was the only currency that could buy respect. He kept delaying the moment when he would have enough to be respected. He graduated top of his class. He did his articles at a prestigious law firm. He argued important matters and spent his days ironing out complicated legal questions. He bought a country house alongside a lake where he could fish. He travelled back and forth to the city, where he lived in a penthouse overlooking the Thames as it flowed towards the North Sea.

After enough time had passed, he realised he no longer did what he loved, which was to think. The ghosts of the gentlemen he had met in the dining halls at the very beginning of his escape had no kind words for his present alchemical work. They were ruled by ideas. He, at that point was ruled by money. It ruled him so completely that even in holy spaces, like the church he attended during his university days, he would approach the Cross to ask for money. This highlighted a part of his life I was more easily able to relate to than his growing up poor: religion.

Even in an impoverished environment there are those who feel the brunt of scarcity more than others, and Christopher's family became the victims of the manufactured empathy of their neighbours.

His mother never had a decent education, and the embarrassment of trying to get one as an adult paralysed her. She thought marrying a teacher would locate her comfortably as a housewife, but instead her husband woke up one morning and tried to gas himself in the kitchen. He was unfortunate enough to survive. At first, the attempted suicide resulted in overwhelming support for the family, but when Christopher senior returned home from hospital and routine settled down again, a fever of unfounded gossip gripped the small town, and they began to remember the events of that fateful morning in an unfavourable light. The family was ostracised, and Christopher's father was asked to leave his job teaching English at the primary school – by the local minister no less, who diagnosed him with profound spiritual poverty and a lack of faith which he would risk spreading by influencing his pupils.

Relieved of his duties, Christopher senior began to drink and spend incessant hours playing the violin, which he had also taught at the primary school. When it became apparent that he had lost all shame and could be found lying under the tree at the public tennis courts after endless pints of beer, the second round of gossip started up, claiming that his artistic eccentricities were what had caused him to try take his life in the first place. People spoke out against being too creative, saying it was unhealthy to entertain the delirious voices in one's head, and even worse to express this through art forms that did nothing for the betterment of your family.

Christopher told me that he came to see church as an exhibition of the vile. He hated the minister and his wretched minions carrying their bibles, the dour prayers, judgmental stares, and the disparaging of drink. It all reminded him of how the community, unable to cope with what they deemed to be the idiosyncrasies of his father's personality, eroded his confidence as a man. They hurt him so they could pray for him, look down upon him as a subject who required God's love.

This was very different to my family. My father's father had been a priest in the Anglican church, so I grew up with the strict formality and quiet competition of organised religion. In my family, religion was a must-have. We threw it on us like a towel after a shower; it wasn't something you could do without, although you could live without it on a daily basis. I knew priests who enjoyed a good brandy but said Mass on Sundays with their hearts fully invested in the Lord. My father grew up an altar boy and then graduated to the choir, the most soulful tenor I had ever come across, and when he regained his speech after his first stroke, he continued to sing in the hospital ward. Religion was neither for the purpose of saving him, nor rectifying his ills; it was just something he did, much like eating. In fact, for us, communing with the divine led us to experience moments of ridiculousness, particularly because of how far my family was willing to go to call upon the spirits.

My aunt Romance was definitely full of flair in this department. A towering woman with a commanding voice, and unattractive by the world's standards, she had self-confidence in spades, and led all our prayer sessions. She had decided to move away from the church of her parents and join those charismatic churches where the pastor taught them to pray in tongues. We all believed her conversion, if you could call it that, it had to do with the fact that she had finally found a church that would entertain her penchant for the dramatic. We Anglicans were suspicious of people who had forsaken their church for other denominations, to the extent that it would have served them best to relocate to a city to attend a new church without having to explain the reason for abandoning the church of your fathers. This was also true of all the Methodists, Catholics and Presbyterians that I knew.

Romance had no such anxieties. She found conventional sermons and church rituals too boring and repetitive for her taste. She thought Anglicanism was too rooted in a certainty not often found in the realities of life; in her charismatic churches, a service would never conclude without there having been some scandal about which to prophesy or pray. There was an urgency to dealing with these problems because God felt, at least to her, present in the here and now, just as she liked it. There were drums during these services and lifting of hands and ululations that would never have been accepted in an Anglican church, and when the moment reached fever pitch, anybody could break off into tongues, that special language of the divine.

My father did not approve of Romance's church; this was often a source of heated arguments. He said he didn't want me influenced by pagan churches, which set Romance on fire. But although she had never had a soft spot for my father, she still valued him as family. His stroke was a family incident, so it was less to do with him and more about healing the family.

So she rounded up her prayer warriors and rocked up at the hospital, but they were asked to leave on account of the racket they caused during their riotous fellowship. Romance, however, would not be deterred. The first night my father was released from hospital, she arrived at our home flanked by her riot club. The prayer session began at first without incident, but it soon became apparent that the Holy Spirit meant business, as the prayer leader, even more boisterous than Romance, flitted from topic to topic in his prayer, ranging from the use of condoms by the youth to the matter of alcoholism. Each topic had a dedicated time to be aired, with all the other warriors agreeing feverishly with his sentiments and short acclamations being shouted loudly in the lounge. When he had rounded up all the ills of the world, he began screaming "Phuma Satane" – out, Satan, out – so loudly I opened my eyes, which met my father's. He was not enraged, as I thought he would be; instead he was bright red from trying to hold in his laughter, his skewed smile quivering. I averted my eyes as the shouts of "Phuma Satane" had me on the brink of exploding with laughter too. Just as we had reined ourselves in, one lady with a long corduroy skirt began hopping around the room as she clapped, breaking out into the dreaded vernacular of tongues. She hopped around my father, clapping and praying until the tail of her skirt trailed into the fireplace and burst into flames. My mother, in a panic, tried to extinguish the fire by beating the woman with her woollen scarf. When this failed to douse the blaze, she ran to the kitchen to fetch jugs of water. The shouts of "Phuma Satane", the praying in tongues, and the burning skirt caused such an uproar, I was afraid the neighbours were going to think a domestic incident was in progress.

When Christopher and I were alone together, relaying our stories to each other like this, I found myself wondering why he had sought me out if he didn't really want to be with me. He knew my whole family without ever having met them. He knew what our professions were, our illnesses and frustrations, he understood the dynamics between us. He asked after them, checking if there had been progress. He even had his favourites, notably Romance.

She found the more obvious parts of our relationship interesting.

"Umlungu?" was her first response, pulling a disgusted face, when I told her about Christopher. I often visited her when I came home for university holidays. "And?" she had asked, her eyes filled with mischief.

"It works just the same."

She had thrown her head back and laughed loudly. "Maybe I will ask Kort-kort if he has an older brother." Romance was working as a housekeeper for the Japanese diplomat that lived down the street from my parents' house. She called her boss Kort-kort because he was much shorter than her.

"You wouldn't want an Asian man, I hear."

"Really?" she had whispered conspiratorially. Then she burst out laughing again. "You guys are lucky growing up the way you do. I would probably shit my pants if a white man proposed love to me.

Absolutely shit my pants. What would I do with him or to him?"

"What you would do with any man?"

"Fokof!" she shouted. "Fokof! And what if he couldn't handle it?"

"Handle what?" By now I was laughing too.

"These!" She slapped her thighs, by now hysterical with mirth.

I recovered from our hysterics and wiped the tears from my eyes. "Well, he is handling mine."

"Ai, but you know you are two slices away from being a chicken bone."

I broke out into fresh laughter, "I am not, what do you think this is?" I said, grabbing the meat of my outer thigh, but she waved me off dismissively.

The chemistry between Romance and Christopher was always odd, despite his liking her. When she ran out of words in English, she would speak Xhosa to him, and he would look to me for a translation. She sometimes used the language barrier to laugh at him. Sometimes while talking to him she would break off and tell me as an aside, in Xhosa, that my husband was very pale, and then laugh. I would then have to come up with a translation to fit the situation, which was not always easy.

Romance didn't care to learn English properly, and she didn't cower because she couldn't speak it fluently. She said "Yes Kort-kort" to everything her employer asked of her without ever thinking how inappropriate it was for her to refer to him this way. She fell back on Xhosa or hand gestures when she ran out of words but given the poise of her demeanour, you could never relegate her to the uneducated classes, even if this was the reality of her life. Her confidence was both endearing and terrifying, and Christopher adored her.

My mother was the villain for reasons I never quite understood. The first time she met Christopher, she had said nothing. She sat in the corner watching my father greet him awkwardly before she stood up and walked to the kitchen to make sandwiches. Returning, she placed the sandwiches on the table and left to sit by herself upstairs. Later I found her marking her students' papers on the balcony, her glasses perched on the ridge of her nose, engrossed in her work. She didn't offer an apology for her behaviour.

"So?" she said, regarding the papers in front of her. "It went well?"

I pulled up a chair and considered the view from the balcony.

The dogs were chasing the pigeons across the lawn, and my father was bent over the carrots beginning to sprout in the garden. The tall trees enclosed us and hid the neighbour's yard from view, but in the distance were rolling hills covered in long savannah grasses that bent with the wind. Christopher had left in a rush for the airport, to meet his brother who was visiting for the week.

I looked back at my mother who had not yet looked up from her work. "You don't like him."

"Does it matter if I do? He is not mine. You should feel lucky that you have a father to approve such decisions."

"It does matter, you're my mother."

"I know what I am, and that is why I have to let you do this by yourself."

"Do what?"

"Grow up."

It was an illicit relationship for much of its duration; not just because Christopher was married, but because he was my professor, whose conduct transgressed the ethics of the university. We nevertheless continued the relationship for well over four years – the whole of my law degree – and then one day, without warning, he broke up with me.

It was a cold windy day on campus, and I met him at the coffee shop near the engineering department. We enjoyed this part of campus; it was mostly empty and the gardens were lush with lawns that rolled out in a rich deep green. It was common to find a student in a deep sleep under the shade of the jacaranda trees, or lovers locked together in feverish reverie.

He had called me the night before to make this appointment. I suspected nothing of his intentions. We had been communicating fairly well and regularly for a number of weeks, which provided me with a false net of security.

I approached him. He was seated in the corner of the bustling shop with his now-finished morning cappuccino, reading the news on a gadget. I forked my hair with my fingers and applied gloss to my lips before I sat down across from him. He looked up.

"Vuyo."

"I'm not late."

"You're not early either," he replied with a distant smile. This was our way of greeting each other because I was always running a few minutes behind. "This is yours," he said, pointing to the cappuccino on the table.

I frowned. "But I hate caffeine. You know this."

"Oh, I forgot," he said dismissively as he packed his gadget away in his satchel. It was then that I knew the purpose of the meeting. Christopher never forgot anything. His memory held onto even the colours of the worst days of his life. He could trace the shape of every object that was part of a scene in his life with such clarity that I was often amazed at how perceptive he was. Even his disappearances from my life were deliberate and calculated.

I remember sitting upright as though I had been called to attention as I watched him. His curly hair was ruffled and his cheeks red from being smacked by the wind outside. He was dressed in blue denim jeans and a grey wool sweater, a crisp white shirt underneath, a picture of understated elegance. His gold wedding band sat on his finger like a swear word as he laced his fingers together and faced me. He had not ordered a cappuccino for himself, so I guessed the meeting would not be long. I stared out the window as I tapped the cup of insult to the injury I knew was coming. It was deserted outside on account of the weather, but the vegetation still made it a peaceful corner of the world. Between us there was a weighted silence as I waited for him to pull the trigger, having already accepted the impending doom of this meeting.

"I have a consultation in an hour," he lied, "so I'll be brief. I have come to the conclusion that perhaps we shouldn't see each other anymore. I cannot give you what you want, even if you currently believe you don't want to get married. At some point you will want to be a priority, and it's best, I think, we don't get to that point. I appreciate of course the dif—"

"It's okay, Christopher. Don't say anymore." I wasn't looking at him.

The ferns outside were shaking violently as a group of students emerged from the lecture hall across the lawn. At that moment I felt truly indifferent. I didn't recognise him. He had disappointed me so many times in the four years we had known each other that this moment was simply a culmination of years of nights spent alone, telling myself I was worthy. I was a final-year student, on the brink of true adulthood, soon to enter the work force with a taxable salary. Him breaking up with me was the final act in severing the bond to my naivety. It was a cruel act, but no more so than many of life's lessons. He touched my hand, the one tapping the cappuccino, and I watched him perform his apologetic soliloquy, nodding my head, even smiling. He said all the mandatory phrases, and I found myself saying them to him as well. We even shared a parting embrace. I watched him saunter out the coffee shop and jog across the lawn and disappear out of my life. Or so I believed.

I left the cappuccino untouched. Walking across campus, I truly felt relieved. My father had just been released from hospital, and was in a rehabilitation centre where he spent his days learning how to smile. An act so simple was now a lopsided affair that turned his playful face into a misshapen sight so painful, you had to look away. I had spent the weekend at his side, listening to his stories of when I was a child and when he first came to the city. He told me of the long buildings, and seeing prostitutes for the first time in his life. I had no idea how these stories related, but they made him feel like himself, so I indulged him. I was leaving home and moving to Johannesburg for work in three months' time, and I figured this was the source of his anxiety. His only child was moving to the city of prostitutes and gangsters to live by herself in an upmarket suburban flat. A place where she had no friends or people he could influence to ensure she was favourably treated.

So I let him ramble, and I laughed when he made what I decided was a joke through his slurred speech. When sleep caught up with him, I would sit reading old messages from Christopher, from whom I had not heard in a month.

The last time we had been together, we had gone hiking. We shared a love for the outdoors, and he had been promising to show me a route he knew I would enjoy. For weeks it was all we spoke about. He gave me advice on the boots I had to buy, and we had decided on a menu for the long hike. The day had met my expectations, and that evening I had lain in his arms content with how we had both grown in this illicit situation, how we had managed to keep it between us; at last, I felt that I could settle for being in his life in this limited way.

When I came home the next day from the hike, my father had been rushed to hospital, where he spent the following three weeks in intensive care. No word ever came from Christopher, and my pride prevented me from reaching out to him. In the turmoil of my emotions, I decided that I had to leave him. That moving to another city meant there would be other men, available men who could take my calls during times of great crisis and suffering. I didn't know how I had let him become so important while I was at best an option. Sadly, as much as I sang the song of more men in the future, I didn't believe it.

Christopher had snapped something inside of me; he knew I didn't think I mattered enough, and that is why he could walk away. The effort of continuing to see me in another city was too much work when before he could see me freely in lectures, even when he didn't speak to me; he could admire me from afar and gauge for himself how available I was. In another city where he had no business, his wife would grow suspicious, and Christopher the Great would be discovered for the scoundrel that he was.

In the four years we had been together, I had thought of bearing his children, wondering for hours whose features they would carry, took joy in the idea that they would have good hair and perhaps my hazel eyes, if not his eyes of the sky. I had hyphenated my surname with his and pictured us going to the bank to discuss how best to obtain a home loan. I had mentally attended work functions and had feigned modesty when he introduced me as his wife, that golden two-worded phrase, yes Professor X please meet *my wife*, at which I would become a charming creature full of wit and life who would engrave herself on the heart of Professor X and his other colleagues. As I walked in the violence of the cold wind on campus after he had left me behind with the cappuccino, I no longer cared that my hair was fluttering in all directions. I realised that this life, where I would be "*my wife*", would not be mine, and it shocked me how deeply I had actually wanted it. I lacked something that would catapult me into that world, and at this thought, tears streamed unhidden down my face in sheets.

In spite of my tears, it was relief I felt when I walked away that day, but the cost was too high. Christopher had enjoyed all of me, but taken none of me when it mattered, and as my father fought to lift a spoon to his mouth, I wallowed in the misery of my decisions.

The world belongs to men. It always has; until that moment, this had never bothered me. They are the only ones permitted to explore the duality of their desires – for home and adventure – while never being called to account for the inventory of damage they leave behind. Daughters of good fathers often believe that they can traverse this truth by living openly and behaving as equals to men – because that is the folly of a father's love for his girl. It gives a daughter enough courage to think she can achieve anything: the best job, supportive friends and a suitable lover, one who will refrain from exerting his given power in the world as a means of control; and in a fair world, this would be true. A father's love hides from his daughter the face of men in their most vile state – the face that weighs its value according to its conquests. For daddy's girls – awful term – disappointment in men is always delayed. It feels like the train you have been waiting for all day, only for it to break down on the tracks. There is nothing for it but to sit and wait for it to be repaired. Repaired never quite to be the same again.

On that cold day though, I found myself contem-plating whether it would perhaps have been better if my father had loved me less, if that could possibly have made me more able to resist Christopher. I would have had more guards around my heart, as some of my friends did. Men love a challenge, it's often said, but against him, I had no snares or defences. My mistake, I guess. It was such a long time ago. When I think of it now, it's not the untamed rage of then that fills me. The touch of melancholy for how that stage of life was engineered enabled the kindness I now have for Christopher. He came back, after all. There was redemption.

My strongest memory for a while after Christopher's funeral was of one of the days just before our wedding.

"Why do you want to marry me, Christopher?"

He was annoyed by my question. He frowned at me with an intensity that disappeared as quickly as it had appeared. We were in his flat a week before the wedding, which had grown from a small affair to a royal banquet. With great compromise, we had finalised sufficient details to take a quiet evening off with no talk of matrimonial rituals. He put his book down and sighed: "Not this again. We've had this conversation."

"You don't want to answer?" I turned my head on the pillow to face him.

"You're looking for that stars and the moons shit right now."

"I'm just asking you a question. You don't have to answer it."

"Of course I have to answer, or I'll pay for it."

I rolled onto my stomach and folded the pillow in half before placing my head back on it. He was on his back, the book he had been reading open and balancing on his stomach.

"So must I start with your beautifully shaped lips or your soft skin?" he teased.

"My father asked this, the first time I ever told him about you. He asked me what the value of a black girl was in a white man's arms – did you know that?"

"Hardly surprising. Do you know the answer to that?"

I shook my head childishly. "But I must admit I've fought off thinking about it because it unsettles me that this is a dynamic of our existence that we can never be rid of."

He bit the inside of his lip. "My father was a racist who knew he didn't want to change. Thankfully he died before the world changed and forced him to be a repressed racist, which would have killed him a lot sooner."

"How do you know you are not? Racist, I mean?"

"I've told you before, I don't know. This matters to you?"

"It seems to matter."

"To you?"

"I'm lying here on this bed with you; I think we should know each other's politics."

"I have black friends."

I punched him on the shoulder and he laughed, "I adored my father. I would like you to understand why I did."

"I already do."

In the early nineties, Christopher had taken a position lecturing at a university bubbling over with student riots in a country that was ablaze. By then he had retired his expensive tastes, and taken up liberal thinking as his area of specialisation. Liberals have a complex position in any revolution. The envy of the oppressed who watch them practice their freedom is met by the guilt of the liberal's open-mindedness. They would, in a minute, renounce their unjust position in this world – but they don't. Altruism is constantly born in situations of great danger, but survival is at its root. Being a foreigner getting a lesson in centuries-old segregation, Christopher chose to align himself with the oppressed because he fancied himself as also having been oppressed by his childhood experiences, and the prejudices of the gentlemen at Cambridge. He taught veiled radicalism in his classrooms, pushing far enough to go against the grain, but not enough to be arrested. He befriended those at the edge of the law, but wasn't materially affected by any sacrifices.

"Maybe I just question the scope of this understanding," I said.

He became pensive and I could feel the chill slide between us that usually preceded an outpouring of his thoughts. I waited. He pulled himself up against the headboard. "All I have ever tried to show anybody is compassion," he said slowly. "It's a useful weapon that is all too often missing from the arsenal of even the sharpest minds. It doesn't lend itself to understanding what anybody at any given time experiences, but it recognises the trials that are associated with being alive. I have been arrogant, so I can recognise it in others; and I have been cruel in order to gain advantage over another person. You know as soon as you meet somebody if they are the type whose light you can put out, but it's never fun when you do. At least for me, it wasn't. I ran through it over and over again afterwards, and punished myself for it. That is all I ever tried to do with my work – to be critical of myself in the world, taking into consideration how that self came to be. It hurts when you invalidate that because I can't, in the end, turn myself into a black person. That I'm not black can't be the answer to me not being able to comment on things that I feel passionate about."

"That's not what I am saying. And it's also not enough to just be aware of it."

"It's a variation of it."

"Maybe." I clasped my hands. "My life is always mutating because of the issues of this country as they relate to how I live in this skin. The euphoria of evolving past these feelings – it's fleeting."

"Then what are you saying? I know what it means for us to be together in this country. I just happen to make money out of studying being contrary to the norm, and I'm not exploiting the plight of black lives as your mother once accused me–"

I sighed deeply. "Oh God, there was that–"

"Yes, that. Your mother and her low opinions of my interventions."

"My mom has her reasons. She wanted me to marry a black man."

He snorted. "Yes, you had found yourself the quintessential black man when I came back to ruin the party."

We chuckled at this. "Leave Sakhile alone, he was a good boyfriend."

"None of my business."

I shrugged, then said: "The horror of our times is that we are forced to make popular decisions when pursuing our personal happiness because of the sacrifices of days gone by. Am I supposed to want to marry a black man because so many people died, or it will make black men feel their existence is justified? I never know. What if I have nothing in common with them? What if I could go on a random public rant where I could tell them that I have nothing in common with their upbringing, their values, their struggles? What if I told them I didn't want to eat the food they wanted me to cook, or watch the television programmes that seems to excite them? Even worse is thinking that I have the right to defend their position in the world because they are who I am supposed to love. I don't want to be in bondage to these expectations. What would you say to all this?"

"I would say that you hate yourself."

A pernicious spirit rose inside of me. "Oh, so you don't worry that you might be accused of having a fetish?"

Christopher despised this accusation, having very early on established himself, at least amongst his white colleagues, as a "k----boetie", someone suspected of cavorting with blacks at their parties and bedding black women. They didn't know he was a married man, who, besides his little indiscretion, namely me, was a principled man. To some extent though, his proximity to the other *was* a fetish for black skin. His being foreign led to a natural fascination with those other than himself, but he chose on the basis of reliability and intellectual prowess. Doubting his ability to discern whether he was acting sincerely or out of curiosity incensed him, and I knew I had hurt him.

"This is complicated," I sighed at the ceiling.

"Vuyo, do you want to do this? These are concerns that are boring, and that we have addressed many times not only between ourselves and our families, but also strangers. I find your rhetoric, particularly at this hour, very disconcerting."

"Frankly, I don't know. There are too many variables that you can't account for. Am I asking for too much?"

I was anxious because Christopher terrified me. It was correct to say that I was marrying him purely at his request. My idea of marriage was my parents' marriage, and that was hardly the sexy couple I believed Christopher and myself to be. My parents had years on them that added more than the weight around their soft thighs. Their contentedness must have once been raging happiness that lit up dance floors and their bedroom. If I had been born into dysfunction, I might have wanted to be married more, it might have held a particular charm; but I didn't want to be married. I just wanted Christopher, but he wanted marriage, and so I was getting married. Therein lay the source of my terror – my easy submission to his will. How far was I willing to move away from myself in order to keep him?'

"If I were feeling more passionate, I think I could settle your nerves somehow."

"Marriage is so traditional. It's unlike you to believe in so fixed and conventional an idea, even though you were married before."

"Deep down I'm a rural Scottish boy."

"Such lies."

"Seriously though, let me attempt to be the boy Casanova in your life."

"I'm listening." I sat up and smiled at him.

"Many choices we have to make in this life don't involve choosing good from bad, but good from good."

"Not your words."

"Give me a chance," he said holding up his hand. "I understand why you believe me to be sceptical of marriage. It was created and turned into an institution to gain control by men over society. It civilised us, and I mean that in the least European way possible. On the other hand, it fails more than it succeeds for more nuanced reasons. When we use pure logic, I have no right to ask you to even consider marrying me, and now I'm not talking about empirical facts." He looked at me.

I stared into his eyes, then touched his chin with my thumb.

My father had passed away the year before we married, having met Christopher only that one time when my mother had dropped the tray of sandwiches on the table and left us to attend to her work upstairs. Prior to that, I hadn't seen Christopher for two years when, as I had feared might happen, we bumped into one another as he was stepping out of a lift at the law building on campus. The night before I had been at Sakhile's flat, browsing the university's website to see if Christopher still offered classes there; it turned out that he did, and had in fact been named a professor. Minutes passed as the face on the website set a reel of memories in motion. There was a danger in returning to where so much had occurred. Fresh pins stung me, only for me to snap the laptop shut as Sakhile walked in from work.

"Black and beautiful" was how my colleague had described Sakhile when she had suggested that we meet for a date. He was a friend of hers from university, and for his sins – being good-looking, intelligent and a qualified actuary – he struggled to meet women. I thought black and beautiful was a hilarious description of a person, but he fitted this banal description, with long eyelashes that formed a cloud over his eyes and thoughts.

In the weeks that followed, he pursued me. Dinner and flowers and jazz music and debates about literary greats. Wine and eventually sex. It was all there, but it also wasn't. There was a hollowness for me in being with him that I ignored, constantly purged into the abyss of shadowed dissatisfaction. He cared. He was present. My efforts to decide who to love had been a failure. Contentment would have to be the next best thing.

The first time I ever made love to Sakhile, it was rushed and disappointing. Passion was stunted by my need to be satisfied with something I had been denied for a long time. It could have been anybody sliding in and out of me, and it led me to resent him when soon afterward he shored up our relationship with declarations of love that were unreciprocated. But I didn't call it that. I didn't have the language for this feeling, the unease that welled up deep in my gut. When we were apart, he wasn't even part of my world. He vanished like a warm breath blown on a mirror despite my furious efforts to love him.

When my father had his second stroke, Sakhile came to see me every single night during the ordeal. He would drive from Johannesburg to Pretoria after a long day of calculating people's life expectancies to sit in a hospital corridor with me. My father wouldn't see me with him; he said it was tradition, which I found hilarious on account of my father being the least traditional man I had ever known. But I understood. He didn't want to see to whom he was potentially relegating his duties, and I equally didn't want Sakhile to believe he belonged in this hallowed space between the two of us. Whatever was left of his faculties, he was still my father.

My father's illness became our common tragedy. He sat with me as I pored through my father's legal documents to ensure that everything was in order should he pass away, and I would say "'thank you baby" in my "'thank you baby" voice.

When I was with Sakhile, it always felt as though I was watching myself from a distance and trying very desperately to bridge that gap by overcompensating. I slept at his place most days of the week, and we cooked special meals on Sundays. Cesaria Evora was our favourite artist, and we both preferred savoury to sweet foods. He went along with whatever idea I had about the strength of our unity.

Romance called out our relationship for the farce that it was, but her reasoning was easy to ignore. She said Sakhile suffered from the same affliction that my father did: being too pretty. In her eyes, a man that pretty was not built for the years.

My mother, on the other hand, adored Sakhile to an unnatural extent. She saw in him the son she could not bear, and his impeccable grooming, coupled with a private school education, made him a catch I had to hold on to. They would often be found running errands that didn't involve anybody else, or she would make a joke that only he would understand. At this, I had to fight from exhibiting childish impudence at the risk of exposing my poor mother who was finally getting her revenge for the years I had been my father's daughter primarily while she grieved.

During those years, my father and I often left her to her own devices in the name of healing. That she had skulked about in the shadows observing us only came to light during those times when she dragged Sakhile about as her handbag, throwing her anger with us at him to carry. At the time, there were words that could have been said to mend this misinterpretation of our intentions, but we had in front of us a man who had lost his ability to move, and so that had become our chief conversation – medication, medical aid, signatures on thousands of papers, cellphones incessantly beeping with notifications of payments due. The fluorescent lights and long white hallways were where my mother and I exchanged our hours for weeks until the morning we stood beside his bed as he passed from this life.

Sakhile did bring a different energy into the house, though. He wasn't emotional, so he could cut through the acrimony that sometimes lay in the exchanges between my mother and I. He had no sense of humour, so Romance constantly treated him as a thing of wonder to be spoken about only after his departure. This often resulted in her sharp tongue being blunted in his presence.

If there was one clear area of misgiving, it was Sakhile's friends. They were nice enough, but were odd in the sense that they hardly uttered a syllable in my presence. Sakhile would later tell me stories of them having raved about me being such a lovely girl. I once caught one they called Stanza masturbating in Sakhile's bathroom. I didn't quite know what to make of it; Sakhile had stepped out for a couple of minutes and I had been left in the company of his two friends. We never spoke of the incident because I was embarrassed for Stanza, but that was as far as my sympathy extended. I guessed that I was the source of his lust, and somehow I wanted to keep that as a prize, which really should have been an indication of a deeper problem. I loved that I was unattainable to him, and yet he was forced to smell wafts of my sweet perfume when I sashayed past him to sit on Sakhile's lap. It was glorious, his wincing and my performed indifference. The reason I came to loathe them was that I felt I needed their attention. It reminded me of my worst days with Christopher, whom I had cut off completely after our last meeting in the coffee shop on campus.

Those first few months in Johannesburg, having no friends, I became the most hedonistic version of myself: walking dangerously on the edge of bitterness that found expression in mildly progressive promiscuity. It led me to the beds of strangers from all over the world, so that within the incestuous pool of Johannesburg professionals, I could maintain the element of mystery about my life.

In those few months I had purged Christopher from my mind. I was free from what he thought or wanted or needed. I let the hair between my legs grow wild because he didn't like it that way. I wore the most expensive wigs – the salary that I earned could support such a lifestyle. The heart that had yearned for his attention was buried beneath the gaudy gel nails that were part of an exhibition to repel any would-be suitor from developing ideas that I needed them in my bed or in my life. Sakhile's friends, however, made me want to perform the way I had for Christopher, which irked me as they were not even worthy candidates for my affections. I enticed them quietly, angered by my need to do so, and they crowned Sakhile as their champion who had nabbed the girl.

The day Christopher crashed into my life again, I had come to the university for an appointment. Christopher never gave a late class, and my personal knowledge of how averse he was to being present on campus after midday had made me confident in scheduling my appointment late in the afternoon.

"Vuyo," he said as he held me by my shoulders. "This is a surprise." I could see that I had floored him.

"I have to go," I said placing my hand between the closing doors of the lift.

"You can't spare me some minutes?"

"Christopher," I responded, stepping into the lift, "I have to go."

When the doors closed, I was convinced that some level of redemption had been achieved. The worst had occurred and it had not crippled me as I had feared. This chance meeting had proven my strength and filled me with confidence in my decisions of the past two years. I toyed with the thought of devoting myself to Sakhile. We would make a handsome couple, sitting in church, paging through our shared bible to the called verse, reading with our hands clasped beneath it. Afterwards, when we had cooked and eaten and washed the dishes, he would pull me against his chest as we ended the week with some mindless American film. This image filled me with contentment; it seemed clear to me where my future should be. I underestimated Christopher's cunning, his will to win.

As light filled my body in anticipation of this newfound direction for my life, I found him sitting on the concrete bench outside the building. He got to his feet when he saw me.

"You waited?"

"Of course I waited. We can't meet the way we did and leave it like that."

"Why not? That is how we left it all those years ago, right?"

"Stupidly so."

"Well, life is different now."

He stared at me. "You look different."

"I am different."

This comment mellowed him for some reason. "Different in a good way."

I intentionally said nothing, and let the moment between us grow awkward.

"Can I see you, please?"

"No. I am with somebody now."

"A gaoler, I presume," he said smugly as he tucked his hands into his jeans pockets and rocked back slightly on his heels.

This was a game for him. The target had conveniently popped up nearby, so he didn't have to work so hard. An insurmountable rage replaced the unicorn who had pranced out of that lift expecting to go home to her Black Like Me lover and our boring existence.

"You don't care about me."

"I do."

"I am not something you get to want when it suits you. I am not a game. I find your disregard for my feelings hurtful and childish, given our history."

I must have shocked him into silence. In all the time we had known each other, he had never allowed me the space to reach a point of verbal violence towards him. It was a side of me he had never seen before. I had felt like I had no right to say such things to him then, and so I was stung into inaction each time I should have been a raging bull. To be meek and agreeable was the only way to have him in my life; it came with the territory of being his secret lover. How could we have been together for so long in such a shallow relationship?

"Disabuse yourself of the notion that I want to see you while you are still encumbered. That I want to see you at all. Be free of that thought." Our eyes locked as these words tumbled out of my mouth.

We had been alone, but now students poured out of the building, emerging from a recently concluded lecture. Turning from him, I disappeared into the crowd and hurried to my car, to safety.

He was still a fetching figure; tall, lean and well dressed. He had grown his hair long, but it only added an earthiness to his appeal. I hadn't wanted to, but I noticed that he still wore his ring. I pushed that out of my mind as I made sure that I placed distance between us as fast as I could.

That night I made love to Sakhile so desperately he asked me afterwards if I was worried about my father.

"Yes, I needed to switch my attention away from him – it's just too much sadness."

He held me close and kissed my forehead repeatedly. But it was no good; it was over between us, had been the moment Christopher had crashed back into my life. I knew I wanted Christopher to feel some of the pain I had carried with me the past two years. I also knew that he still mattered, and the fact that I did to him as well emboldened me. I allowed him to seek me out. I punished him, but also tried to love him as I had originally intended.

"I hurt you," Christopher now said again. He pulled his knees up and the book that was balancing on his stomach slid precariously to the edge of the bed.

I pursed my lips. "And yet in a couple of days..."

"Vuyo, people can gather all the data in the world, but none of that replaces the simple truths. I want my union with you to be at the highest level that it can be because for many years I couldn't give you that. In the end, the break up was as clumsy as it was inevitable. Now I just want to marry you. That's all I want. I didn't get to that conclusion by being rational or even worse, romantic. Maybe I'm being impulsive. If that's what unsettles you, then my plea is for you to trust me."

"What do you mean by that?"

"Just trust that I am sure about what I am asking you to do."

"You asked somebody else once. And with the same certainty."

"I also meant it then. I left you because I wanted to mean what I had said to her."

"You got to have us both then, untainted."

"I didn't create the world, my love."

"You benefitted from it, though, and she is out there without you, in spite of your promises."

He breathed in deeply. "When we moved to South Africa, she changed somehow." He went on, his speech uncertain. "It was at the height of the Truth Commission, we were young, I was working all the time, and she was terrified of the anarchy she believed was about to ensue. She watched these events unfolding on the news, and I had to reassure her. I grew tired of consoling her, and I think that germinated the seed of her resentment. We never recovered, not even as the violence settled down. She wanted something that I didn't understand."

"She wanted you to care about her feelings."

"I did."

"You did not, you soothed her fears, you consoled her – to use your words – and then you walked right back into the world she feared. You did the same to me, except I didn't have rights as she did, so I perhaps deserved it."

"Tonight you seem intent on injuring me."

"I'm telling the truth. It is hard for me to lie next to you like I'm a victor. I am not proud of the girl I became in order to be with you, and a part of me will always squirm in pain when confidences of infidelity are traded by my friends."

"It's because you have a view of yourself as some celestial being, where your virtues are as rigid as the lines of a page. You are like your mother in this way."

I laughed weakly: "That's a first." A seriousness fell upon me as I ruminated over what he had just said, "Perhaps I am. I love her, you know. When we lost my sister, my worry for her was bigger than my worry for myself, and difficult as it is to admit, there is relief in my heart each time I remember my father went before her. She is a more complete being than he ever was. He needed us, she only ever had herself – it's a strength I wish to inherit."

"Do you love me?" he asked, as he turned his back to me and placed his feet on the wooden floor, his book crashing onto it.

"Yes." I touched his bare back. It was warm and the contrast of my skin against his ached on my fingers. He felt as near as he did far. "But I don't need you."

There was a long silence.

"When we were younger, she – Sinead – was the only girl who could hold my attention. I vowed that it would always be that way, no matter what, but by the time I decided to pursue you, I no longer knew who she was. Even though we were happy. That was my struggle for the longest time. I was happy, but when I was with you it felt like a very real thing of its own; it didn't feel deceitful, it felt right. It came down to who I was responsible for, and at the time it wasn't you. Our rendezvous, for a lack of a better word, made me realise I wanted more: more life, more travel, just more – and even with that feeling, I convinced myself I was in the wrong. I was just being childish. Only to learn that she no longer had or yearned for the capacity to love me. She always did want that slow parochial life. I no longer did, and to be honest, I don't think I ever did, I just wanted her. In the end, nobody was willing to change their minds or delay their needs. It was a stalemate."

"Do you not worry that I might want out someday?" I added, "I'm much younger than you and I have a few good years ahead of me."

He laughed at this and turned to face me again. "The whole point is that it lasts as long as it can. I am not so scared this time around – though I can't even be sure that my bride loves me. The dread of failing won't make me lose sleep, which could be good for us, I think: we can relax. No pressure to be soulmates."

"I sort of had it in my mind you would be my boy-friend forever. Husbands have gained quite a bad reputation throughout history."

"And wives."

"I suppose we could create our own brand of misery."

He paused and smiled: "I will never leave you."

"Again."

"Yes. I will never leave you, again."

My only reply was to kiss him lightly on the lips and nestle against his shoulder as he returned to his book.

We were married the next week.

For days after the funeral, that was all I thought about. Sitting in my room at my parents' house paging through our wedding album, wondering if I had made that day up in my head. Spending countless hours inert on my bed and then on Sundays dressing up for Reverend Sindi to come and give me communion after spending hours praying for me. I just didn't understand what it could have been for – to spend all those years in sad confusion only to set myself free – then be given what I wanted only to enjoy it for four short years. This thought looped in my head as the days became months.

Vuyo

I have been telling you all along about the days of my life. Do you find that now you know me or my troubles? Do they remind you of a song? There is joy in finding the end of the road, but what of the road? One can think of it as something arduous, something to traverse or endure, but so many sing its praises – or embrace its challenges, or longing for freedom from the strain of the ties that bind.

I am not such a person. For me, it hurts to find limitations where there should be the expanse for expression. To know oneself is to be a part of a people.

Before our generation, perhaps it was the norm to be what was ascribed to you: the way my parents would casually say, "We are black people" or my mother would say, "She is a January." There is no space left in the completeness of the sentence, no room for doubts or questions. The words take up all the air in the room.

Now the question of who I am has answers in the making, but they are far from clear. Maybe by now I should be able to boldly lay claim to an identity, but to my mind what should follow that is the termination of my life. There would no longer be any reason to reach forward, to unlearn and re-learn, or to undo what has to be dismantled.

This is the confusion of our times. Our elders want us to live by definitions, but behind definitions hide histories of some or other person's prejudice. The labels our elders put on themselves had the power of reach. They were aspirant war cries about how to reconcile the person who walked in through a door with the person who walked out.

I bear no such burden, but I bear burdens still.

I have ghosts, but they are my guides. I am a widow, but my husband left me his seeds. I am black, but my understanding of the world is white. I am Hlubi, but I tell people I'm Xhosa. I am educated, but I know nothing about life. I am loved, but I feel completely alone. I am Christian, but I believe in and pray to what are called my ancestors. I am beautiful, but I feel inadequate. I am African, but I am well versed in the knowledge of Europe. I am critical, but live according to convention. For me, knowledge has only exacerbated my inertia, opening up the roads less taken and leaving me unsure of which path really is the one for me. I'm half of all the truths about me, which makes me feel unworthy of the wondrous gift of life that bows to the wind born from firm decisions.

I wish I was strong and mysterious.

Often I feel pliable, too malleable. Governed by fear so overwhelming, it gives me the appearance of immaturity. Everybody else seems to have better ideas about how to exist than me; it's that foolishness that accepted an affair as the standard of love, being cheated on – or rather, with – as acceptable. This is not a sermon dedicated to highlighting virtue, but I need to illuminate the depth of the confusion of a life without a clear path.

Similarly, I am used to rejection. I have told you of some, my mother choosing to mourn my sister rather than to love me; Christopher, many times; but one notable one came early in high school. I chose a tribe of friends, as one does at that age, and due to some social faux pas I unknowingly committed, I was excommunicated from the tribe. They took a vote, and forbade one another from being in my company. Of course this was juvenile; but it was not obvious to me because it was a pattern of my existence. It felt definitive.

Find compassion for me in your judgements of my formlessness. Be kind when finding that you are short of patience for my woes. I am sure I am not alone in the insecurities with which I am riddled. I have used everybody around me as a crutch, in spite of my mother's warnings against doing so. She tried more than anybody to extinguish my neediness. She tried to make me a January when my yearning was to be myself.

To be frank, I could do with less free will, because all I have done since I knew of time has been to grieve its passage, constantly struggling to clasp at it but finding my hands balled around emptiness, searching for home in everything.

Home has a familiarity to it that can be found elsewhere, but is difficult to replicate. One can have many homes, all found along the path to clarity. When in transit, it's hard to know how long to remain rooted to a place. It's unlike being on vacation when the borrowed shelter is accounted for from the start, and the experience has a natural apex that declines along with the sentiments attached to it as the borrowed time draws to a close. In transit, one must make the severance with the hope that the timing meshes with the shift to follow on the continuing journey. The difficulty is that such shifts are predicated on the uncertainty of life. Built into transitions is their inherent expedience. Someone will suffer for you to learn, and someone will reap the benefits of that learning. In this way, we can say that life has meaning.

Home, however, is something quite apart. It is the end place. For rest. For solace. Rest is needed all along the road. Solace grips the soil as the roots of learning take hold. Anywhere and anybody can be home until their mission is accomplished; but once all is accomplished, one should be home.

I am of the generation that for the first time in centuries is native to this land and unafraid to call it home. Yet so many people want me to "qualify" for this; they burden me with the obligation to be grateful for the opportunities that someone like me now has.

So many fathers' and mothers' bones form the foundations of my freedom, and their families still feel the cold of their loved ones' absence. They miss them at dinner time or when *that* song comes on the radio. They wonder if they are at least dead, and not lost. How else can they have reconciled themselves with a country that now has a good story to tell?

Yet in between, there are millions like me. Trapped in the cubicles of capitalism's factories and offices, churning out a new country and swallowing our complaints that some say are cushioned by privilege. No matter our individual horrors and the complexities accompanying them, we say nothing because someone else almost always has it worse. Even our memories are questioned and accused of being sanitised or inauthentic. Stereotype is the foundation of all prejudice, so I can't simply exist as myself, as that would mean so many things are untrue.

So I hope that one day I will find the words. Maybe then you will hear me.

Sunday

Great-grandmother, heal me.

Full circle, what a strange term. To name something complete that was always complete.

The great-grandmother birthed the grandmother who birthed the mother who birthed the daughter who birthed the babes.

Our love is what keeps us bound in a world content with brokenness.

Great-grandmother always used to say, "Even if we are at each other's necks, at least we are facing each other." Proudly she would add, "We are the first crops of the harvest. Our backs remain unbent even though they are tried. Nobody who comes to you can hurt you if that kind of love has been washed over you."

"You will live."

I resisted.

"You will live."

I relaxed in the water.

"You have no other choice."

Great-grandmother spun wool in the evenings to stitch the shawls with which to shield us from the world.

She wrapped one around me now.

Vuyo Aitken (née Fani)

I open my eyes in the water. The sun's beam is weak on my face, hidden behind the sullenness of the sky. I hang in the water, paddling my legs to keep from sinking. The waves steadily knock me in different directions in a regular rhythm. There is water all around, but far in the distance, I see the shore. I bob around in the water and feel the pain that now aches in my belly. It is growing in urgency, but the will to return to more solid ground has not yet found me. I have to speak to my great-grandmother and ask her for the wisdom of the elders. I don't know what world my children will be born into, and it scares me to imagine it.

Now I know I should have come here from the beginning. It was from this shore that all our history, our nation's story, of mixed identities and deep hurts began.

I am cleansed now.

Christopher is dead, but his heirs will inherit the land – the land of our fathers who came to reside here according to various political dispensations, but are now bound by blood in my bloated belly. Theirs will indeed be a future filled with challenges, but to blight hope with afflictions is the way of our parents. I want a new way.

I watch the shore for long minutes as I flap my arms in the water and an owl circles overhead. An omen, I think, and close my eyes. "Great-grandmother, speak to me now from your grave."

"What will you have me say, child?"

"Inside me, they both grow, a boy and a girl. Fatherless. They will be alone in this life in a way that my love cannot shield them from. Speak to me so that I may be able to speak to them."

"In the age of our elders, children disappeared at the hands of owls. The owls hid outside the villages watching for those who did not heed the teachings of their parents about the dangers of straying too far from the path, or finding joy in the things of the night. The owls snatched these children to hide them in the mountains. Today we can still hear them if we shout their names down into the valley.

"Not even the best warriors of the land could find them when they called out to them and their echoed cries called back. The elders were distressed by the prevalence of owls, and the stupidity of the children who ignored what was known. Many wondered what had happened to the children. Some said the echoes were screams of ceaseless torture to haunt the parents for their negligence. Others said the children had become owls, but because they still had their spirits locked within them, they found themselves back at the villages of their birth. Unable to curb the nature of what they now were, they too stole children.

"The elders rode out deep into their forest on the backs of leopards who hunted in the day, a rare breed that escaped the long rifles of the hunters who sought these animals as prizes. They came upon a clearing in the forest; in the middle, old trees stood pushing themselves back into the land. The trees made terrible sounds as they crushed their ancient roots, which had married each other beneath the ground to form a mesh of thick symbiotic vines feeding on the fertile earth. Above the trees stood a cliff from which a song could be heard. Craning their necks to look upwards, the elders saw a wall of bodies of small children, defiant, with glowing eyes that terrified all those who gazed upon them.

"The voices seemed now to be in the distance, having retreated from the face of the cliff. Arrows flew down towards and past the elders, piercing the water that rose from under the trees to emerge as a wide river. From the river, a small girl with black eyes and dishevelled hair stepped forward and asked the elders what their presence in such a place could mean. When the challenge of the owls was told, the small child said this to them:

> There is a song of mourning I know. It speaks about the contours of a faraway land in the south. A land of isolated people who came sick from their places of genesis, and grew strong from the richness of the earth. But now the people are sick again. The illness that was long cured

when they first arrived in the land now plagues it.

To sing the song, a troupe of girls must walk out to the River Styx and sing to the water, to the souls on the other side, and to the boatman who stands ready to announce the names of those called by their elders. The young boys must follow the girls. They must stand behind them and throw arrows over their heads into the river and pierce the water so it may release its powers to cleanse the land. Together, the young girls and boys must bind their hands and hum the melody. They must drown the parents of all the children acquired in the service of owls. Not a single one must jump into the water as their parents are washed away into the great expanse of the ocean and back into the unknown from which they came. The children must not worry themselves with guilt; their parents understand the sacrifice. The owls were once our allies, but they have since forgotten their promise to our creator, and for that, the ages will bear them little kindness.

It is the time now for the green sprouts of germinated seeds not of century-old trees. That is why you see them sinking into the ground. We must cry out in pain for all our children lost to the mountains, or whose spirits are trapped in owls. But what we stand to inherit once some of the links with misplaced wisdom from past generations have gone is far greater than the chaos that will ensue at the severance. The first sunrise after the restoration, look to the east for the eagles: they will carry the resolution for that which bought you here.

"The small girl walked back into the river, and the elders returned to the village to tell all that they had seen. The ritual was performed, and a fortnight later, the villagers woke up to the calls of eagles. They sang a song that sent the owls fleeing into the mountains. The eagles cursed them to become symbols of danger and death, thereby upholding the ancient pact between the elders and the animals of the forest in which the owls were bound into the service of others instead of themselves."

"Great-grandmother, I don't understand."

"Life and affliction are breathed into us all in equal parts at birth, even though we are perfect creations. We must all live with this truth. Times have changed, but things that make up the hearts of men never will. Put in our children the obedience of the eagles, and they will soar. Abide by it yourself and you will be healed of all that has come to hurt you."

I felt my great-grandmother's embrace in the water. It gave me comfort, and then I found myself remembering the sweet smell of lavender steeped in my clothes. The long verses my mother crafted well into the night for her anthologies rang out to me from the ocean, and I heard my father hum to the tune of a classic jazz tune he had heard in his youth. I smiled as I watched Romance fill the space of a room. I wanted our innocence as a family to envelope me in a world that took so much pleasure in demeaning and reducing us to blackness or maleness or femaleness – or *something*. Christopher's death revealed the urgency of life to me. I missed watching him, witnessing his charged energy and an approach to life that most of us ignore as we gain years and resign ourselves to the sameness of routine and the eventuality of death.

I opened my eyes and saw that the current had carried me back to shore. The ocean spat me out onto the beach, and I felt the pain of my children fighting to enter the world more sharply. The waves licked my feet as I lay back to see the sun fighting through the clouds.

The ocean delivered me just as the first fishermen were loading their nets into their boats. I frightened them, I could see it on their faces. I must have appeared to be something from a fable, magical and mystical. They backed away from me when I called out to them, and some ran away up the sand dunes, not prepared to risk an encounter with a witch.

I had been so foolish! My children were going to die before they had drawn breath. My mind was racing. I was angry that Christopher wasn't here. Husbands are supposed to be present when their children are born. I began to cry, first from the pain of my contractions, then in self-pity. This time, a guard of men appeared, some dragging their nets behind them.

"She's pregnant," one said in Afrikaans, and I heard another swear loudly and say, "No, she is giving birth." The second voice came close to my ear and asked, "Were you in an accident, Ma'am?" I shook my head, the pain racking my body and vibrating through my legs. I turned my head to him and whispered: "My children, help them."

The man stood in alarm and shouted for the men in the distance to search the beach for shipwrecked children. Then he knelt down again. "Shhh." His coarse hands gathered my scattered braids into a single column. His presence gave me the strength to focus. I was a mother. It was too late now for any other task. There was no time left. I had come here of my own volition. Long before this moment, I was meant to be here.

The panic all around was increasing, with the fishermen shouting and shoving each other. I closed my eyes as my tears streamed. The voices continued to bicker, and another man came forward, too young to be of working age, but dressed for hard labour. I was calmer now, just trying to encompass the pain as the water licked my feet. The wiry fisherman who had gathered my braids whispered in my ear: "My dear, we need to help each other to do this thing. It's too late for hospitals, you understand?"

I nodded and instinctively clasped his calloused hand, rough with leathery skin and knuckles like the rings of a tree. I couldn't tell if he was young or old, but the weather had battered his face. I thought of Ou Takkies, right by the sea, my grand-uncle who was said to have loved the ocean. This man's eyes were as kind as Ou Takkies had looked in Ma's wedding photos.

The man eased me up slightly and lay my back against his thighs. My hands dug into the sand. The young fisherman now stood between my parted legs, staring with either shame or guilt at what confronted him. I heard the old man issuing him instructions, and with each contraction he moved to position himself better.

There was only pain now. The older fisherman bent his head, and sang to me:

> *Down by the water, down by the water,*
> *down by the water, that's where mama waits for me, she*
> *said that's where she will always be,*

down by the water.
I had gone away, so far astray, so far I was too afraid to pray, but in the winds echo, somewhere in the bay, she sang to me and I heard her say:
Down by the water, down by the water, come so we can fix your way.
Here you can always stay, mama's love feeding you each day, down by the water.
I have come here now, on my knees with my head sober enough to bow, with all the strength my body can allow, I am here, come to me, down by the water.

He sang the song with a sweet sadness that made me ache for my mother's stern face, the face that was my own.

The other men were standing far off, keeping guard or distancing themselves from the unfolding scene. The great expanse of the ocean lay before me, and in my bones I felt all of my ancestors there, past and present, patiently waiting for the changing of the guard. The old fisherman was still singing "Down by the water" under his breath as he stroked my braids in the distracted way in which men convey empathy.

I don't know how long the birthing lasted. I only knew of the passage of time from the movement of the sun in the sky and shadows growing longer. The growing length of the shadows provided some reprieve from the glare of the sun. The water had retreated far from my feet and the sand had dried.

I began to anticipate the arrival of my children as I dug my feet into the sand. They would be orphans of a kind, but inside them coursed the blood of a dynasty built from the ashes of a forgotten family name high above the many bends of the Thina River as it flows to the sea. They had the blood of a martyr, a religious man, who perished for his belief that hatred corroded the spirit and inspired generations after him in a small rural town where nothing ever happened, but where freedom now reigns over its surrounding rolling hills. They had the blood of a boy who lived in the shadows, wrestling with confusion and the fires that burned in and around him. They had the blood of their father who challenged the day with his every breath and refused the straight lines of convention. They had the stories of our people, their struggles and pain, their resilience and strength. I pushed through the pain to birth my children at the point where divinity changed hands from mystical waters to solid earth

The young fisherman at my parted legs was sweating, until after a pain that lasted and lasted, I saw from his wide eyes that I was crowning. The older fisherman confirmed this with a stern question, and the news was affirmed with a vigorous nod and a wash of relief when in the next moment, a sharp cry produced shouts of victory and applause.

I grabbed the old fisherman's arm in the midst of his excitement: "There are two of them."

He was confused. I repeated my words less urgently, and he bent down again to cradle me and shouted commands to the young boy now covered in my fluids and blood, after putting my wailing firstborn on the sand, high up against my thigh so that I could feel him as he wriggled in the blinding light of the sun.

For the second child, there were no songs, just anticipation. The patience of the strangers was approaching its limits, for they were men of the ocean who preferred the predictability of the ocean's boundless fluidity. What was before them now had the familiarity of domestic life. A birthing woman was outside of the realm of minds of simple men who knew enough about the mystery of life to respect it, but preferred the challenges of the ocean.

Feeling their impatience, I tightened my grip on the old fisherman. He looked out briefly over the ocean, thinking possibly of the day's losses, then he bent his head again to stare at me in pity. He didn't share his thoughts although he had fashioned his mouth to speak. I was going to beg him to not leave me, but a wave of pain rushed through me and I pushed out the second baby, then collapsed back panting, my children wailing by my side.

The young fisherman ran down into the ocean, and for a second, the waves engulfed him. The other men shouted praise out to him as they applauded. The old fisherman stood and walked up the sand dune to where his boat lay, its push down to the water having been abruptly halted. I saw his small frame bent over the green distressed wood of his boat, and when he returned he had with him long strips of gauze wiring. The babies were wailing incessantly now, and he clumsily handed me the second one – a little girl, I now saw – as he tied the gauze around the navel of the first. He sawed through the umbilical cord of my son and handed him to me as he took my daughter, unintentionally with more care than he had the boy. He worked on her umbilical cord until it fell off, then handed her to me and sat back on the sand, his legs drawn up and his elbows resting on his knees.

The sounds of wind and water around us were singing in chorus but it was also quiet, as though it were deep in the night and the magic of darkness had cast a spell on the earth. I was a mother, but had no idea what that meant, or would come to mean. Yet I was certain of my abounding love for them. The white dress in which I had baptised myself was now soaked in blood and bits of tissue. I was an open wound, my breasts swollen, but I could not suckle my children until I offered them properly to this life.

I searched for the old fisherman whose head was still bent in either relief or prayer. "Ou Takkies," I said attempting to raise my voice, but even the energy for that had drained from me. I raised myself and placed my children carefully on the sand, their tiny fists unfurling. The beams of the sun must have been searing their tender skin without the comfort of cold salt water to balance the elements.

I stared at them as though they were no part of me. The girl had her father's eyes of the sky, and her balled fist opened up and clung to my index finger when I reached for it. It was so sudden, I burst into tears. The boy had my amber eyes, Groot Pa Katje's eyes, with which he gazed at me in a moment of serenity. They were earnest with the compassion one would offer a stranger in hard times. I kissed them on their foreheads and gathered the afterbirth and cords, which had been covered with a raffia bag.

The old fisherman hurried to my side. "I have to do something," I said resolutely, aiming to discourage being dissuaded, but he was an ocean man – he understood rituals. The young fisherman was marshalled to watch the babies, and the older man led me to the water. The waves crashed and unfurled more loudly, and I waded into the waters, my dress soaked in blood, and the pains of birth beating through my body, my muscles fatigued from labour and the emptying of my womb.

I stopped when the water was at my waist, and placed my hands in the water and opened them, and with each wave rocking me up and down, I watched my placenta and their umbilical cords floating away. I stood praying, and the old fisherman kept a firm and steadying grip on my arm as a precaution against the derangement he suspected on my part.

I turned to him: "In the days of old, we buried our umbilical cords where all our ancestors were born so that when we returned later in spirit form to take up our place in the Lands of the Undying we might be recognised and welcomed by our own. It has been a tradition for every January born to have their umbilical cords buried in the garden at Groot Huis, but three Januarys have come instead to be by the sea. It is only the sea in its infinite and great expanse that they came to be at peace with the workings of the world; and the land has never settled them the way in which tides of the great sea does. When I, my mother and Romance die, we will lead our people to new habitats to rest. Places that don't shackle our movements or value us by some measure borne from the workings of lesser, cruel beings. Our only misfortune is that we were not born into this freedom, and we taint it with our burdens of a past life. Unlike them, today my children have been born in the majesty of limitlessness. Hear me, God, that my children may know you. Inam, the one who is with God, born fighting to be first just like his father. Liso, with her eyes of sky and my heart, threaded brows just like mine – I send you out into the world to be blessed by the infinitude of all that has informed your creation."

The fisherman washed my face and I felt his callouses against my cheek.

We made our way back to the beach and my babies.

Overhead I saw three eagles circling us. An omen, I thought.

Acknowledgements

Years ago, in my adolescent years, I decided that I was going to write a book. I had read enough of them, and my writing elicited enough positive reactions from those around me, to warrant the belief that perhaps such a feat was within the realms of possibilities for my life. Attached to that was of course the overwhelming feeling of insecurity that often accompanies any creative process. The will to continue was buoyed by all the people in my life. They have spoken into and for me during the long decade or more that it took to create this moment – a published book.

I dedicate this book to my maternal grandmother, Noluphato Ntsimazana Mlobeli, who, lit up by the embers of a dying fire, whispered in my ear that I had interesting ways of relaying stories. I was ten years old then, and at that point in my life, had only met her a couple of times. It was her conviction in my supposed talent that arrested me: I felt like she had exposed my deeply held secret – my love of stories. She saw into me. She saw me. I thank her and my grandfather for being loving and simple people whose home was the peaceful centre for all of life's turbulences, and the canvas for my dreams.

My parents: Tata for always knowing how to enjoy and tell a good story. There is not a moment in my life when I don't see a frame of you caught in raptures of laughter at the climax of a story. You taught me the art form by how you indulge in it – so authentic and clearly articulated, wrapped up with purpose intended to connect our experiences in this life. Mama: you taught me that all dreams need the foundation of discipline. To love what you do is important, but to be disciplined in pursuit of it and to grow in its evolution is another, and you taught us how to be disciplined by example. You have always been a constant and reliable example of grace and dignity. As a unit you have set a standard so high for my life that at times it can be overwhelming, but I am thankful for how deeply your love has inspired me.

Thank you to my other parents, Momncinci and Tatomncinci for always being "just down the road". As I get older and realise how complicated it can sometimes be to move together harmoniously as adults, the relationship you have with my parents is something I am grateful to have I witnessed.

My siblings – and siblings for me includes a huge network of people – who were my first audience. My immediate siblings read all the drafts of my many attempts at books over the years, and lovingly steered me towards my own voice. It is a powerful thing to be loved because it is the mirror long before you have the courage to look, or even see; and here, with you in my life, I am always seen. I thank you all for the conversations that blend our varied perspectives with my personal convictions – which I am always forced to challenge because they are not permitted to exist lazily or without proper qualification.

This book is also dedicated to my nephew, Sigurd Siegemund, who, since his birth, has elevated the notion of what I thought of as beauty. His arrival bought to the fore how the hands of time are designed to propel us forward in unseen but powerful ways. To be given the honour to love someone into shape is so profound for me that I wanted to create something tangible he could hold as an outward expression of what is deep inside of me for him; to have no doubt of his value in spirit or form.

My friends. That is the sentence, and it is complete and whole: my friends. First of all, to dare to interpret yourself to a stranger is an act of extreme courage, but to be accepted after the attempt is generosity that never fails to render me weak. All of you were bought into my life by God; I couldn't engineer such meaningful interactions on my own. I wouldn't have the wisdom to know what I needed and from whom – the fact that in my basket of goodness I am always being sent exactly who I need at precise moments in my life makes me eternally grateful that I didn't have a hand in your presence in my life. It is always appreciated.

My love. Thank you that your ears are long enough for my worries and for being so fiercely confident in what is possible in this life; this widens the scope of my dreams and fortifies my resolve to achieve them. What words I have for you belong in less viewed spaces, and I'm doubtful even then of their quality in expressing the depth of my gratitude.

To Helen Moffett, I believe I can replicate this achievement again in coming years because of what you breathed into me when you touched my book, and me.

To Jacana Media: Bridget, Lara, Megan, Kelly-Ann – all of you have played a part in bringing *Christopher* to life. Bridget, thank you for backing a voice that even I hadn't used yet. I have stalked Jacana for years, so to me our marriage is something I didn't question, as I have been in the shadows, waiting, yet doubting my ability. Thank you for giving my creation a safe home.

In this book I have referred to histories that might injure or offend some people. It is not my intention to trigger traumatic feelings that are a part of someone's real life experience. I wrote this book to highlight how profound such a history had on my understanding of who we are as a people; to address how little I or my culture featured in the spaces I inhabited outside of my home, and where I formed ideas about my identity. All references to trauma are meant to illustrate those moments when my perspective shifted, and are ways in which I worked through my feelings of being erased in certain contexts, and having to conform in others. If it is clumsily done, please find mercy in your critique, which I will accept in lieu of understanding the genesis of my perspective.